Ruxandra Cesereanu

ANGELUS

Translated by Alistair Ian Blyth

Afterword by Marius Conkan

DIÁLOGOS
BOOKS

Angelus
by Ruxandra Cesereanu.
English translation by Alistair Ian Blyth.

Printed in the U.S.A.
First Printing.
10 9 8 7 6 5 4 3 2 1   15 16 17 18 19 20

Book design: Bill Lavender.
Cover art: Angela Rotaru. Thanks to Humanitas Publishing (Bucharest).
Author photo on back cover by Catalina Flaminzeanu, copyright © 2015.

Library of Congress Control Number: 2015935161
Cesereanu, Ruxandra
Angelus / Ruxandra Cesereanu
with Alistair Ian Blyth (translator)
p. cm.
Includes Afterword by Marius Conkan
ISBN: 978-1-935084-85-3 (pbk.)

DIÁLOGOS
AN IMPRINT OF LAVENDER INK

TABLE OF CONTENTS

PART ONE

PART TWO

ANGELUS

PART ONE

OF HOW PEACEABLE AFFAIRS ALL OF A SUDDEN TAKE AN UNACCUSTOMED TURN

The former empire had frayed like a yellowing doily, so much so that its once celebrated capital, named simply Metropolis, was and yet was not a space like any other. There was nothing particularly eccentric about it, but rather it was fitted to the way in which the Homeland, having just crossed the threshold between millennia, with a wolf's paw in the twentieth century and a rat's tail in the twenty-first, put on airs of being hallowed ground, ripe for fresh events. And so when the three angels descended upon Metropolis they were straightaway noticed. They were identical, garbed in jeans and tunics, as well as blue capes, in fact not so much blue as azure, and their long, curly chestnut hair was tied in a ponytail. They had elongated eyes, the eyebrows seemingly plucked and penciled, and their necks were long, like a flamingo's. Oh, and above all, an essential detail given the course of the events about to unfold, they were mute; they were without speech. They were not deaf or blind, but they were mute. They did not fall from the sky all in the same place, but rather each ended up in a different part of Metropolis, like a bird bereft of legs and forced to land wherever it could. One of them fell into the middle of a routine parade inside the capital's Fortress, and so he was arrested on the spot, having been mistaken for a spy. The second fell inside a pharmaceuticals factory, and in the ensuing confusion he was taken to be the Dutch negotiator who didn't speak the country's language but who was handling a transaction with the foreign parent company. Given that the negotiator in question had been nicknamed the Flying Dutchman, when the second angel plummeted straight into the main tablet-bottling room, the workers quite naturally mistook him for that foreign investor in their Sacred Homeland. None but a girl from the country, toiling with great dispatch as she sorted pills, grasped that the young man with a blue cape and hair tied in a ponytail could not possibly be Dutch, but must have come from some far more mysterious realm. And this is why, after waiting for the others to return to their tasks and put the visitor out of mind, she led him away by the hand, shut him inside a locker and made a sign for him to wait there until she finished her shift. And the angel understood. But even had he not understood, it would not have made any difference. The third "individual", as perhaps I ought to call him, although I shall correct myself and say rather the third "angel", ended up among the clerks of the National Bank, and so he was straightaway mistaken for a thief. A guard frantically sounded the alarm and as quick as a flash the angel found himself arrested by some bruisers in camouflage uniforms. In short, this is how things stood: three angels had dropped out of the sky and onto the Metropolis, descending for some unknown purpose, and two of them had been arrested, while one alone still remained at large, although it was not clear for how long. All that day the girl from the country, who worked at the medicaments factory, thought about the golden man she had concealed inside her locker: she was in no doubt that he must be an angel and she was determined to protect him from prying eyes, to hide him away. And so after her toilsome shift came to an end, she waited for the others to leave and in the semi-darkness opened the locker inside which she had sequestered the visitor fallen from the heavens. She took him by the hand, put a kerchief on his head, and dressed him in a yellow plastic mackintosh, for rainy weather, scrunching his blue cape into her carpetbag: she was in luck, because the clouds had broken, releasing a shower perfect for concealing an angel. She would give him back his cape once they reached her house, where he would be able to reveal himself before her in all his glory. She took the visitor by subway, traversing the entire city, despite the curious glances the other passengers cast at the stranger. Then, she took him by bus toward the edge of the Metropolis, until they reached her ramshackle house, where she lived with an aged aunt. She was now wary of that aunt, as if she were the very devil, because she knew that if the old woman got wind of the visitor's identity, she would spread the word and the emissary from above would be arrested in a trice. After sneaking him into the house, through a window, and after some brief small talk with her aunt, the girl shut herself up in her room with her distinguished guest. First, she toweled him to dry off the rain, and then she gave him back his blue cape, which was rather rumpled after being stuffed in her bag. She decided to give him something to eat, but quickly changed her mind, knowing that such messengers do not ingest food; at the most, they drink water, but nothing more than that. Then, the girl quite simply lost herself in admiration of the golden man who was now revealed in all his splendor. She fell at his feet and thanked him for making her the first to whom he had revealed himself, to whom he had made himself known. The second angel could not speak, he was mute like the others, as I have already made plain, and so he said nothing, but merely blinked wearily. The girl understood all there was to be understood and hastily undressed him, before tucking him up in her own bed, while she herself curled up on a chair, to keep vigil. Perhaps things might have taken a romantic turn, or perhaps not, which is more likely, given that angels are sexless, even if they look like men. In any case, the second angel's fate was only temporarily more fortunate than the others', because at the crack of dawn the girl's aunt, as she puttered around the house with a broom, sensed that odor which only angels emanate: a fragrance of deep red incense with a tang of caramelized sugar. The silly little aunt burst into her niece's room and espied the unusual guest asleep in the bed while the girl watched over him. Affrighted, she shrieked at the top of her voice. Before the girl and the angel knew what was happening, a number of neighbors had already rushed across the road, they too espying the strange guest. Taking him for an unclassifiable criminal they pinned him down, despite the girl's protests. A brief telephone call was made to the police, who were already abreast of the situation: a rumor was circulating in Metropolis that two strangers had landed from some unknown place and were causing the authorities a headache, and so if yet another one had turned up, then it seemed only normal, numerically speaking. But what and who were these strangers that were baffling so many heads in the erstwhile empire? Were they spies or terrorists? Could they even be extraterrestrials? What was it that they wanted? The president of the country—an unctuous type, who had no truck with angels, if I may put it like that, since he had never been in the habit of praying when he was a child, being an atheist, and because he did not put much faith in the Church, but only in the Nation's Political Corps, as he liked to say in his speeches—avoided making any allusion to the three visitors for the time being. Rather, he decided to wait until such time as he would be handed a full report on the interrogation of the three that had tumbled out of thin air, a report that was to be drawn up by the competent organs, i.e. State Security, which had enough working sections and specialist departments to elucidate the enigma. Indeed, the Ministry of the Interior issued special orders for all agents to keep their eyes peeled, to scour Metropolis for any other potential individuals with blue cloaks and chestnut hair tied in a ponytail that might be lurking; such individuals would be easily detectable inasmuch as they were completely mute. They were to be arrested on sight, but without being roughed up or inflicted any bodily or mental injury, as the emergency orders specifically indicated.

After interrogation, these men, if hominids they were, and even if they were something else entirely, would need to be studied thoroughly by the Homeland's scientists. The agents scoured the city for a whole week, but there was no trace of any other individuals with blue capes and ponytails: the native citizens did not have such sartorial habits. It is true that the strangers who had plummeted from some unknown place did have tunics akin to peasant smocks, and this somewhat muddled the calculations of the researchers at the Ministry of the Interior. Oh well, what can one do: foreigners in love with the local customs are not unheard of, and this to a certain degree softened the native view of the three golden men. They wore tunics. But was this because they wanted to go native or because they were trying to pull the wool over the authorities' eyes? In this respect, things were rather unclear, and so people would have to remain vigilant and cautious. A week went by and the authorities concluded that there were no other strangers akin to those already captured, and therefore the interrogation could commence. Theretofore they had held the three in quarantine, in a kind of prison hospital, lest they infect the general populace, although no one knew what kind of infection they might be carrying. Might there be a disease called *long-hair-in-a-ponytail-itis* or *blue-cape*? In fact, it was all very complicated, and this is why they all affected to be suffering from acute deafness. For the time being, there was no question of bringing up *angelitude* or *angelicity*; the authorities avoided such unscientific, un-political terms like the evil eye. For a week, the warders had tried to feed the three strangers, even forcibly, through a tube, believing that those creatures were on hunger strike, but in the end they became convinced that the unexpected guests had no need of sustenance in order to live. Could they be fakirs or yogis? They ingested only water, the same as anyone else, but this they did more from politeness than any real need. Nor were they adverse to cow's milk or even a bottle of distilled alcohol, something not at all angelic, but which at least endeared them to their warders. Although they were angels, they seemed very mimetic angels, as a professional nitpicker might have observed. But given that for the time being no such nitpicker was on hand, let it be made plain that as far eating was concerned, the three strangers ate nothing at all. And as for drinking, they drank only to humor their warders, since they had no need of liquids. And so, after a week of quarantine, what had to come to pass did indeed come to pass.

A Telling Interrogation: Neither Terrorists, nor Spies, nor Extraterrestrials

To cross-examine the interlopers under suspicion of being angels the Interior Ministry set up a commission comprising three chief interrogators, all of them captains, each in charge of three lieutenants. And so, no fewer than twelve men, each answerable to State Security, worked around the clock on the interrogation. Once again, strict orders had been issued that the three unidentified individuals should not be maltreated or threatened, but merely studied, in slow-motion as it were, and, as far as possible, tapped of any information useful to the Homeland and damaging to its enemies. No specific mention was made of God. The only objects on the table in the interrogation rooms were, as you might expect, notebooks, typewriters, rudimentary computers, and, of course, huge carafes of water, together with glasses, as well as a few pots of coffee and porcelain cups, to meet the liquid requirements of interrogators and interrogated, although the latter, we should recall, seemed desirous neither to eat nor to drink (although this stands to reason, as they were, after all, rumored to be angels). In the end, they dispensed with the glasses of water and everybody, captains, lieutenants and three angels alike, kept handy only pots of coffee and tea. Black coffee and tea were to remain stalwart, indispensable liquids throughout the interrogations. From the outset, however, all of them, great and small, found themselves at a major impasse: how could the angels communicate, even if they wanted to, given they were mute, regardless of whether they were mute from birth or mute merely by circumstance? The Minister of the Interior, informed of this fact as a matter of urgency, could do no more than scratch the tip of his nose and tug his earlobe. How was he to tell the President that the three interlopers from on high could not in fact be interrogated? Heavy was the burden on his shoulders, devilish the task. In the end, however, the impasse was overcome thanks to one of the lieutenants engaged in the interrogation. He remembered the girl from the country who had sequestered the second angel, the one that crash-landed in the pharmaceuticals plant, the girl who had taken him home, crossing the whole breadth of Metropolis. The interrogators established that the three captives had perfectly functioning eardrums, and so the only impediment was how they might express what they had to say otherwise than in words. They summoned three doctors specializing in the language of the deaf and dumb, and these experts began to communicate with the strangers, haltingly at first, but then at a cracking pace. They also summoned the girl who worked at the pharmaceuticals plant, and she straightaway recognized her golden angel: he had a small mole beneath his right eye, unlike the other two that had tumbled out of the blue. The interrogators and the doctors all took note: the three angels were identical, but nevertheless there were little details that made each one distinct. They looked as alike as three drops of water, but even so, they were different. The girl was able to communicate with the second angel with remarkable ease: he responded to her using precise signs. These signs were neither expansive nor solemn, but playful. After a while, the physicians were able to unravel the sign language employed by the visitors, and so the girl was sent back home, but not before being informed that if she breathed one word about what she had seen and heard during the preliminary interrogations, her life would take an unpleasant turn. The girl nodded obediently, but before she left, she made the sign of the cross and fell to her knees before the second golden angel. After that, the medical interpreters set about their task. They did not manage to get much out of the three individuals, however. They were obliged to communicate with them as best they could, and their findings, which were passed on to the interrogators, went something like this: the three angels did not know exactly why they were in the capital or why they had been parachuted there. Of course, "parachuted" was merely a convenient way of putting it, besides having an appropriately military ring. Quite simply, they had been picked, although it was not clear by whom, and sent on their way, all three of them, garbed as they were, without being entrusted with any specific mission, without being told what exactly it was all about or why the capital of the proud Homeland had been selected in particular. But the three strangers had been assured that the purpose for which they had been sent would be revealed to them in good time, after the state authorities regained their composure and all the hysteria died down. Naturally, this answer, no matter how many nuances it subsequently acquired, was unsatisfactory, and so now the interrogators' investigation files were brought into play. The first verdict, that they were terrorists, was quickly discarded: it was clear that the angels, if angels they were, had no weapons. They did not know how to handle a machine gun or flamethrower, and nor did they have any proclivities in that direction. Maybe if they had been handed a grenade they would have known how to throw it, given the necessary pointers. The second verdict, that they were spies, was also swiftly ruled out: the angels were mute, they spoke no language of any kind, neither the preeminent native language of the land, nor any other; which is to say, the three spoke no human tongue, because they were incapable of doing so. However, the captains tasked with the special mission did wonder whether the strangers were merely confidence tricksters, of which there is no shortage in this world and who roam around, turning up when you least expect. Lately, it seemed that people of that ilk had taken up residence in the Homeland in droves. Ultimately, even if, at a pinch, they were indeed angels, why could they not also be fraudsters, although this might not be obvious for the time being? The captains did not yet have any evidence. Then again, the angels were well-behaved, serious, grave even, but without being overbearing. They were dressed casually, and only their blue capes betrayed something unusual, something in the way of a holy mission, albeit one that was unfolding in slow motion. But how holy? Not least, the strangers had not resisted arrest, had not been violent, but on the contrary, without putting on seraphic faces, they seemed to be playing along flexibly, like pawns in a game not even they fully grasped. They smiled almost continuously, but without ever laughing, without making hieratic gestures, without making the sign of the cross, without lifting their eyes to the heavens, without seeking the One who had sent them, if indeed He it was. The only thing it was possible to say with any clarity was that the interrogators, despite their exceptional commission, and despite the urgency of their task, had not come to any real conclusion: they had no idea who the three supposed angels might be or what they were doing in Metropolis. Nor were there any real grounds for keeping them under arrest. On the other hand, it would be ill advised to let them roam the city at will. Likewise, it was not possible to expel them from the Sacred Homeland, because that would risk a religious scandal of global proportions. The Interior Ministry did not know what to do, and nor did the President. Once again, one of the industrious lieutenants came up with a daring idea: what if they were to administer truth serum to the three strangers? Let the reader be in no doubt that this truth serum was the very same drug that many other nations have also developed, experimenting on the sick in asylums and on prisoners in the grim jails that teem with such specimens. It was that same serum whereby the person injected succumbs to alluvial delirium and tells the whole truth and nothing but the truth, even about what he had sucked from his mother's dugs, as the interrogators liked to boast. No sooner said than done. The angels did not put up any resistance to being injected with the truth serum, but their compliance was sooner neutral, although the skin on their arms did blister slightly, which alarmed the physicians, given that they had been obliged to damage the flesh of the unusual visitors, especially in the event that they did prove to be angels after all, angels with full rights (not that it was clear what such rights might entail). For this reason, the blisters that erupted on their arms after each injection were immediately treated with an infusion of chamomile, in order to salve the vesications as expeditiously as possible. Then, the physicians and the interrogators waited and they waited, but in vain. The visitors slept for a long time. They did not emit any sound, as would have been natural or expected. But after all, they were mute. They did not so much as even mumble to themselves. But they did gesticulate in sign language: interpreting their message, the medical specialists declared that the strangers knew nothing, and that their signs abundantly proved it. Probably not even God was much in the habit of speaking, suspected the Interior Minister, on learning the latest news about the distinguished captives. It is true that after they had awoken from the sickly sleep brought on by the ineffectual truth serum, the strangers had consumed enough coffee to stay awake for a whole lifetime. But they had drunk that complimentary coffee only to humor the interrogators, because if it had been up to them and their real needs, they would not have ingested liquids of any kind. Then, on the final lap, one of the canny lieutenants had come up with another idea, a hypothesis that might just save the day: what if those quasi-hominids were extraterrestrials? His superiors (the captains), his colleagues (the lieutenants), and the Interior Minister himself laughed heartily: never had they heard such bunkum. How could they possibly be extraterrestrials? But, of course, after the failure of the interrogation, the strangers would still have to be stripped of their clothing and examined down to their very DNA. Even their fingernails and the hair on their heads would be scrutinized under a microscope. X-rays of their whole bodies, teeth included, would have to be taken. But that related to medical procedures. Extraterrestrials? Not a bit of it! The exceptional Commission made up of captains and lieutenants dissolved themselves forthwith, given that they were of no further use and the object of their labors had itself evaporated. The Interior Minister shrugged, not knowing what else was to be done, but the President was obliged to prepare an official declaration and appear on national television: a large number of the capital's inhabitants had learned of the fall of the three angels, and so matters could no longer be covered up, although they could, of course, be manipulated in the State's favor.

THE SMOKESCREEN SPEECH OF THE HOMELAND'S HUMBLEST CITIZEN

For his televised speech, the President knew that he would need to wear a special outfit: before doing anything else, he decided to have himself made up like a simple rustic and to wear a peasant smock, similar to the angels'. The President also knew that he would have to comport himself in a natural way if he was to have the desired impact on the nation's viewers. In the end, maybe the strangers were nothing short of manna from heaven for his next electoral campaign. Why should he not use the opportunity to take them under his protection?

"Dear friends," he began, with a preoccupied mien, "I would like you to grant me a few moments of your time so that I can impart to you some important news: upon our city, the Metropolis, there have descended some citizens that some believe might be angels. We don't know whether they really are angels or whether they are something else, but without us necessarily being irreligious what we can say with our hand on our heart is that we are all human and in consequence we all have the right to believe or to doubt as the case may be. And so let the believers believe, and as for those who do not want to believe, they are still citizens of the Homeland." At this point in the presidential speech, the cameramen sniggered: had the President been tippling? Was this any way to address the nation? The director of the national television station shushed them indignantly, and a few clipped lugs were sufficient to quell the impertinent lads behind the cameras. "Dear friends, like many of you, I too wonder," continued the President, with fresh rhetorical wind in his sails, "what these angels might be and why it is we see their like so rarely, if ever. There is no exact answer to such a question," concluded the speaker. "Angels are enigmas. Or, to put it another way, they are miraculous creatures. How then might they be glimpsed, touched or even perceived? In no wise," decided the President, speaking to the nation with aplomb. "And nevertheless, sometimes they give us a sign and even reveal themselves to us: in dreams, as a rule. Well, at such times they amaze us, they astonish us, because we do not know how to perceive them or talk to them." The President's wisdom was glaring, and the intellectuals watching him on television were impressed by the skill of whomever had written his speech for him. Who might it be? "And because we don't know how to communicate with them, the angels don't linger among us for very long, but reveal themselves only rarely, out of the blue, and then return to their own world and their own affairs. But what are the affairs and the labors of angels? Dear friends, as you will already have surmised, the angels generally toil for the prosperity and the good of mankind, but their work is invisible. This is why we cannot judge the work of these creatures. We can merely admire it, nothing more. We can gain an inkling of it. We can sense it, whether directly or indirectly." Here, the cameramen nudged each other again, and once again they were dealt clipped lugs. "But who is it that sends the angels? Obviously, this is a question that even a child in nursery school could answer. Nevertheless, I shall not answer it, because, dear friends, I do not wish to appear arrogant: as the nation's elected leader, it is my duty to be the Homeland's humblest citizen, to embrace humility. And so I humbly say to you, with my hand on my heart, that I do not know who sends the angels. Why they are sent we already know, but who sends them is, I think, something best left inviolate in its mystery, without our putting troubling questions." At this point in the speech, even the intellectuals were left slack-jawed. The President was a staunch atheist, as everybody knew, but even so, his speech was now washing over them from all directions at once, now defending angels, now claiming that it was not possible even to speak of them, because he had to be humble.

"And so, without being indebted to speak of Whom sends the angels, or not, I would now like to talk about something else much more important, namely, about how the angels reveal themselves, when they do reveal themselves, only to nations and peoples that have an important word to say. In our case, if it turns out that the three newcomers are indeed angels, then it is on the sacred soil of the Homeland that they will have appeared, probably with some particular purpose. But what this purpose might be is something that we shall all have to discover, dear compatriots, if and only if we have patience. And there is also need of rigor—" and here the cameramen laughed out loud "—there is need of faith and above all patriotism. For, without a love of country not even the angels, if angels they be, will be able to be understood. And if they be not understood, there will be a risk of their being mistaken for dangerous entities. This might give rise to strife, polemic and envy. Dear fellow citizens and compatriots, I have but one request to make of you: let the coming days be a trial period for the three foreigners dwelling in our midst, as well as for us as a nation, in particular those of us living in our intrepid capital. Let the nation know that the descent of the three visitors might be a patriotic test of all citizens, as well as a challenge of unknown import. This is why you should be vigilant, but not violent. The Army and State Security will also be vigilant, likewise the Government and Presidency. Let there be peace in the world, and let our Mother, the Homeland, preserve us forever and ever!" The President concluded his epoch-making speech to the applause of the director of national television, to the titters of the cameramen, and to general stupefaction among populace, proletariat and intelligentsia alike. There was no doubt about it: the President had thoroughly astonished both those who had voted for him and those who had not. His speech, simple and yet convoluted, was to drive the political analysts out of their minds. As soon as the broadcast was over, they commenced to pick apart the text of the presidential discourse. Was it a cerebral, emotional or sensual speech? Was it about angels in the strictest sense of the word, or did the term angels in fact camouflage something else: a military plan on the part of the President, an international plot, an attempted coup, an extraterrestrial invasion (in which case, the idea put forward by the lieutenant on the exceptional Commission would not have been farfetched after all)? Had the President's atheism gone awry? Had the premier had a revelation to alter his unbelief? Had he had a vision on the road to Damascus? Had someone converted him? And if so, what was it that the President had converted to? This was not at all apparent. Why had the three strangers descended upon the city of Metropolis? What was so special about this city that it could elicit such an unusual event? Might not Metropolis arouse envy and rivalry, and thus risk being bombed, even destroyed, wiped from the face of the earth? What if the strangers were not ordinary angels, but angels of the Apocalypse? What if the President had found out about this and did not know how to inform the public without causing panic? Why had the putative angels landed in Metropolis and not some other city? A flurry of questions throbbed in the heads of the political analysts and journalists, each eager to decipher the enigma of the presidential speech and make a splash in the media. Might the very word "angels" be magical, bewitched, dangerous? Was it not a word like any other, one absurdly invested with powers not guaranteed by any reality?

WHAT USE IS THE APOCALYPSE AND TO WHOM?

The first thing that happened after the presidential speech was that the capital's common people, but also a few intellectuals, asked themselves the following: even though the Apocalypse talks about four horsemen, might they not have been thinned out and reduced to just three? And if so, might not the strangers who had descended upon Metropolis be those very horsemen of the Apocalypse, albeit fewer in number? Naturally, the people who asked themselves such questions were believers through and through, zealots even, and could descry signs in whatever they saw, inasmuch as Metropolis might be beholden to all the nations of the earth for whatever was to come. It was no longer merely a question of the Alpha and Omega, but also a third holy letter, regardless of whether this third letter would be heard at the same time as the trumpet specific to the Apocalypse. Did not those three angels, if angels they were, resemble that apparition in the sacred book of John, whose hairs are white like wool and his eyes as a flame of fire? True, the strangers were without speech, and here there was a genuine problem of dissimilarity, so that the voice of thunder and the mouth out of which goeth a sharp sword did not have much in common with the newcomers. On the other hand, those who had descended from the heavens seemed to be telling the natives not to be afraid, because they brought with them keys of life aplenty, even if the keys of death were not to be denied. Nor was the sacred number seven to be found in the strangers' advent: whichever way you totted it up, the number in question did not come to light. But the Apocalypse need not go by the book. It would be more human for it to adapt to the times, and so the capital's inhabitants continued to investigate whether the creatures suspected of being angels were or were not the messengers of the Apocalypse. But which Apocalypse? The year one thousand had come and gone, the year two thousand likewise, albeit not long since, and the citizens of Metropolis, the same as other citizens the world over, already found themselves in the third millennium. Might the Apocalypse be slightly late? Might it be arriving presently? Anything would have been possible in a metropolis such as the one of which we tell. The inhabitants only had to be patient and not to be disheartened: something was surely afoot in the capital of the Homeland, something revelatory was about to happen, and perhaps in the end many would end up eating from the tree of life, if they repented, spurned temptation and believed unto the death. But what about the second death, was that still on the way or not? It might be believed that the sword from the holy mouth of the Apocalypse would cleave many, but something was not quite right, as I have said before: the supposed angels were mute. And so it was unknown where the new pillar in the temple of God or the new crown of life might be. The eye-covered creatures of the Apocalypse were four in number, not three. Where were the white, the red, the black and the pale horses, where the riders with the bow, the large sword, the pair of scales, and the power to kill by the wild beasts of the earth? Where were the white robes of the chosen? The strangers wore only tunics, jeans and blue capes. Their jeans were not even worthy of mention, as they were wholly inappropriate to any apocalyptic interpretation, being reminiscent of the repudiated days of hippies *sans frontières*. In the capital, the sun had not turned as black as sackcloth of hair and nor had the moon turned blood red in living memory, not for hundreds of years, apparently. The stars had not fallen unto the earth, and the islands had stubbornly refused to move out of their places. And in any case, where were the dens and the rocks of the mountains where the city's inhabitants might have hid themselves in the event of an Apocalypse? There were no dens or rocks of the mountains anywhere nearby. But the members of the intelligentsia were ruminating on why it was that the sun was said to have become black as sackcloth of hair. The angels' hair was not black, but auburn. Was it some kind of trick? And why was it said that the heaven departed as a scroll when it is rolled together? Whose scroll was it and what did it say? Was it man or beast that had been flayed to make the parchment? The sackcloth of hair and the scroll were truly prodigious enigmas. They raised too many questions, and those questions threw no light whatsoever on the identity of the three strangers. And besides, this world has four corners, not three, and so the angels, if angels of the Apocalypse they were, ought to have come from the four ends of the earth and, more importantly, they should have been bearing seals. And they ought to have announced who and how many were those who would no longer hunger or thirst, or be withered by drought. But the inhabitants of Metropolis had not heard any trumpet and they had not had any hailstones or blood mixed with fire, and nowhere in the former empire had there been any apparent slaughter. As for the strange star named Wormwood, it had not revealed itself to anyone. Eagles had been spotted here and there high in the sky, but that was hardly unusual.

Swarms of locusts had occasionally invaded the fields of the Homeland and even people's houses, but they didn't have hair as the hair of women or teeth as the teeth of lions. Nobody could recollect having heard mention of the name Abaddon, the angel of the bottomless pit. Perhaps there had been fire, smoke and brimstone, but not in any systematic fashion. But all the same, it might be said that the three strangers did look like a rainbow, and their faces were radiant, but they hadn't invited anybody to eat a holy book. The most important thing was something else entirely: where was the famous Beast of the Apocalypse? The crowned Beast that swept the stars from the heavens with its tail, and which had the number of a man: six hundred and sixty-six. The Beast was nowhere to be found. And what about the lake of fire and the feast of birds? Yes, thrice yes, the false prophets would all be devoured in the lake of burning brimstone. But let us not conclude this chapter with the incendiary words of the author of the Apocalypse, even if some might interpret that this is what the preceding knotty tale was all about. Rather, let us end with the famous words of the Evangelist, for it is exactly as he says: In the beginning was the Word. It will always be thus. Even if the angels are wont to keep silent.

LOOKING FOR WINGS AND OTHER ANGELIC DEFECTS

The strangers could not be released on to the capital's streets until an special medical commission had carried out a thorough examination of them, and so the President himself delegated the Head of Experimental Laboratories to pick experts from every field to perform all the necessary tests on the three, albeit without causing them any physical or mental distress. No sooner said than done. First of all, a generalist doctor examined them, after having them strip off all their clothing: he made a note of the fact that one angel (the second) had a small mole under his eye, but the others had no particular distinguishing features. The first doctor also had to do something very predictable, but no less risky for that: he had to look for wings or wing substitutes. The strangers had bodies like any other human, without any trace of wings—not so much as a stump or any downy fluff between the shoulder blades. The scapulae revealed no hint of any wing socket, natural or artificial. The generalist doctor sighed with a certain amount of relief at not having had to be the one to announce any shocking news. All the same, he did not exclude the possibility that the three might still be angels. He tested their knee reflexes with a little hammer, made them bend over and touch their toes, and checked the musculature of their arms and the soles of their feet. Everything was normal. Then it was the turn of the radiographer, who did discover something, when the visitors passed through the whole gamut of sophisticated apparatuses: the third stranger had only one kidney. The brain specialist was prepared for anything, and so he did not wonder when the tomogram showed that all three strangers had unnaturally developed cerebra. Such unusual growth was not entirely unheard of, however, and there were plenty of other cases throughout the Homeland. Nevertheless, he made a meticulous note of it in the clinical observation file, refraining from any undue speculation before completion of all the other medical and scientific tests. The ophthalmologist was surprised merely by what beautiful eyes the visitors had, and the otorhinolaryngologist pointlessly verified what everybody already knew: the angels had perfect hearing; they were not deaf. The cardiologist recorded a much stronger heartbeat than normal, as well as a seething of the blood in the arteries, but this might also be explained by the fact that the visitors were being subjected to a certain amount of stress due to their treatment at the hands of the authorities. The supposed angels had no lung ailments: they did not smoke and they did not cough. Again, they had no liver problems, something of a paradox given that they took no nourishment, although their stomachs were small and bunched up. The urologist established that even the visitor with only one kidney was in perfect health, inasmuch as that one kidney, being gigantic, did the work of two. The dentist observed something amusing: one of the three visitors, probably the first, the one who had landed in the middle of the military parade, had no wisdom teeth. At least now it was possible to tell them apart: one had a mole under his eye, another had only one kidney, and another had no wisdom teeth. The andrologist, having made a discreet examination, found that the gentlemen, although not unusually virile, were neither hermaphrodites nor androgynes; they were a little anemic and a little callow perhaps, but still men. The dermatologist recorded in the clinical observation file data about the strangers' white skin and its golden sheen: it was rather like raw silk. But apart from that it was still an eminently human skin. The psychologists called upon the assistance of specialists in mutism: yes, the visitors were mentally normal, even if they appeared to be innately autistic. They did not, however, dwell upon the fine details of this supposed congenital autism. It was also the psychologist who declared that the three who had fallen from the heavens must be triplets, or cousins at the very least. Then it was the turn of the logopedics specialist, who checked the placement and elasticity of the tongues in the strangers' mouths. The tongues were normally positioned and of normal size, and yet did not articulate words. There was a mystery here, which the logopedics specialist declared that he was unable to elucidate. Finally, the DNA experts delved to see what they could discover with their state of the art microscopes. The three visitors' DNA was more tightly coiled than normal, like the kind that used to be found in more primitive humans, but nothing more than that. As for the visitors' hair, the dermatologist had forgotten to say that it had the same consistency as the skin with the golden glints, like raw silk, except that it was more of a bronze color. They had wonderfully thick heads of hair, such as you find only in peasant women who wash using homemade soap. Everybody now realized why the strangers wore their hair in a ponytail: if they had worn it loose, it would have tugged their heads back and altered their poise. In conclusion: were they or were they not angels? The doctors, staking their reputations, declared that the visitors supposed to have descended from the sky were hominids. Ready for anything, President swallowed this news without astonishment. He was just about to make another official speech on national television when the Capital's Police informed him that a huge crowd was marching through Central Square, demanding the release of the angels that had graced the city at the dawn of that new millennium. There was no turning back: the President would have to rethink his speech and the Government, too, would have to adapt to the new situation. As a matter of the utmost urgency.

THE MOTLEY CROWD AND THE SLUM PHILOSOPHER

At first, the crowd gathered peacefully in the Central Square, among the stalls selling various junk: knickknacks, binoculars, fur hats with earflaps from the time of the former empire, aviator caps, sunglasses, insignia, and so on. There were also pointy witches' hats, devil statuettes made of grey plaster, all kinds of soft toys, amber jewelry, icons, vodka miniatures to fit jeans pockets, Fortress key rings, and other tat. The crowd was motley and vociferous: there were peasant women who had come to Metropolis after hearing of the descent of the three strangers suspected of being angels; high-school teachers; engineers; rockers; Satanists; dancers; brigadiers wearing overalls; blind opera singers; those nostalgic for bygone days; truant schoolchildren; and many more. There were people selling berries in plastic cups, bunches of wildflowers, slices of pizza and fizzy drinks. Beyond the Square, on Heroes' Boulevard, the pedestrian crossings and underpasses were clogged with people. The population was restless. Some had come with colored balloons, others were blowing soap bubbles, others were throwing confetti and grains of rice, like at a carnival or wedding, and still others were wearing pinned to their chests pictures of martyrs cut out of the newspaper. There was expectation and agitation. In fear of random terrorist attacks, the capital was swarming with police, as if it were under a state of siege. Then, the first cry went up: "They're our angels! Ours and the Homeland's! Give us back our angels! We want our angels!" The capital's inhabitants and those from the surrounding areas did not really know why they had gathered en masse, but the first of the slogans, which had been more like a throwaway remark, made it clear to many. Yes, that was how things stood: if the Metropolis had been lucky enough to receive the blessed strangers, here and now, then why should the nation and the masses not benefit from their coming, even if they weren't classic, textbook angels, even if they didn't have wings, even if they weren't angels at all? You could no longer use the word "angel" with the same meaning as in the past, as the President himself had said: ultimately, the word "angel" could mean whatever was required, as long as it implied salvation. It was not known why or how, but a large part of the capital's population had realized that it was no longer appropriate to employ the idea of redemption as a means of understanding the purpose for which the strangers had been parachuted into their Homeland. Redemption was going too far. The days of idealism were long gone. The notion of salvation was sufficient. But salvation from what? Well, salvation from everything: the world needed an outlet, not just Metropolis, but the whole planet, Greenland included. If others had been graced by strangers suspected of being angels, they would probably have declared a national holiday with all the festive trappings. Obviously, other nations would have first of all made sure that the visitors weren't mutants. "They don't need visible wings, because they have inner wings," one of the capital's famous intellectuals then shouted, the Slum and Tavern Philosopher, who was very popular with the public for his columns in *The People's Gazette* and notorious for his inveterate tobacco habit. He had a pronouncedly native look, with his eternally unshaven face, his shock of hair, his bloodshot eyes and his ancestral, venerable pipe, which was like a talisman, always in his mouth. "We all have inner wings: external wings are only for the blind." "This is the last thing we need," thought the Chief of Police, worried about the swelling crowd, "now prophets and cranks are sprouting like mushrooms after the rain." But ultimately this was only to be expected: people needed explanations and prophecies, regardless of whether they were founded in reality or preposterous. The devout little old ladies from the capital's outlying villages were already murmuring an improvised incantation about seraphim and cherubim: eyes with wings, wings with eyes, nay, wingless eyes. The Chief of Police nearly burst out laughing, but his subalterns were looking at him with serious faces, and so it wasn't the time to make light of things. The crowd was droning a churchy melody and had begun to slither in a slow, snail-like dance. "We all have wings," shouted the Slum Philosopher through a loudspeaker, pipe in mouth. Where had that loudspeaker popped up from? What a boon for a rabble-rousing philosopher prone to irate prophecy! The crowd was on the march. "We demand a healthier and more prosperous life!" the shout went up, all of a sudden. "Great," the Chief of Police said to himself, "from angelic to social and union demands." "We want a clean Homeland! Down with corruption and gangsterism!" The bit about "gangsterism" took the Chief of Police by surprise. "That's an odd word," he told his anxious subordinates. But they knew that already. "We want a people's court for everything that doesn't work in this country!" Now the policemen really pricked up their ears. Could the demonstration for the angels' release be turning into a revolt? There had been people's courts in the past and things had not turned out well, quite the contrary.

The Chief of Police wondered at this blend of belated revolutionary fervor and naivety on the part of the chanting crowd, massed together like a flock of belligerent sheep, and straightaway realized that the angels had been nothing but a pretext. But a pretext for what? For another revolution in the Homeland? No question of that. It was just old women's talk. "We want our autochthonous angels," another shout resounded in the Chief of Police's ears. "Autochthonous?" he wondered. "What's that all about? This is an uprising of intellectuals and professors," he concluded, musing aloud in front of his subordinates. "Listen to that—autochthonous angels. Look what happens if you let the wrong people publish in *The People's Gazette*, if you give people free speech. Where's the censorship of bygone days? Censorship was a fine thing when it was wielded purposely. Our nation has started to go soft in the head lately," thought the Chief of Police with a feeling of disquiet, "people have got it into their heads that they are the elect among nations, that they are the chosen. Not one of our historic dictators would be of any use in the third millennium, because the idea of revolution has been smoked down to the stub, and the stub is what you toss away last, that's what you do. This is how things stand," he said to his subalterns all of a sudden, "if those sheep and frogs keep on bleating and croaking much longer, we'll turn the water canons and tear gas on them. We're well equipped, thank God." "Will we be deploying anything else?" asked one of the other officers. "Not at all, just the water canons and the tear gas. There's no need for bullets. Don't make any arrests. There's no point. But if you feel like it, you can use the rubber truncheons, at least for the sake of practice." "Will you give the order now?" "Let's wait a little longer, to hear what else they'll shout, what they'll surprise us with next. Let it reach the critical moment, then we'll get clearance from central command." The crowd was shouting disjointedly: "We want equality for all! We want angels for all! We want it all for us all! Baa, baa, ribbit, ribbit. We want interviews with the angels, pictures, badges, banner and T-shirts." "Those idiots haven't realized that their angels can't talk, that they're mute," the Chief of Police chuckled to himself, but then he was taken aback at his own words: he himself had called the strangers angels. "Damn it, they've got me saying it now! Swarm them!" he ordered in annoyance, "Cordon off the crowd. Intimidate them, but don't resort to serious violence. Rubber truncheons at the ready, forward march!" The battle lasted less than half an hour, after which the crowd, their eyes streaming from the gas, their backs smarting, withdrew from the Square, scattering down the streets that led off the broad Heroes Boulevard. Nobody had been left in a coma. Nobody had lost consciousness. The crowd had been given a moderate thrashing, enough to numb and daze them. The demonstration was over. Nobody felt like shouting about wanting the angels any more.

THE ZEBRA-STRIPED TIE OF EL LEADER MAXIMO

In his luxury flat on the cosmopolitan Boulevard of the Sun, the president of the Nationalist Party was getting ready to intervene in what he called a "patriotic affair". The matter of the so-called angels greatly perturbed him. He was sitting in his gigantic white-leather armchair, with a brandy purchased from the delicatessen, the only beverage that could satisfy his refined tastes, and a bowl of zakouska, occasionally sucking on an ivory cigarette holder in which was inserted a fine Cuban cigar. And he thought and he thought. He was wearing his silk-lined white plush dressing gown. Suddenly struck by a micro-revelation, he summoned one of the pageboys on duty and ordered him to fetch his dappled jacket, white trousers, and zebra-striped tie, his preferred attire on those days when he appeared in front of the cameras of the television station he owned and which was watched by around a third of the capital's population, which is to say, by those who believed they were the authentic indigenous core of the Homeland. Indeed, the television channel was called For a Brave New Homeland (or Ef-bee-en-aitch, as it was known in the capital's working-class districts). The limousine, likewise white, was already waiting for him at the door, and so El Leader Maximo, as he was nicknamed, given that he resembled, albeit very slightly, a dictator from a faraway land in another continent, flung himself within, as if onto a four-poster bed, and drove off to Ef-bee-en-aitch. It was not for nothing that he adored Cuban tobacco: it was part of his albeit infinitesimal likeness with a dictator known as the Terminator. The Ef-bee-en-aitch staff had already been informed of his coming and so they interrupted the broadcast of jokes and proverbs to make ready the studio for the lightning appearance of El Leader Maximo, whose speech commenced thus:

"Compatriots, the catastrophic comedians who currently conduct our country want to turn our homeland into a dunghill of democracy. The politicians in power, those men of the crypt, those polluters and poisonous mushrooms, want to cast us into the ravening claws of mysticism and masonic conspiracy. Behind their obscene manoeuvres can be found, as you very well know, the crucifiers of Christ. Compatriots, we must exterminate the dead wood and the degenerates, the cesspools and the corrupt, the apostates and the vipers, the conmen and the crooks! Cast them out of the Homeland! The monkeys need to be shut up in a zoo and studied, and then their corpses need to be buried, lest the stench pervade the Metropolis. The executioners of the younger generation must not be allowed to proselytize. The time has finally come when there is no longer any room for rubber men and gelatinous goons, and the suckers battening on the nation's body must be crushed. Let us be allergic to the cancer and leprosy in the Homeland; let us become vigilant and competent surgeons. There is something rotten in the state of our Metropolis; our Metropolis reeks of putrefaction. What then is to be done? What is to be done with the rust and the decay of politics, with the rabble, with the dishrags, with the shit-eaters? The power and the grace are in our hands, compatriots, and so we must liquidate the ignoble bacilli-infected bastard of a Constitution, we must heal the gangrene and the syphilis in the body of the nation. The Government is a wild beast, but we are the tamers of that beast that is controlled by secret conspirators, by parasites and villains. The so-called elected President of the Homeland, but in no way elected by you, has blunted fangs and is vulnerable to lice. But above all he is the human trafficker of your souls, beloved compatriots! What are those angels? Who other than the Good Lord could explain? But for that we need a crusade on behalf of our indigenous soul. The piracy and looting at the sacred heart of the Homeland must stop! We don't need foreign angels, wearing blue jeans, because we have our own Orthodox angels. Away with these export angels! Away with the public enemies of the Homeland!"

The speech of El Leader Maximo was interrupted, however, at this point by none other than his chief adviser, while adverts for indigenous milk, indigenous cheese and indigenous alcohol wallowed over the screens of Ef-bee-en-aitch. "Maestro," the diminutive chief adviser timidly whispered in his ear, for diminutive he was in comparison with the podgy Leader, "the supposed angels were dressed not only in jeans, but also in peasant smocks, and so they might also be a tad aboriginal, at a pinch, if anything can be proven." "Listen here, you troglodyte," roared El Leader Maximo, "why didn't you tip me off sooner? I'm paying you for nothing. You Caiaphas! Incompetents, I'm surrounded by incompetents, on my word!" "No matter, maestro," the diminutive chief adviser ventured, "we'll rectify it somehow. All you have to do is add a brushstroke here and there, and we're home dry." And then he whispered in his ear for another minute. After which the televised speech of El Leader Maximo resumed. "Beloved compatriots, it is not fitting that a state monopoly should be imposed on the angels that have descended upon our proud Metropolis. The angels do not belong to the corrupt and defective State, but to us, to all of us. For the redemption of the nation, the angels must belong to the people. And so I ask you once more: what are angels? They are what they ought to be, in other words, a visiting card, a crossroads, a state of ferment, by means of which either we are saved or we perish. The end of the world is nigh, so it is rumored, and, therefore, let us repent! Citizen of the Homeland, do not taint your soul and do not succumb to lechery. Do not sit at the same table as the devil and do not make yourself one of his servants and acolytes. My sheep, my little lambs, my flock, beloved compatriots, I promise you each one angel for each of your souls. If we repent, then God will redeem our Mother Homeland and send angels for each of us. The present Government has discovered only three angels, and the President has been incapable of saying what they are in fact. I promise you millions of angels, raining down on the Metropolis and the Homeland. I swear on my soul. I swear on my family. I swear on anything you like." And here ended the speech of El Leader Maximo to the cheers of the personnel at the Ef-bee-en-aitch station. The diminutive chief adviser was jubilant. The Leader himself was flushed with the excitement and virtual splendor of it all. "Did I bowl them over?" he asked his underlings. "Maestro, you are unequalled and unbeatable. So help us God and may we win the elections."

IF YOU HAVE ANGELS, WHY NOT USE THEM?

The speech on Ef-bee-en-aitch had been viewed by a larger audience than usual, precisely because the capital's inhabitants had been expecting El Leader Maximo to make a nationwide spectacle of himself. The President of the country flew into a rage and downed half a bottle of the strong stuff, cursing and slapping his staff. The Chief of Police chortled on the sly with his subordinates, remarking that El Leader Maximo would either end up in the nuthouse or as the next president of the country. The workers of the capital's outlying districts were excited, each hoping an angel would climb down his chimney or be lowered down on a rope. The old biddies in the villages near the capital wept for joy. But somewhere in the Metropolis a calculating, pragmatic brain was at work, watching, listening and drawing a wholly different conclusion from El Leader Maximo's speech. That brain belonged to the head of Caravan, the Homeland's largest advertising agency. If you have angels, why not use them? This was what the senior exec known simply as the Boss swiftly intuited. And so, his mind was already whirling like a spinning top. First there would be ads for mobile phone companies: What's yours is yours, an angel for everyone; Man to man, angel to angel, angel to man; Get more out of life with an angel (guardian or not); Live the moment here with an angel. *In Touch with Life*. Then he thought of the avalanche of potential soap powder ads: From superangels to supermums; The scent of the nation's angels; Removes stains even from angels; Dirt is good when you've got an angel to wash it; A drop in an ocean of angels. But when it came to alcoholic beverages, he would have to give the matter some serious thought, because it was dangerous to overdo it there. All the same, his brain was ticking at a hundredfold rate: How refreshing! How angelic! Probably the Most Angelic Beer in the World; It looks angelic, it tastes angelic, and by golly it is angelic; The Angel of Beers; Angelic stout is good for you (that was a particularly stupid one!). And so on, and so on. Then, cosmetics and suchlike stuff, because women might be more sensitive to the winged creatures with human faces than men: An angel in your perfume, because you're worth it; Healthy skin is vital even to an angel; Discover the secret of real beauty alongside your guardian angels; Eternal youth with your angels of the third millennium; Your natural first choice, an angel for your teeth; The best treatment for angelic dandruff; For healthy hair, an angel's just the thing! Obviously, the adverts that required the most mental mastication would be the ones for foodstuffs, as the three strangers did not eat anything, while the natives stuffed themselves. And so: Chocolate moments with timeless angels; Delicious as a chocolate angel; The minty freshness of an angel's mouth; Spreadable cheese, *passion pour les anges!*; Traditional recipes in the world of angels; Angel's milk for happy babies; Mouth-watering angel ham; More angels, more energy; Live life to the max with angels; The refreshing aroma of angels; Mineral water for thirsty angels; Tasty, nourishing, angelic. And as for other products and services, the possibilities were endless: A radio station for millions of angels with functioning eardrums; The paper for house angels; Our readers are cleverer than angels; The newspaper written and read by angels; Loans guaranteed by angels; The softest furniture at angelic prices; Smile with the angels and you'll be in heaven! The number of things that could be invented and inventoried was endless: ketchup (Give hell a miss with a ketchup that spells angelic bliss!), motorcars (A car spacious enough for all the angels in heaven!), computers (Log on with an angel!), bodyguards (We're your guardian angels, every which way!), sexy lingerie (Angels need to be pampered too!), expensive watches (Angels don't waste time!), vacuum cleaners (Bust astral dust with angel power!), photocopiers (Copies only original angels!), toys (Angels-r-us), life insurance (Your future's more secure with an angel), exercise bicycles (It's time for a change, get fit with an angel!), marketing (We'll sell angels for you), telephones (Phone now, the angels are on the line), petrol (Quite simply more angelic), real estate (Apartments for luxury angels). Advertising didn't necessarily require logic or grammar, the Boss told himself. In the end, the most natural thing in the world would be to make an advert for my own company: A Caravan of angels! Technology for a lifetime.

BLACK HOLES, WHITE HOLES

The members of the Metropolis Academy had set up a commission to investigate the authenticity of the three strangers. The commission was made up of mathematicians, physicists and chemists. Surely the chemists ought to be able to discover, in the case of the so-called angels, a formula containing a smidgeon of uranium? Nobody knew for sure. The truth was that the chemists played a derisory part in the proceedings: with their Mendeleev Tables in front of them, they did not quite know how to apply them in the given situation. Heigh-ho, the days of the alchemists are long gone and today's chemists are nothing but wretched realists! And so the mathematicians and physicists on the commission soon got shot of the chemists, so that they could debate among themselves undisturbed. For, the mathematicians, with their jam-jar-bottom spectacles, and the physicists, with their shaven egg-heads, were already pondering an idea: they were all but convinced that the arrival of the three strangers had some connection with the theory and structure of black holes. They were fixated on the idea. They could already picture galaxies strung together like beads and in some cases even superimposed upon one another, which had been pulverized in the Big Bang, but also remained in the form of interstellar dust, linked together by an umbilical cord. Of course, it was hard to determine how the universe had actually come into being, but it wasn't as hard to unravel the way it had evolved. But it was possible that the so-called angels might originate from collapsed stars, inside which time would have come to an end, although the light of the stars in question would not have been destroyed, even though they were dead: it was possible that their light might continue to function, having been pulverized and enclosed in a gravitational field. And having come this far, you could not help but conclude that it was a matter of black holes. Not just one black hole, but lots of them. The boundaries of black holes have always been difficult to trace and precisely for this reason, when lots of black holes had the opportunity to merge, their energy could produce inconceivable things, including a new temporal dimension: thus, time did not disappear, but was propelled and propagated differently. And thanks to the non-disappearance of time and the information stored therein, all kinds of things and events might have come into being, such as new, quasi-human life forms and types of intelligence. But then was not the risk that the three strangers might be precisely what nobody wanted them to be, i.e. extra-terrestrials? Not at all, decided the mathematicians and physicists of the Homeland in unanimity. All human beings are quanta of energy, and the three envoys (no matter whence they may have come, fallen, plunged, slid, etc.) were no different. Their muteness did not necessarily point to an extra-terrestrial dimension, but was relative. Then, it was already known all too well that black holes were only partly black, inasmuch as their matter might emerge and be transferred to other structures. Naturally, not all the universe was made up of black holes, but the scope of such structures was, in terms of their energy and substance, of such a nature as to give rise to hope rather than despair. The scientists of the Metropolis were excited: if their theory were accepted by the President and the Government, then their discovery would be illuminating, and the angels would be decreed to be intense and innovative forms of energy and living matter. But not extra-terrestrials! This simple and elegant explanation, at odds with the convoluted times, was not to be abandoned! The mathematicians and physicists did not even need the three strangers to be present in order to debate the future of humanity: the trio in jeans, tunics and azure cloaks were sooner a pretext for a trenchant scientific discovery. Life was hard, and these angels that were connected to black holes had a beneficial and miraculous purpose of their own, although terms like miraculous ought to be avoided by mathematicians in particular. The physicists and their relatives, the biologists, suspected that the supposed angels might be connected not only to black holes but also the reversal of the greenhouse effect. Like in a fairy tale, the Homeland's illustrious scientists stayed behind closed doors for three days, in an amphitheatre equipped with measuring devices, computers, astronomical telescopes, notebooks, microphones, tape recorders, etc. They scribbled down equations, but these proved to be of not very much use, and so they abandoned them, although at one point they had succeeded, almost in a delirium, in writing an equation as long as an intestine, which caused them to exclaim, protest, quarrel and shout at each other. Perhaps the banished chemists would not have gone amiss after all, since they would have been able to consult them on the matter of molecules, but now it was too late: if they were out for glory, then they had to pursue it by themselves! True, those remaining in the amphitheatre even drew a diagram that ought to have proven why the universe must have not one but many versions of a story. Here, as everybody must admit, regardless of whether he or she is up on cosmic matters, the formula for imaginary time invented by that paralyzed, brainy foreigner on the other side of the world came in very handy, and the members of the Metropolis Academy required no persuading, as they plunged straight in: yes, imaginary time was a bridge between black holes and the descent of the so-called angels. Naturally, nor could the theory of relativity and plenty of other gimmicks be overlooked. But what was at stake was something completely different: if the universe merely existed, without having come into being out of nothing, from the void, then it meant that substantial energies such as the supposed angels also merely existed, and it was only civilization and our Christian perceptions that made us class them, falsely, as supernatural. Let it be clear, the mathematicians and physicists of the illustrious commission did not necessarily believe in God, but nor could they be said to be one-hundred-per cent atheists: they belonged to the sect of opportunistic relativists and probabilists. At one point, the oldest among them put the question differently, irritating and inflaming the others, old-timers and whippersnappers alike: what if the suspected angels were part of a gestating time loop, with the mission of being a cocoon for it, conserving its energy until the loop unfolded and flowed to the edges of a black hole, whence they were spat out at random, then descending on our proud capital? Some members of the commission burst out laughing, some were set to thinking, and some, the majority, saw red, given that the one thing that was clear to everybody was that the angels hadn't landed in the Metropolis at random! For, it was known that black holes capture light, but what exactly goes on inside a black hole is not known. Just as multiple universes might exist in parallel, so too might multiple black holes function in parallel, creating a corridor of energy that might have sucked in lots of things, let's call them things, without them being able to get out again except following a gravitational collapse. Nevertheless, black holes were merely partial prisons: information did not completely disappear inside them; there might also be leaks, but these leaks could only materialize in parallel universes. The oldest member of the commission then went back to his obsession: might not the three envoys originate from parallel universes, where fragmentary information leaking from black holes might be reassembled? This was an eminently cosmic fact and excluded any extra-terrestrial origin on the angels' part! One of the physicists came up with another idea: the angels might have the same energetic consistency as stars, with the principle of collapse also being functional in their case. But as plenty of people know, the universe either expands or contracts: if the angels, possessing the same kind of energy as stars, depend on such cosmic motions, then it means that they too are either expanding or contracting. Except that as far as they were concerned expansion or contraction would translate as follows: in terms of their visibility or invisibility, their descent to earth or conservation of an energy akin to the stellar substance up there in the sky. This new hypothesis, coming from the lips of the rebel physicist, awakened fresh envy. The big bang, stellar collapse, black holes, oh dear: the Academy removed its protective hand from the shoulders of the commission of mathematicians and physicists (the chemists, as we have already mentioned, having been banished), dissolving it as a matter of urgency after three days of torturous debate in the amphitheatre. It was about time too, the commission not having reached any valid conclusion. It was incapable of defining what exactly the angels were. The members of the commission had voted in every possible opposing way and no stable verdict had been forthcoming. Scientifically stable or mentally stable? Nobody knew. The only thing that remained valid was the uncertainty principle of quantum mechanics. But what if the angels did have something to do with black holes? Nobody had thought of that.

THE MIDGET AND HER TOYS

The Metropolis was by no means languishing in torpor and slumber, however: somewhere, a woman tiny in stature, but gargantuan in ambition, was already hatching a plan whereby to capture the minds of the capital's littlest inhabitants. The woman was nicknamed the Midget and she turned out to be nothing more or less than the director of a chain of toy factories. And this chain, as may easily be divined, went by the modified name of Midgling. The minuscule woman could already feel a pang in her brain at the piles of money she was convinced she was going to make: t-shirts depicting the angels' mugs, footballs, sunglasses, baseball caps, plastic handbags for little girls, bicycles, stickers, and so on. But more than anything else, the Midget was already thinking of a project for matching dolls, brother deliverers, three in number, whose story would make them meet Barbie and, at a pinch, her male counterpart, Ken, although the latter would have to be slightly diabolized. Success would be guaranteed. Obviously, the three brothers would have to be quite muscular, martial artists and maybe even into cinematographic interstellar battles, which would suit the taste of children not only from the Metropolis, but also children throughout the Homeland. The Midget also had in mind a slideshow featuring the three angels, to be shown in the main window of the central toyshop, where prospective purchasers would be able to play with the dolls in question at leisure. The diminutive but ambitious woman had recorded all the speeches about the three newcomers: she knew that there was a risk that they might not be angels or might only be half- or quarter-angels. But the one-hundred-per-cent reality did not matter, only the realism and lifelikeness. For her, as manager of Midgling Industries, it was manna from heaven: manipulation gave her a huge thrill, it incited her to be not only a woman, but a superwoman, a giant, an amazon, even a Walkyrie. It is not hard to guess that the Midget, in her childhood and thereafter, had read everything there was to be read on the subject: she had realized that her life had to unfold strictly for little people, not for big people, and so she had decided to become a specialist even before she left school. She had then taken advanced courses in advertising; she had worked her fingers to the bone to make a name for herself and to prevail, always teetering on very high heels to make up for her fairy-tale stature. Some teased her by calling her Thimbelina, a nickname that infuriated her. She preferred to be called the

Midget: in that name there was a kind of dignity and grandeur and it suited her sense of herself as a harsh and hard-to-satisfy mistress. After she became the owner of the Metropolis's toy industry she gave up wearing high heels: she was coquettish, always dressed in a tailored suit, made up like a doll, but she no longer risked breaking her neck by teetering on high heels, because she no longer had to prove anything to anybody. And now the arrival of the three strangers, which had stirred up the populace, the Government, the President, the Academy, the Police and many other authorities that had not yet had their say (but were going to), had prompted her to take action. She was hardly going to sit twiddling her thumbs and let such a challenge pass by! She did not even need to see the three strangers with her own eyes; what she had discovered here and there, from the speeches, was enough, because her imagination was without limits or obstacles. After all, it was thanks to her imagination that she had survived and forged a career; and not just any kind of career, but one that was meteoric: she was envied even by the tallest top models of the Metropolis, blondes almost seven feet tall, and it was rumored that even the country's first lady was jealous of her success. The Midget had no intention of dyeing her hair: she was a fiery brunette, which is why she used bright red lipstick, to create a startling contrast. As for the supposed angels, she was rather disappointed that they had chestnut-brown hair tied in a ponytail, but there was nothing she could do about that, those were the facts of the case and she would have to employ her genius at improvisation, to captivate the tots she craved to bewitch. Inasmuch as she lived only for this: to delight the little people to whom she felt akin, at least thanks to her diminutive height. She set about researching tales about angels, she even reread the Bible, she made notes, and she compiled file cards: once only had three individuals, natural-born angels, ever appeared all at the same time. She was convinced that the newcomers to the Metropolis could only be triplets, regardless of whether they had been sent by Who Knows Who or had been born of some flesh and blood woman. This is what that diminutive woman liked to call God: Who Knows Who. She didn't necessarily believe in Who Knows Who, but nor did she necessarily disbelieve: sometimes it was not a bad thing to believe in such risky things. But for her, Who Knows Who was gigantic in stature, and that annoyed her terribly. And then, all of a sudden, precisely because she was thinking intensely of how she might make the three triplet angels intelligible, the

Midget realized that she must also, almost inevitably, think of a doll to represent Who Knows Who. She rejected the likeness of a white-bearded patriarch: by no means. Who Knows Who would have to be a midget compared with the three angels that had descended to the Metropolis! Yes, she was a genius: she was a visionary, that diminutive heroine of ours! At least that was what she thought. Who Knows Who might even be the Midgling! Then, she rummaged in her mind to select the material from which the threefold doll might be manufactured: plastic, glass or rubber? Better rubber, so that the angels would be elastic, springy and likeable. Their faces would be grave, that was only natural, but their bodies could be flexible, like a contortionist's, especially given the angels didn't have wings! In that way their bodies could function like jack-in-the-boxes, like merry spinning tops. The three strangers were mute, true, as was plain from the official speeches, but the diminutive woman was already thinking of housing a recording in their rubber bellies, a recording that would imitate the flutter of angels' wings. She didn't quite know what the fluttering of cherubim's and seraphim's wings might sound like, but that could easily be solved, if her imagination was up to the task, because anything in the whole world can be imitated. And so the Midget foresaw that her magnificent toys would not have bodies plain and simple, but bodies covered with feathers, even if they did not have wings. That would be the cunning solution to the dilemma of the three strangers' angelic origin. But what kind of feathers should she glue to the rubber bodies: hen's, duck's, goose's, swan's, eagle's, raven's, crow's, dove's, sparrow's, turtle dove's? The tiny woman opted for sparrow's feathers, which seemed the most practical and realistic: sparrows could be found in every yard. She herself put together a mock-up of the intended slideshow, as well as a prototype for the angel-doll, although she still had one matter to resolve: whether they would be male, hermaphrodite or androgynous. The Midget decided that they would be of every kind, i.e. male, hermaphrodite and androgynous: the factory would produce three series of angel-dolls, the first being males, the second hermaphrodites and the third androgynes. She wasn't interested in the angels' sex: tots didn't think about stuff like that, and the owner of the Midgling chain was almost wholly indifferent to the matter. But as a manager she had to be shrewd and efficient, and the three series of angels met every taste. She had no intention of putting angelesses on the market, as that would have been fatal. A female-sex angel on the market would have caused dissatisfaction in the minds of the children, as well as in the minds of the grown-ups. Ultimately, the Midget did not rule out that parents sometimes played with their tots, and consequently would play with angel-dolls. The last thing she came up with that evening, night and morning, during which she was het up in her striving to excel, was the turnover and number of products. The turnover that resulted from her basic calculations was huge, and the number of angel-dolls was projected to be in the millions. Even if angel-dolls remained in stock, they could still be put to good use: she would donate the unsold leftovers to the homeless and to orphans. The former would use them as fuel for their fires, and the latter might, perhaps, find in the dolls substitutes for what they had never possessed and could never possess.

KYRIE ELEISON: THE PATRIARCH TOILS FRUITLESSLY

Within the Fortress of old Metropolis, the Patriarch and his advisers were worried and pale-faced as they waited, sunk deep in velvet armchairs in the office of the primate of the local Church: what was to be done about the torturous and unprecedented situation in which they found themselves? The Patriarch had sent a spy to the interrogation of the three strangers, but the spy in question had not managed to gain any enlightenment as to the origin of the invaders. But as the whole population knew and suspected, the Patriarch had to make a statement, to react, at the very least to elucidate whether the strangers were angels or not. Of course, a commission of theologians with erudite and lucid minds had already been convened as a matter of urgency, just as the authorities had hastily convened commissions of their own in order to unearth the truth. But as he waited for the aforesaid theological commission to give its verdict, the Patriarch sat chatting nervously with his inner circle. He kneaded his hands like a helpless old man, and indeed he was an old man: he had notched up around one hundred years. He would have liked to die in peace and not to have had the ill-fated arrival of the three strangers turn up out of the blue in his dotage, but there was no turning back now. He had to make a speech; he had to issue his blessing or his anathema. And he had no appetite, no appetite at all, either for the one or the other. His advisers gazed at him pityingly: a great burden had indeed landed on the Patriarch's shoulders. The Patriarch was being tested by Who Knows Who (as the owner Metropolis's toy factories called Him). And so the Patriarch was a kind of Job in the present situation. My dears, we all know that angels are what they are, messengers of the divine hypostases, warriors against the creatures of darkness, and wardens of the tollbooths of the afterlife. We know equally well what humans are: creatures fallen into sin. And best of all we know what God is. Thus began the Patriarch, reluctantly, to address his advisers. Angels are creatures with souls, but without matter, who intensively and willingly participate in God's work, whence the question: can angels exist independently of the will of God? Can self-contained angels exist? They do not exist, my dears. Inasmuch as angels are celestial creatures to whom God closely reveals Himself, allowing Himself mysteriously to be known to them. Angels are guides and rescue erring man, they rescue him from the unholy, leading in the paths of the truth. But above all angels are gifted with being able to mediate divine visions and revelations, but only for holy men. It is they who mediate between God and man; they are the energies whereby men learn the meaning of contemplation. They are God's heavenly army. They announce the holy and redeeming order. To my mind, we do not necessarily need to examine whence the name angel originates, but only the content of the fundamental term. The heavenly order says that angels are what they are, in the likeness of God. Let us avoid confusion and not seek any other rationale than the root of the powers of which we now speak, as they are superior beings. And we may say one thing with our hands on our hearts: angels are abundantly divine in origin, they come from the Almighty, they are complete and perfect. Wherefore let us not oppose them, let us never deny or contest them. Sublime is the divine mystery and hard to fathom! And so too the angels, who are the first servants of the Almighty. Let us therefore bring our spiritual eye to rest upon these spirits and through them proceed with our life upon this earth, without seeking any final explanations, because there is no absurdity in perceiving angels, even if there be contradictions in our own souls with regard to them. But the variety of angels also bears witness to this fact: for, these creatures are of both fire and air, and both the one and the other are equally endowed by God, and their power is that they transform something into something else, a man into a different kind of man. The angels resemble the human species; they have eyes, nostrils, ears and mouths, they have eyebrows and eyelashes, they have teeth and arms and hands and legs and feet and trunks, and they are usually garbed in luminous raiment. And they also have girdles and staffs and lances and sometimes they appear in the form of a lion, bull or eagle. And as is known all too well, angels have wings, or rather, these are the legs whereby they fly up and then down, when they have business among mankind. But their wings are not heavy, just as they themselves are not heavy, and they weigh almost nothing, inasmuch as God has endowed them with lightness and with disobedience to gravity and gravitational fields, as they fly swiftly and outside time. And then it is known too that they are golden, silvery or brazen; or else they are colored like the rainbow, like topaz or emerald; but this is more complicated to explain, and so I shall leave it for another time. The last and most important thing of all is that they bring joy and happiness. Thus concluded the Patriarch his supposed meditation on the angels in front of his astonished advisers: for, he had done nothing more than to summarize and belabor the well-known Pseudo-Areopagite of antiquity. The Patriarchs words were actually lengthier and more higgledy-piggledy than that, but we have decided to shorten the linguistic manifestation of his anguish regarding the coming of the three strangers. And so things were as tangled as could be: not even the Patriarch could find any answer regarding the three who had descended upon and to the Metropolis. And the guile and dilemma were all the greater given that the Pontifex Maximus in Rome had sent prying messengers of his own, who were due in the Homeland and Metropolis on a working visit. When then was to be done? Three, yes, three cardinals were about to arrive in the capacity of emissaries extraordinary from the Vatican, for a privy audience with the Patriarch and his advisers. What could they want?

AT THE SPITTED TAVERN

Obviously, the authorities were the most entitled to elucidate the arrival of the three mysterious strangers, because they and only they could legitimately give a precise, rigorous and coherent speech. But things don't always work out like that and they don't only depend on smart-arsed official voices. For which reason, a convoluted reality often seems easier to untangle in unofficial, even marginal circles, where it is not prophets and theologians and politicians that drive the debate, nor even scientists, but rather pariahs, whose portion is leftovers and castoffs, wind and rain, homelessness and inadequate nutrition. What I have been trying to get at in this un-rhetorical toing-and-froing is that not only the centre of the Homeland and the Metropolis was meditating atrociously on the still-sealed secret of the three supposed angels, but also the periphery, the broad and welcoming periphery wherein had taken shelter all kinds of individuals whose tongues were well able to wag in their mouths. And the place in question was a huge covered market, which the new inter-millennial times had converted into a tavern with countless nooks, sufficient to accommodate at least a quarter of the Metropolis's habitual drinkers. And that place was known, in both the official and the unofficial parlance, as *At the Spitted Tavern*, even if the name made no sense, given that it is, after all, impossible to place or imagine a tavern on a spit. And what was consumed most avidly at the so-called *Spitted Tavern* was the beverage most approved by the authorities, one able to satisfy every tippler forever and ever: rum, strong, dry, highly aromatic, deep brown rum, which loosened the tongue and manufactured fervent, combative speakers, capable of debating every burning issue of our sinful world, at least intermittently. Hic, hic went the official refrain of all the mouths in the *Spitted Tavern*, hic, hic, and thrice hic, may the Lord bless all the hiccupers and hawkers versed in the ways of rum, for many were the things that liquor soothed and many were the things it engendered in the minds of creatures maligned or quite simply desirous that they might be heard and that they might infinitely give voice, for the world was so full of failures and faux failures that it was hard to tell them apart: and with rum inside them, they all looked the same. But why should we not be open and admit that perhaps the marginalized more than anybody else might be able to come up with the perfect theory about the angels? Quite so! Why should we not give them a chance? For which reason let us proceed to listen to the voice of the tipsier among us. Well, yes, everybody knows they're angels, but nobody's ever seen 'em, a voice burst out, albeit not out of the blue, a voice that seemingly incited to rebellion. Let us call him Drunkard One. I've travelled the length and breadth of this here Homeland and I know the Metropolis like I know the inside of me own pockets, but never yet have I seen an angel, including any that fell from the sky, and that I swear on the holy relics of my patron saint! I've never yet found myself in the company of angels, although I've visited every watering hole and drank whole oceans, and as for imagination, that's the one thing you can't say I don't possess in abundance. But whether they've passed me by or whether I haven't been able to spot 'em, I can say with me hand on me heart that I don't believe angels could be anti-human. What do you mean? interposed another drunkard, whom we shall hereafter name Drunkard Two. Nobody said anything about anti-humanism, where did you come up with that, man, where did you come up with an idea so daft or, to put it another way, an idea so outlandish? Hic, hic, I agree that we can't discuss it in ethical terms, because angels are beyond morality: whoever sees 'em and if he does see 'em will be crying his eyes out, more like, with tears of gratitude. Sometimes the man who sees 'em will be overwhelmed with pride, and that's worse, a harder burden to bear. Give it a rest with your anti-humanism, it hasn't got anything to do with how the traffic cop tells the driver to take a left or a right! When and if you see angels you can go whatever direction you like. But you'll barely be able to keep your legs under you, let me be clear about that. Not at all, said Drunkard One, making a strong comeback: leglessness doesn't come from seeing angels, but from a hangover and the misfortunes of a hangover, because after all that rum, the liver is knackered! Maybe the nerves are knackered, especially if we're talking about delicate creatures, interrupted Drunkard Two. You can turn left and right at the same time, interposed another rum-drinker, whom we shall name Drunkard Three. It's all vanity, vanity of vanities, listen to the words of Ecclesiastes! We're listening, why not, we've listened, said Drunkard Two: but if an angel were ever to show himself to you in a crowd or even right here in this tavern, what would you do? I don't know and it's not very clear to me right now what I'd do, said Drunkard Three. I'd cling to him, confessed Drunkard One. Just like that: I'd mount him, let him carry me on his back for a while, because that's the only way they can be angels, by helping people in their misfortune.

Not a bit of it, Drunkard Four, who was also on the ball, declared: don't mix up the self-contained, the independent angels with vast missions, don't mix them up with the guardian angels. The second kind are vagabonds, but more tangible; you can catch them with a bit of effort. But the others, the pure angels, are untouchable: you can see them, but you can't touch them. They don't even have internal organs, opined Drunkard Five: they're made of non-human stuff. And what's more, angels are always singing: the guardian ones don't sing very much. They don't even dance. And they don't go to the pub. So, don't start getting a taste for what you can't have or touch. What's that, is one of the jabbering wise men of this here tavern of ours trying to say that angels are superhuman? Merciful Lord, do not forsake us, forsake us sinners not! But, said Drunkard Four, casting himself into the vortex of words: I say it's a natural reaction when confronted with a vision of an angel to curl up into a little ball and try to vanish as quickly as you can, as a way of making sure you're still in your right mind. In other words, better not to utter a word, not to lose your senses, even if you don't make the sign of the cross, and maybe even to have a quick drink, so that you'll be able to go on living as before. Let's not exaggerate and let's not gloss over the situation, interposed Drunkard One, the initiator of the discussion, holding an earthenware mug of rum. There's no point starting a fight about it or breaking glasses. A few backhanders wouldn't go amiss, but without breaking any furniture or heads. And so step aside brawlers, this is a serious discussion. There's no room here for drunken disgust and puke, even if that's exactly what we are. If the whole world were pampered by angels, where would we end up? Above all else, there'd be no more heroism. Then there'd be no more hope or despair. No infamy. I'm sick of cunning words and hidden meanings, burst out Drunkard Three. And I'm ashamed to have to say it, but that's the way things stand: we're ridiculous, all of us. Impotent. I don't intend to hold a moment's silence for my unhappiness, or for anybody else's, but I'm sick of everything and everybody, including angels. Even if you could summon them just by tooting a horn, it still wouldn't be any good. I wouldn't be any good at all. If an angel were like taxi drivers, even a surly one, but still have the speediness of a cab, then how good it would be! But I don't hold out any hope. I don't want to compose any odes or declaim any laudations. I just want to be left in peace and to collect my obol of rum. I'm talking now to all the topers of the *Spitted Tavern*, be they proletarian or not: spit yourselves, brothers, but before you kick the bucket don't forget to put a farthing in the church collection box for all the illusions that can't be refunded. Because lies are not for sale in the shops and you can't get any receipt for what you pay for them. What clarity of thought, chortled Drunkard Two, oho, your majesty, better you give your head a good shake, to get rid of all the whims and fancies. Maybe there exist drunken angels like us and only for us. They'll probably be more primitive and brutal, but maybe there exist greenhorn angels adapted to our needs. But they don't reveal themselves to the unbeliever. Don't be annoyed, brother, but you're down on these angels harder than a policeman's rubber truncheon when he pushes us into a corner and gives us a thrashing if he catches us at dawn after we've finished our ethylic business and are just leaving the tavern. You can't do business with angels, not that's there any need to. With angels you negotiate to a certain extent and that's all: you negotiate what you have to do and you negotiate how not to pay too much for what you have done and didn't do well. There aren't very many great villains, just small and medium villains, and so any negotiation is permissible and realistic. But what is it our souls yearn after and pine for? Look here! you're talking just for the sake of it, butted in a host of other Drunkards. I feel like cursing. I feel like going on a drinking binge for days on end. And I don't even know why. And I feel no shame. But what is transcendence? said Drunkard Six rousing himself from his lethargy. What is transcendence if it isn't the act of distancing yourself from mankind? What is the physiognomy of God and his angels? asked Drunkard Seven, hiccoughing. Why does God insult us by sending us angels, as if we weren't capable of looking after ourselves? Because ultimately, angels are all mixed up. Ineffable, incompatible, undesirable. They're not at all undesirable, roared Drunkard Eight: everybody yearns at least once in his life to make contact with the angels. It's part of the problematics of anthropology, he further prattled. Maybe we're talking too seriously about such things, but let's not leave it up to the national folklore either. Given that angels don't possess a temperament. Yes, that's right, I'm telling you, sozzled citizens of the Metropolis, the individuals in questions don't possess a temperament, even if they do possess character. Angels are unimaginable, but not necessarily utilizable. They are akin to the bird kingdom. To birdies. Or to pussycats. Almost the whole of the *Spitted Tavern* tittered at that. Perhaps angels are parasites. Perhaps that's why we're gossiping about them. That's why we get as drunk as pigs and wake up in the gutter and only after three days are we able to start all over again, banefully giving free rein to our gullets. I say that it all comes down to the original sin, interrupted Drunkard Nine, that's where all the misfortune originates. Life is a whore, as we all know. Our souls are sick. But drink eases and soothes. It allays and pampers. And it's the same with the angels. They're also a kind of strong drink. Heh, heh, heh, and hic, hic, hic, chuckled the sozzlers of the *Spitted Tavern*, at least there's never a dull moment, at least we've got something to talk about, at least we're not all on our lonesome, even if the sadness can't be shaken off. Long live the blessed land of the jabberers! As chance would have it, all the interlocutors, be they failures or not, were the cream of Metropolis's intelligentsia, scribes and painters and singers of rock crossbred with other musical genres, and so even if the matter was not elucidated, at least they had been seen to be busy and to discuss, in a manner that all might understand, the question of the angels temporarily residing in the regions of the Homeland that had broken away from the former empire. And so help us God, said Drunkard Ten, at closing time.

IN THE LOWER WORLDS: PURE MATHEMATICS, EUCLIDEAN GEOMETRY AND CHAMPAGNE

Somewhere in the lower depths of the Metropolis, someone, just who we shall find out presently, a rather omnipotent and influential character, was gleefully rubbing his hands together. Then he stroked his beard, stamped his hooves, and flicked his tail. So what you're saying is this: there's a rumor that some angels have arrived in the area, right? The Devil-in-chief was not particularly swarthy and nor did he glower menacingly, despite his being depicted like that in the classic theology textbooks and in children's coloring books. Tell me, lads, have some puny angels really turned up on our turf? The wee devils fidgeted bashfully, abashed, not knowing what exactly to tell their boss. That's more or less right, one of them ventured to say, avoiding a clear answer. Some puny angels, weirdly dressed and mute to cap it all. He-he-he, chuckled the Devil-in-chief, liking what he heard: if they're mute then they won't be able to give tidings of any miracles. And nor perform any. He-he-he, gone are the days of angelic exploits; nobody believes in revelations and illuminations nowadays. Fortunately, the human race has grown rational and materialistic enough to believe only in two plus two equals four, as distinguished philosopher Descartes put it. Pure mathematics and Euclidean geometry. Well then, well then, said the Devil-in-chief getting back to the matter in hand: and what do the priests of our brave Homeland have to say about it? They haven't really said anything about it, Wee Devilkin made so bold as to mumble. So what you're saying is that they haven't gone out on a limb with a diagnosis! What about the other know-it-alls and everybody else? Well, not even they know what to make of it. What about His Nibs, what does he have to say? the boss asked his underlings, glancing heavenward. He hasn't said anything either, reluctantly said the diminutive page known as Wee Devilkin: if His Nibs sent them into the world, then He sent them and that's that. Take heed, knave of hearts, thundered and fulminated the Devil-in-chief, mind you don't hoodwink me! On my word, said Wee Devilkin, but I wouldn't dare, Highness. And how is it going with the political conniving? Badly, Wee Devilkin went on, because the politicians have no idea what's going on. You mean to say, mused the supreme devil, nobody knows anything, nobody understands anything, and nobody dares define things as they stand? Wholly unsatisfactory, amigos, His Highness went on, in the only earthly tongue said to be angelic (or at least according to some emperor whose name His Highness could not quite recall). Hitherto I haven't heard of anything out of the ordinary, and that is no good at all. Nothing about wings, or feather down, or ascensions, not even a botched ascension. You've got me all confused, amigos, because you've tucked your tails between your legs. I need to have a wee glass of champagne and meditate on the angelic question in peace. What am I supposed to do, muttered the Devil-in-chief to himself, the world is going to hell in a handcart, nobody believes in anything any more, not even I believe in anything, nor do my knaves, nobody in the blessed world! The drunkenness and deformity, the weeping and wailing! Ugh, vanity and infamy and wasted time! There's too much overcrowding in this world, exclaimed the Devil-in-chief, too many things have been going on, and now these puny angels have turned up, those losers, nobody has the faintest idea what they're about, because they don't even have a carryall, a token, a sign. And as for those hominids, it's the same as ever: you can whack them over the head and they still wouldn't get it. The boss broke off the thread of his magisterial thoughts, suddenly remembering the champagne. Am I to understand that you no longer obey my commands, you worthless knaves, you wretched underlings! Bring the champagne, before I give you a good hiding! And French champagne was brought, a bottle of Veuve Cliquot. The boss opened it with his hands, rather than his tail, despite what those with an overactive imagination might have presumed: he uncorked it himself, to make sure none of it would spray out, as usually happened when the champagne was opened by novices. After the first glass, he smacked his lips, after the second likewise, and so on. Do angels take pleasure in sunrises and sunsets? the Devil-in-chief suddenly found himself wondering. What, if anything, do they yearn for? I reckon they're fellows who haven't got sick of life yet. Hmm, yes, the boss loved the word "fellows". The champagne had put him in a good mood and relaxed him: the world was less parched and dry. And so what if the hominids were as thick as two short planks, duh, maybe they were just daft and feather-brained, you at least had to allow them that much. Oho, the Devil-in-chief was a bit tipsy and for that reason, and that reason alone, he asked himself in amusement whether the devils themselves had in their virtual arsenal any angels, swart ones, naturally. Well, are we those angels of darkness or not? the chief asked himself, rather sadly. For, as they say, a devil is not the same thing as death, although he might be.

That's right, said the Devil-in-chief to himself. He might be, but he's not. *Enfin*, said the chief, whom the champagne had Frenchified, it's not appropriate for me to be contentious. On the other hand, I ought to experiment, do a few lab tests: those pantywaists that have turned up in the Metropolis are ripe to be put to the test, and I can't be bothered with contemplation, but rather negation, may I be struck by the apoplexy if I'm not! That last thing he said was just in jest, as there was no question of the Devil-in-chief himself ever being struck down by the apoplexy. His Highness never went berserk. And, nota bene, he was no fraudster, but as sincere and as honest as the day was long: one half of the visible and the invisible world was his and his alone. The other half, duh, could be anybody's at all, even the Heavenly Father's. If angels really do exist, the Devil-in-chief said to himself, it means that the hominids of the Metropolis must be completely stuck-up if they're incapable of recognizing them. And even if they were hauled off and baptized in the waters of the Jordan, they still wouldn't believe it. Something didn't smell right; there was something fishy going on in the Metropolis (yes, all that stuff about there being something rotten in the state of Denmark was stale news!). And don't get me started on the subject of predestination, because I'm not in the mood. But it's true that those losers that dropped down on the Metropolis inspire me, yes, that's the effect: they fill me with inspiration. They could be my muses, for a time, he-he-he, bleated the Devil-in-chief, it's the least they could do, given I'm no fisher of men. But don't let anybody mention the name of Satan, because I can't abide him. Here at my place the darkness isn't all that bad, it's an ordinary kind of darkness, I can't see why everybody has to exaggerate it. The chief knocked back the last drops of the champagne and ruminated once more on the thoughts that had been absorbing him lately. Maybe it wouldn't go amiss to send a few of his cleverer adjuncts to find out what those wretched angels were up to. To get a whiff of them, to find out where they're coming from, as it's clear to me that nobody wants to make any straightforward statement about them. What I need is a clear and honest report, so I can know how things stand. Because if they're well and truly angels, then it's totally unacceptable, and I'll say it again so that you'll get it into your thick skulls: un-ac-cept-a-ble! Wee Devilkin, it's an emergency, listen to my orders: harness up a few adjutants and go and see what's going on with those angels that have descended on the Metropolis. Right away, Your Highness! But there's no need to take anybody with me.

I can manage on my own. He-he-he, chuckled the chief, I knew you were a hard-worker. Get on with it then, lad, and come back with a proper report, because I'm really curious. Wee Devilkin nodded and scarpered in the blink of an eye, taking one of the channels to the surface of the Metropolis. And the Devil-in-chief chuckled: I'll soon see what's what, and if I get into bother, then I'll chuck in the job and retire, I swear. Hmmm, blue tunics and hair tied in ponytails, it doesn't smell good at all, even to me, and I like the stench of sulfur and burning coals. Then, after the knave and the rest of the little devils were gone, he started to come out with all kinds of onomatopoeias in his own inimitable style: beh-heh-heh, crr-crr-crr, slom-slom-slom, and so on.

SOMEONE ALL-KNOWING AND SOMEONE ALL-UNDERSTANDING

Precisely because an expert opinion had to be issued, and given that the Patriarch and his advisers, as we already know, had proven incapable of doing so, they—although it was not at all clear who they were—had set up a commission of expert theologians to provide a verdict and a diagnosis to enlighten the entire population. But this nth commission or committee was to be as exclusive as could be, since it was made up of just two people: the Homeland's most celebrated theologians, both resident within the walls of the Metropolis, as was only natural. One of the famous theologians was known unofficially as the All-Knowing, while the other one was nicknamed the All-Understanding; but as to how they had earned those nicknames or who had dubbed them thus or when, nobody knew, the answers to such questions having been lost in the mists of time. Of course, it was suspected that they had been given those edifying nicknames because of their wisdom. Not the super-celestial origin of the angels is to be the topic, began the All-Knowing, in his thunderous voice: because that relates to perfection. The topic is to be merely which category the three young men in blue tunics belong to: if such they be, are they cherubim, seraphim or archangels? Let it be so, agreed the All-Understanding, in his reedy voice, that is, the second theologian: although, most estimable confrere, we ought also to elucidate the meaning of angels, not only their titles: which is to say, do they flame, are they superabundant in wisdom, are they unswerving, are they subtle? Let us not forget that angels are endowed with the property of cleansing with a purging flame or with roaring water and that they are usually surrounded by rays of light. And nor are their doughtiness and courage at all negligible or to be dismissed. They are neither capricious nor tyrannical, effectuating only that which divine commandment has assigned them to effectuate. And their belts of sapphire, for a part of them is girded with such an accouterment, say much about them, likewise their lances and axes. And brass is their metal of predilection, and then precious stones. Sometimes they ride in chariots of fire; sometimes they go on foot. They set their mark on people's foreheads and even wound them, or they prophesy to them, and many other things they do, and in particular they may snatch the fortunate up to heaven. Colleague, interrupted the All-Knowing just as thunderously: let us move on to more difficult matters, which is to say practical matters, and let us leave theory aside.

Otherwise we might go on for days and we have no time to lose. In our hands lies the answer that the Homeland is waiting for, and so it is no joking matter and nor any occasion for idle chatter. But, interrupted the All-Understanding, his face rather flushed: I was merely laying the groundwork. The ball has been served, the All-Knowing decided on behalf of them both (in private the All-Knowing practiced that sport known as ping pong), and so let us make judgment and issue our statement: are or are not the three strangers angels, regardless of what kind? Well, they're not, said the All-Understanding in a quiet, choked voice: and they are not because they lack something essential, that is, wings. Do not be over-hasty, colleague, the All-Knowing warned and rectified him. There are, as we know all too well, angels that do not have visible, apparent wings, but that does not make them angels any the less. Some might have two, others four, and others six wings. They might also have no wings at all, but it wouldn't be the end of the world. And they might function without them, without the classic accessories, thanks to the fact that, as evidenced by the Holy Scriptures, the angels are by no means few in number, but rather they operate in cohorts, even if only one, two or more descend to a particular place at any given time. Let us not generalize, but rather particularize, the All-Understanding contradicted his collocutor: who and what are the three that have descended to our holy Metropolis and why is it they have come, if they be what they are? Correct, agreed the All-Knowing. Although they had reached agreement, and things ought to have taken a comforting turn, the All-Knowing, known for his Paracelsus-like bent, suddenly began to stray from the subject at hand, following some bizarre logic of his own. The angels are creatures of Him the Most High, wherefore they derive from Him and thus they have the four elementary qualities whence all things originate: that is, they are dry, moist, warm and cold. They are volatile spirits, but also sincere, patient and perseverant, in harmony with Perfection. They cannot be improved, inasmuch as they have already achieved perfection, precisely because they originate from the centre of the heavens, just as humans originate from the centre of the earth. But what is going on here? exploded the All-Understanding, otherwise a mild theologian. Were we asked to form this worthy commission so that we might rant and rave officially? Or so that we might reach a stable verdict whereby we elucidate matters? Colleague, replied the All-Knowing, do not interrupt; hear me out. There are no measurements for angels, inasmuch as they are not repositories of seed, they are not born of one another, but rather they are born of the will and energy of God, wherefore the law of movement does not apply to them. But nonetheless, in them there is a seed of chaos, and this seed is named Archaeus: it is imponderable and often intangible. The prime matter of the angels is rays of sunlight and only secondarily rays of moonlight, this being the reason why angels are masculine rather than feminine. Enough, shouted the slender All-Understanding: I'm dealing with a lunatic here, the All-Knowing is a lunatic who has pulled the wool over everybody's eyes up to now. And having said that, the flushed theologian, the second in the order in which we presented them, quite simply took to his heels, thereby disbanding the nth commission to have been convened with the object of reaching a logical, healthy verdict for the sake of the entire population of the Metropolis and the Homeland. And the doors of the supreme conference room, where the two had been ensconced, slammed shut. The All-Knowing did not break off his speech, however, which had only just got going and was now scintillating and racing at breakneck speed: What is the life of the angels and what might be their death? God is fire, therefore the angels too are creatures of fire, and so when they touch humans it takes place by means of fiery fusion. Only the Son of Knowledge can comprehend such things, because the universal seed of Saturn, Jupiter, Mars, Venus, the Sun and the Moon has endowed him with reason beyond visibility. As for their armor of bronze and the gold they emanate, these most likely belong to Mercury. But are the angels or non-angels that descended to our Metropolis entities of fire? They do not have armor of bronze, their hair is blond, true, but . . . The All-Knowing babbled for another few minutes, and then the helicopter from the Metropolis Emergency Hospital landed nearby and almost an entire platoon of nurses and doctors bundled him away, since it was serious, very serious indeed, if one of the official theologians from the commission of religious experts had lost his mind. A diagnosis was not reached immediately, but everybody suspected that it would go something like this: a prolific panic attack. The All-Knowing had gone insane precisely because he had been a member of the commission in question and precisely because he was required, by official mandate, to declare whether or not the strangers were angels, and if so, what kind of angels they were: seraphim, cherubim or archangels. The human condition is an enigma greater than the angelic condition, said the All-Knowing, in conclusion to his babbling, as we has borne away with feigned gentleness by the nurses and doctors: because God has never doubted His angels, but He has doubted humans, the reason for that being that humans have asked Him awkward, insolent questions, inappropriate, unwarranted questions, for which there was no fitting answer. Humans thus tried to find their own salvation independently of God, and so the hymning angels were no longer of any use, hence their absence on earth. Hallelujah.

THE NOSE AND THE ANGELS

The most famous *nez-parfumeur* of the Metropolis was known as the Uncle and was the son of a French grandmother and a native aristocrat from the capital of the Sacred Homeland. Brought up next to a private magnolia forest on the outskirts of the Metropolis, it is no wonder that the Uncle's nose had achieved an extraordinary refinement even in childhood and that as an adult he was to create the celebrated Metropolitan perfume, as it was called, a perfume used by the capital's most exacting ladies. At the famous dinners lauded as banquets in the celebrity magazines, the exacting ladies perfumed themselves with nothing but Metropolitan, which had revolutionized the art of scents: it was captivating and provocative, it had a hint of mystery, with woody base notes of cedar and sandal, mingling with amber, musk and, above all, oh, above all magnolias cultivated and picked in the foothills of the Himalayas, transported by airplane to the Sacred Homeland and unloaded at the main airport. The reason Metropolitan had cornered the market was also because it conjured up the image of a rather dangerous, dominating enchantress able to intrigue the sharpest masculine spirits. It was a perfume that went well with dark greys, with black or violet and deep green. The capital's women had begun to use it, not only at banquets and galas, but also at interviews for high-powered jobs. One thing was clear: only well-versed temptresses should dab themselves with Metropolitan. True, other expert noses had pronounced that Metropolitan was quite akin to the famous Magie Noire or equally celebrated Opium brands of perfume. The latter was marked by an aroma of jasmine mingled with mandarin, coriander, cedar and above all the incredible and magic taste of ylang-ylang. And it was as explosive as Metropolitan wished to be, full of suspense, adventurous, sophisticated, used especially by tigresses capable of devouring men, of terrifying them, even. Like its admired but also maligned relatives, Metropolitan had to be seasoned with silk or satin dresses that clung to the body, because the effect it strove to produce was one of sparks. The Uncle had been applauded on the open stage, the women of the capital in particular and the women of the Sacred Homeland's high society in general adored him, they had declared him a god, and he felt coddled and spoiled by his adorers. His home was always full of huge bouquets of flowers from his female admirers, women addicted to Metropolitan perfume, who sometimes even drank it in secret. But in time, something strange happened: at the height of his dazzling success, the Uncle became melancholy, the glory disturbed and bored him, his brain was already tortured by another temptation, and what that temptation was we shall see presently. Was it not possible for a perfume more tremendous than the much-lauded Metropolitan to loom on the horizon? A perfume that could truly drive both women and men out of their minds, an ineffable, intangible, invisible, inexpungible, unbeatable perfume. It had already been a year since the Uncle had withdrawn from the world, ruminating and meditating intensely on what he hoped would crystallize as a new universal and cosmopolitan challenge to his parfumeur's nose. Early in the morning he would consume liquors of every kind, and by lunchtime he would be drunk on the glossal aromas that made him believe he was in the very belly of Paradise. He languished in the huge greenhouse where he had planted a miniature forest of magnolias, which reminded him of the ancient matron of his childhood, the essential forest whence everything had originated, his parfumeur's genius and talent and charisma. He had no living relatives, he was unmarried, he had not adopted any orphan child, he was alone with his perfume and the crazed female admirers who unceasingly sent him bouquets of flowers and, lately, boxes of black chocolates and cigars, although the Uncle did not smoke. But under pressure from the media and mystical frenzy surrounding the arrival of the three strangers, the Uncle came up with the idea of creating, oh, what a challenge, the long-awaited perfume, which, it went without saying, would be called *Les Trois Anges*. And thus it was that he came spectacularly back to life, shutting himself up in his laboratory among his test tubes of floral aromas, among his exotic tree barks, among his chemicals and essential oils. However, there was something else that the Uncle required for his *Les Trois Anges*, without which it would not be able to become the perfume of not only the century but also the millennium: he required a piece, no matter how small, be it only a flake, of skin from one of the three strangers, for a true, alchemical perfume cannot be complete without that something. The Uncle, the same as everybody else, had already learned that the strangers' DNA was rather odd, albeit not extra-terrestrial or anything other than humanoid. And he also knew how hard it would be to obtain even so much as a cuticle from the finger of one of the supposed angels, supposing any of them was in the habit of biting his fingernails. The famous parfumeur could get his hands on a cuticle later, but what mattered now was the floral and chemical base of *Les Trois Anges*. And so the Uncle set to work sampling and testing aromas, coaching scents, enriching and rarefying streaks of heavier odors. For the time being, the one thing he knew for sure was how *Les Trois Anges* would be packaged: the perfume bottle would have to be azure and shaped like a single wing, with the tips of its feathers splayed. But what if the strangers who had descended upon the Metropolis did not have wings? The thought did not daunt him at all; it was no obstacle for such an exceptional, magisterial nez-parfumeur. There wasn't even any need for two wings: one was sufficient for the iridescent bottle that was to contain the ambrosia named *Les Trois Anges*. The carousel or carnival of aromas excited him intensely: he was truly like a god; his nose was in fact an omnipotent and solitary sex, which needed nothing more than aromas. And now, yes, this was the challenge, if he were able to manufacture the precious liquid, would he not be a self-contained Demiurge? Does not God send His angels among humans? So too the perfume *Les Trois Anges* was to be sent into the world, among mortal men and mortal women, the translucent creation of that nose of genius known as the Uncle. He had to isolate each of the scents, to hybridize them, to adapt them, and to engender the scent of all scents, the sole inexpungible scent of paradise. No sooner said than done. The alchemy was to last for days on end, and so all that remains for the storyteller in the shadows to do is to condense the history of the invention and manufacture of the much-desired perfume. What the Uncle selected first of all was wild lily, which even King Solomon had praised: but this was not just any kind of lily, but a lily-tuberose, crossed with iris and capable of lending a velvety texture to the hard, biting scent. The Uncle knew all too well what sounds the aroma would provoke—sighs of nostalgia and moans in the shadows. It was a formidable, engrossing, persistent scent. Then he chose lemon flower, with its sharp, acidic harshness: this was the scent of a pungent mystic harmony. Then he selected haughty hyacinths, whose scent penetrates the very throat, whether it be inhaled from near or afar. The aromas he had already conjured up he augmented with a waft of peach, as this was the aureole required by such a consecrated cocktail. The gentleness of lilies-of-the-valley could not be omitted: the sigh of such a scent was sharp in its languor. A flat note had to be added, however, and so the Uncle added a vaguely piquant hint of basil, as much as a transparent fibril of down from an angel's wing. What the celebrated parfumeur was looking for was a muted, secret sensuality, nothing blatant, given that angels are sexless. He then admixed a partial aroma of magnolias (it went without saying) and plum flowers, and a glancing effluvium of white freesia, the alloy in question being suited to creatures that link heaven and earth. He employed mimosas as scented pigmentation, as it were, like false freckles on a lady's face. Blue poppy was likewise required, but only a slight nudge, nothing more, as it was exotic and ravishing. The same as in the case of the legendary Chanel No. 5, the Uncle knew how to use linked aldehydes to lend roundness to the scent and an etheric breath. And to do that you had to be a genuine master chemist. He trod softly with minor mixtures of amber, musk and frankincense, and did not forget to call bashfully upon sandalwood, and also the controversial ylang-ylang, in atomized rather than lethal doses. Oh, and he also required the merest cuticle from the sacred flesh of the supposed angels, and then the perfume would be ready. Phenomenal, exclaimed the Uncle. Abyssal! Magisterial! Godly! he did not flinch from crying aloud all alone in his laboratory. I shall be the emperor of all noses. I shall.

NUMSISFANGLINDTRIN

Leaning over his desk, with dozens of slips of paper covered in old words written in spirals and snaking twists, inscribed in all kinds of sophisticated inks, the famous Linguist of the Metropolis was tinkering with an unknown language. Thitherto he had studied dead languages, being particularly preoccupied with Cyclotimic Caldaean. He had also studied tripartite Spanish, given that there was a suspicion that it might be a remnant of the language of angels, as the private secretaries of the former emperors were wont to gossip. But not a bit of it: he had not reached any major or even minor result. He had even visited orphanages for retarded children, hoping that he might be able to intuit a divine language in the garbled speech of the mentally deficient, since in the world of men there were no creatures more seraphic. The linguist was renowned and had Sanskrit and Hebrew at his fingertips, ancient Greek was a bagatelle, hieroglyphics were as easy as playing skittles, and he juggled Japanese as easily as he did Chinese. He even knew the language of the Eskimos, and he was reasonably competent at deciphering the scripts of the Aztecs and Incas. Modern languages were chaff to him; he only felt at home among ancient tongues, with the exception of Spanish, a weakness he had picked up from *Don Quixote*, the only novel he had ever read from cover to cover and which he knew by heart. But all his reverence for ancient languages went down the drain, much to the amazement of the other scholars, when the erudite old man—who in fact was not very old at all, but rather, having reached the age of sixty, at the height of his powers—learned of the descent to Metropolis of the three strangers suspected of being angels. For, the Savant became completely obsessed, fascinated by the thought that this and none other was the moment to discover or, if it came to that, to invent the language of the angels! As far as discovering it went, he knew there was no chance of that, and so all that remained was for him to invent it himself. And then the Savant had a revelation: without any archangel, without any mystic light or fluffy halo, without any thunderous voice, without any highly specialized dictionary! For the first time ever he discovered within himself the word he had been looking for: NUMSISFANGLINDTRIN. But let us try to be scholarly, however, and let us not torture the poor reader or put her up against the wall, killing her with cerebral exertion: NUM was the particle for feminine substantives, SIS for neuter, FAN for masculine, and the ending GLIND was valid for all verbs. Qualifiers would all be accompanied by the prefix TRIN. When we speakglind of Godfan, letglind us not doglind so in the trindeceptive wordssis of trinhuman wisdomnum, but only through the powernum that the Spiritfan has bestowedglind. Letglind us not ventureglind to sayglind something about the trinmysterious Godheadnum that is trinhigher than beingnum, other than that which hasglind beenglind revealedglind to us in the trindivine imagesis. For the trinformless and trinpristine essencenum of trinimmaterial thingssis cannotglind beglind comprehendedglind through trinmaterial thingssis. Godfan isglind trinincomprehensible comprehensionnum. He isglind the essencenum and lifenum and ressurectionnum. And His Powernum isglind the causenum of all the thingssis that existglind. It was obviously a difficult language, a language impossible for ordinary people. And so the Savant decided to simplify it and to create a single letter for each word: M for feminine, N for masculine, S for neuter, RI for adjectives, and G for verbs. Let us then repeat the discourse invented by our Savant. When we speakg of Godn, letg us not dog so in the rideceptive wordss of rihuman wisdomn, but only through the powern that the Spirin has bestowedg. Letg us not venturegto sayg something about the rimysterious Godheadm that is rihigher than beingm, other than that which hasg beeng revealedg to us in the ridivine images. For the riformless and ripristine essencem of riimmaterial thingss cannotg beg comprehendedg through rimaterial thingss. Godn isg riincomprehensible comprehensionm. He isg the essencem and lifem and ressurectionm. And His Powerm isg the causem of all the thingss that existg. No matter how much he would have liked to attach a just one letter in the case of adjectives, he had had no choice but to adjoin an intelligible whole syllable. Yes, in this instance, the language in question had come up against a stumbling block, and that was why what was required was not only the consonant R but also the vowel I, in order to soften the harshness of the transition to the rest of the word. It wasn't great. And nor was it very brilliant. Then, the Savant thought of the one thing he could still do: he thought of the way Don Quixote spoke. The language of angels could only be matte and as slippery as ice. A language caught between light and darkness. But neither God nor the Savant had any business with light. What was also required was darkness, albeit a luminous darkness. Naturally, the strangers captured in the Metropolis had straw-colored hair, but that was not enough. Something else was needed.

And that essential thing was their language. But the supposed angels were mute, and the Savant had forgotten all about that. Although their mouths were functional and they did not suffer from any disease of the throat or tongue, they were mute. Eureka! cried the Savant. The angels, if angels they were, could in no way be mute. They quite simply refused to speak any other language than their own. This is why they had said not a word under interrogation. This is why they had not spoken to the people who had captured them, or even to the girl who had hidden one of them in her house at the edge of Metropolis. Eureka! The language of angels did not have to be invented: it already existed. And in order to discover it, all the Savant had to do was to make the three strangers speak. But what if they were not angels after all?

TEMPTAT AND SERAPHIC CHOCOLATE

As the reader will have been able to realize unaided, the descent to Metropolis of the three strangers had troubled the minds and souls and thoughts of many, from the President to the Government, from State Security to the Patriarch, and so on. Even the taverns, as we have already seen, were swarming with ideas and intuitions. Not to mention the scientists! And the masses were buzzing busily like bees around the city's squares. And so let us be permitted to continue our examination of the general reactions of disturbance, amazement and morbid or healthy fantasy, exploring less-familiar areas. Everybody knows that every self-respecting metropolis, the Metropolis of the Homeland not excepted, has its delicatessens, the most special of which are the chocolateries. Well, in Metropolis that place was called Temptat. Nobody knew where the name in question had originated, but the suspicion was that it was short for temptation. The owner of Temptat was unfortunately also the leader of an execrable political party, but only he had had the money required for such an investment. On the other hand, the chocolatier-in-chief of Temptat, a true genius, was a mild, slender gentleman with a pleasing bald patch, a hooked nose, and, not least, studious-looking spectacles. He had proven to be not only an expert in chocolate of every variety, but also a man of erudition. He was nicknamed Chocolax, thanks to his bonhomie, inasmuch as he resembled, like it or not, a cartoon character. Perhaps the lady or gentleman reader will divine what I am about to say next: Chocolax, worthy scholar that he was, on hearing the astounding news about the presence of the three strangers in the Metropolis, immediately rummaged through his famous library in search of that late-mediaeval treatise that discussed the theology of chocolate. Quite simply, he recalled that treatise only now, quite suddenly, after the arrival of the supposed angels. It was a treatise written in Latin, sponsored by none other than the Inquisition, which sorrowfully pronounced that chocolate might represent a vice transplanted into Europe from across the Ocean, from the faraway Americas. That the Church should be prudent in regard to chocolate, particularly during fasts, even if pregnant women and brainless children and oldsters in their second childhood craved the stuff immoderately. But let us not invent words and sentences so lightly, but rather let us quote with assurance, for in the treatise in question may be found the following: *unless this brown matter come from God Above, and we unworthy mortals are not capable of discerning such substances sent to us by some channel obscure*. Yes, that it what it said in the famous treatise. Chocolax was convinced that the said channel obscure, a channel paradisiacal rather than infernal or cursed, was named chocolate. For which reason he smiled all-knowingly and at the same time cryptically. To him, the art of chocolate had always been a challenge, a goad towards knowledge of both this world and, at a pinch, the next. Perhaps there was something heretical in the belief and intuition, but Chocolax sensed that things were otherwise and that is why he had become a chocolatier, an unusual métier not to be found on every street corner. He was a specialist in every kind of chocolate, particularly those kinds mixed with dried fruits: but only now did he sense that the day had arrived when his mastery would be put to the test, thanks to the three strange messengers who had descended upon the Metropolis. Yes, he interpreted their coming as a special sign to him alone, a sign made by somebody or other, by a metaphysical or perhaps pataphysical entity. Or else, why not, it was merely a mysterious sign and nothing more, like so many other things in this world, but for Chocolax it was sufficient: he had divined that it would be fitting for him to manufacture a new chocolate, which would be named precisely that—Angelus! And so there was no turning back, he was obligated to create a new aroma, a new flavor of chocolate. Not in order that he might become more famous than he already was, but in order to pay homage to the three that were suspected of sundry things, including angelhood. In any event, Chocolax was firmly convinced that the trio with the azure tunics had quite a lot in common with the angelic hypostasis. And the fact that they had no wings in no way counted against them: I hope you heard well, estimable readers—it counted not at all! And so the master chocolatier hastily retreated to his laboratory, where dried fruits from all four corners of the world lay sliced and cubed in their transparent jars, and the chocolate powder was heaped in huge, fine pyramids on mother-of-pearl trays. Likewise, he brought to bear the herbs and spices with which he had always laced his confections in varying doses: pepper, chili, mustard, thyme, desiccated pinecone, nutmeg, coriander, juniper, allspice, paprika, and rosemary. He was aware this time that it would have to be different, and so the first blend he selected was one of pepper and pinecone. Then he added a few mustard seeds and some nutmeg. Nor did he forget to sprinkle in a little acacia honey. But the most important ingredient of all was yet to come: the brown nucleus of chocolate filtered through creamy milk. Then he added some diced dried mixurn fruit and powdered apricot stones, mixing it all into a fluid bar of chocolate. He tasted a little. It still needed a little pepper, and perhaps even a few more mustard seeds. The mixture then had to be bronzed in the oven: the aroma of the mixurn fruit rose to the surface, blistering the thick chocolate like crocodile skin. In that quasi-divine mixture, master Chocolax intuited the very substance of the Metropolis itself, his miraculous, depraved and insane city, as well as the coming of the three angels, for now he was sure: the three men in blue tunics were indeed angels. As for the name of the new and enchanting chocolate, in which mixurn and pepper and pinecones and apricot stones and mustard and nutmeg and acacia honey and a mystic hint all intersected, the name had been decided from the very outset: Angelus!

WHY DO ANGELS FALL?

At the Cirkus! At the Cirkus! Thus spoke the fancy posters, which showed the face of a clown with a red wig and eyes made up a vivid blue. The seven-feet-high posters sprawled over every morris column in the centre of the Metropolis. At the Cirkus! At the Cirkus! The circus owner knew perfectly the tricks of advertising and why a circus would never go amiss in a metropolis. For more than twenty years he had been the supreme manager of the Metrocirkus confraternity, during which time he had purchased all kinds of exotic animals from the most unlikely of places: camels from Abyssinia, giraffes from Sudan, crocodiles from Egypt, royal peacocks from India, hippopotamuses from the Ivory Coast, rhinoceroses from the Gabon, gorillas from Tanzania, elephants from Bangladesh, polar bears, penguins, seals and walruses from Alaska, tigers, leopards, lions and jaguars from various famous regions of Africa, giant parrots from Peru, condors from Tierra del Fuego, and cobras and serpents from all over the world. At the Metrocirkus there were also huge aquaria with sharks and whales, as the owner had found tamers even for the sole specimen of great white shark to be found in the former empire. And then, of course, there was also a gallery of freaks: bearded women and women with plaited hair all over their bodies, one-legged men, Siamese twins joined at the head, three-foot dwarfs and eight-feet giants. But up until then the owner of the Metrocirkus had never thought of angels. Taking note of the excitement that was gripping the inhabitants of the Metropolis because of the arrival of the three newcomers and realizing the increase in business he might be able to achieve, Signore Metrocirkus, as he was known, secretly decided to act in such a way as to bring the three putative angels, or at least one of them, to the Cirkus. He did not yet know whether he would have to contact one of the three in person or whether he would be able to send a messenger, let us say his tiger- or his crocodile-tamer. But it was clear that some kind of tamer would have to be sent. Naturally, he would have to settle on a substantial fee and an appropriate contract, even if he were able only to secure the services of a single angel. What ultimately mattered was the advertising! And he would also have to give serious thought to getting a sturdy set of wings for them. They would be made of feathers from northern geese, as these were the most durable and resilient. Resilient to what? the reader might ask. Resilient to falls, because angels fell from the Heavens above quite frequently, as far as Signore Metrocirkus knew. Of course, they or he would have been able to fall onto mattresses, but the professionals at the Cirkus did not countenance the like: if they fell, then they were either injured or killed; the circus owner did not allow accidental falls. He did not permit errors on the part of any of his acrobats or even his tamers: not one tamer had ever been injured by an animal in his custody. Nevertheless, angels were prone to fall, as this was one of their meanings, and so the wings would have to be thick and dense, to protect them from any serious injury. Signore Metrocirkus quickly summoned one of his wardrobe ladies, the ones who saw to décor and the acrobats' costumes, and described to her the wings he envisaged for his future angel act. In the end he had reached the conclusion that he would only be able to handle a single angel, as hiring all three would create managerial problems. He had plenty of money, but he did not have enough bodyguards to protect the wearers of fake wings from the crush of the crowd: Signore Metrocirkus knew all too well that if he managed to hire one of the suspected angels, the inhabitants of the Metropolis would trample each other underfoot and possibly even kill each other just to get a look at a falling angel or to touch him. But what if none of the three men with the ponytails were interested in the Cirkus? Impossible, decided Signore Metrocirkus. It was impossible, because he alone was aware that in the end the authorities would release the three from the Fortress. There was no way they could keep them in prison, because they were not guilty of anything. Nor could they hold them in the experimental laboratories, because they had examined them already and not been able to find anything deadly or dangerous. They will soon be released, and I shall have to be ready, Signore Metrocirkus said to himself. He pictured a satin costume with blue pearls and lace on the chest and sleeves, and he moaned with pleasure: that was how he craved to garb the contracted angel, because that was how he had imagined his guardian angel must look, the guardian angel he had never had, neither as a child nor as an adult. But what if he could create a guardian angel for himself? Was not that his secret thought? Signore Metrocirkus shed a secret tear and then got a grip on himself, giving an awkward cough: he was the absolute circus owner, he could not allow himself such moments of effusiveness and abandon. But even so, the idea of the guardian angel remained there like a toy sword protruding from the top of his head. Ultimately, if none of the three strangers wished to be hired by the Cirkus, having found some better occupation, then Signore Metrocirkus would still keep the costume for the relative and putative angel and he would still dream his dreams, regardless of his important and highly visible job. Yes, yes, he would still go to sleep alone in his elegant trailer, upholstered in velvet and devilskin, he would still fall asleep embracing that angel costume. But until such an outcome, one not at all to be discounted, there was still a long way to go: it was still possible that one of the three strangers might agree to be hired as the official angel at the Cirkus, which would augment the company's esteem. He would teach him to walk the high wire without a safety net, oh, yes! For that reason, the signore would even be ready to change the company's name to the Flying Cirkus or the Pedestrian of the Upper Air! But were his thoughts themselves not roaming the upper air? Was he not giving away the sparrow in his hand for the crow in the bush? The wisest thing was for him to say what his forebears had said: we shall live and learn. And this is what he did say, muttering it under his breath, like a banker taking advice from a board of invisible directors.

AN UPSET STOMACH AND CHAMOMILE TEA

As I have already announced on a different occasion, the Pontifex Maximus intended to send no fewer than three cardinals to investigate the said delicate angelic matter in the Metropolis. The reader will no doubt recall this dangerous announcement. Consequently, the three illustrious messengers, as much messengers as the three they had come to examine, checked into the Metropolis Hotel, the capital's most luxurious, situated near the Fortress, taking secluded suites well guarded by the hotel staff, so that they would not be disturbed by journalists or other prying eyes. The Patriarch and his advisers were promptly informed and warned: the guests had arrived and they were impatient. All-Understanding, the celebrated theologian, was also informed, inasmuch as he alone had remained to man the barricades, since All-Knowing, the other famous theologian, had lost his mind due to causes unknown during a discussion on the topic of the angels, a discussion intended to be providential. And nor did the cardinals sit twiddling their thumbs, but discussed among themselves the questions they were going to ask. In the first place, they intended to demand to be shown the three specimens rumored to have descended from Heaven, although they were convinced that no such thing would happen. And indeed, for such a thing to come to pass was out of keeping with the direction of the times and the situation, for which reason it did not come to pass, despite the insistence of the three cardinals. The Pontifex Maximus was waiting for news as soon as possible: his envoys would have to come back with a firm verdict—otherwise it meant the earthly World would no longer be under control. There were already all kinds of uprisings and rebellions among not only the faithful, but also the priesthood. And the Pontifex Maximus felt responsible: he had discovered that the Muslims were also interested in discovering the origin of the three angels, and the Jews were not sitting idle, but had sent out spies. Even the Hindus were in a ferment of rumor. The whole of Christendom was being put to the test! The Pontifex Maximus asked himself: if they are indeed angels, why did they turn up in the Metropolis of all places? This was the most painful question. And the answer, no matter what it might be, looked just as agonizing. But let us return to the cardinals sojourning in the capital of the Sacred Homeland. They arrayed themselves in their famous red robes and skullcaps. They lightly pomaded themselves, so as not to smell of old age and an exhausting journey. And nor to be redolent of stiff, inflexible theology. Then they set off to the Fortress of the Patriarchate, where they were awaited with trepidation, being conveyed by official limousine. The city's inhabitants lined their route to watch in perturbation, as the entire population had by now learned of the arrival of the envoys of the Pontifex Maximus. After they had been served coffee, dainties and even the local pie, after they had exchanged the customary greetings and wishes for good health and prosperity, the Patriarch invited them into his private office, adjoining his private chapel, where none but the nine bishops he shepherded were waiting, along with the multi-talented theologian known as All-Understanding. His secretary-in-chief was also there, Inkpot, as he was called, which is to say, the man in charge of the Patriarch's inkpot. After they had all finished clearing their throats, the cardinals engaged in the chatter appropriate to such a high occasion. The Pontifex Maximus is highly alarmed at the news that the three said angels have turned up here, said the first cardinal. For, their arrival is much more dangerous and may be far more lethal than if they were not angels. This we already know, agreed the Patriarch, together with the nine bishops. And the secretary-in-chief busily wrote it all down. Can they really be angels? Might we be allowed, with your reverence's permission, to catch a glimpse of them, even if only from afar? asked the second cardinal hesitantly. We do not know what they are, we do not know yet, interposed All-Understanding, we are still examining them, studying them, we shall see. As for catching a glimpse of them, it is impossible, even from afar, as they are for the time being in the custody of the Sacred Homeland and the authorities. And what is your verdict? interjected the third cardinal. Given that we must deliver news of the situation to all Christendom. We all know very well, blustered the Patriarch: we may learn the mode of being and the actions of the angels only from the Holy Scriptures, as only therein can we be enlightened. Consequently, we shall have to verify the similarity between the appearance of the three distinguished guests and what there is to be said about angels in the Holy Books. Only in this way shall we be able to understand that which is higher than us. All these things we know, replied the first cardinal. The Pontifex Maximus also knows all these things. How else might we explain angelic reason, given that it is not wholly accessible to us? The learned have no need of such explanations, inasmuch as we are inured and mystical clarity is sufficient. Thus spoke the second cardinal. Mystical clarity? exclaimed All-Understanding. But how initiated are we, and how prepared are we for mystical clarity? In the meanwhile, sensing the tense mood, the secretary-in-chief regarded the others fixedly. The very mystery of ineffable godhood is hard to unravel, added the third cardinal, by way of reconciliation. The lively intelligence of flesh-and-blood creatures such as we ought not to dwell in puzzlement, but to find the appropriate consonance between things, said they, signaling their agreement and inclining their mitered heads. The Patriarch himself then interrupted, saying: it is not permitted to those who know God to identify the angels except solely by means of the angels' likeness with God, or, rather, by means of their imitation of Him Above. Of course, agreed the cardinals, except that their nature and appearance are various. For, there is not only one kind of angel, but many are the kinds. Consequently, it is meet that we ask: of what kind are the three that have revealed themselves in the honorable Metropolis? What kind? Not even we ourselves know, stated the All-Understanding. We have not had the perspicacity to be able to discern what kind of angels they might be, because, I repeat for your subtle hearing, we do not yet know whether the newly arrived strangers really be angels or not. But how long might it take before it is possible to determine whether or not they be angels? asked the increasingly impatient and irritated cardinals. Nor do we know this for sure, but we hope that time will be patient with us, answered the All-Understanding. But I do not wish to bore the reader with such insipid dialogues, but rather to tell her only that the two camps dueled with humility, sometimes false humility, for as long as they dueled, they inclined their skullcaps and miters, they muttered, they frowned, they flushed, until the Patriarch brought the proceedings to a close in strangely triumphal wise, as follows: the Tradition of the Holy Books speaks of myriads of angels: perhaps among these myriads might be included those who have just arrived in the Metropolis. One thing is undeniable, namely, we mortals cannot overlook heavenly creatures. Their blessed hosts are numerous, outstripping our human and material numbers, for they are spiritually guided only by the intelligence that transcends earth and heaven, blessedly bestowed upon them by the giver of divine wisdom, by the principle of all things. *Dixi.* That having been said and settled upon, albeit paraphrased from the celebrated theologian Pseudo, and in no wise representing the Patriarch's own words, the cardinals rose to their feet, bowed politely, and made their way out. They were swiftly conveyed to the Hotel Metropolis in the same limousine that had brought them thence. They did not sleep the whole night, but stayed up conferring with each other. The next day, the Patriarchate's special airplane flew them through the upper air to the city where the Pontifex Maximus was awaiting them. The Pontifex Maximus impatiently wiped his spectacles. In conclusion? he asked. Nothing, the trio of cardinals replied in unison. Nothing is known. It is not clear what the individuals are. The Pontifex Maximus heaved a sigh of relief and asked to be served chamomile tea, as a remedy for the upset stomach he had been caused by the so-called angels.

METROPOLFILM AND ANGELIAD

Metropolfilm was the name of the huge film industry that existed in the capital of the Sacred Homeland, as something of the sort had to exist, otherwise what the hell kind of magnificent capital would it have been? The studios were at the edge of the city and housed in dozens of huge hangars, inside which the sets were changed at whirlwind speed depending on which of the hundred films produced there annually was being shot. Of those hundred films, only a dozen were delivered to domestic and foreign audiences, the rest being abandoned during production or their scenes being recycled for subsequent films. The brain of Metropolfilm was a massive magnate with a huge gut and a mafia-style hat, constantly chewing on a cigar: rather predictably, he had been nicknamed the Brain with the Cigar. We shall call him the Brain, to make it quite clear whom we are talking about. The Brain had a number of bodyguards, as he was not only a billionaire, but also mixed up in a series of dodgy businesses, some of which were controlled by none other than State Security: businesses connected with high-class strippers exported over the borders of the former empire, the girls in question being recruited from among the two-bit actresses drawn to Metropolfilm. The Brain himself decided which of them would cause a splash as stripteasers fatales. Metropolfilm produced films of every kind and calibre, from folkloric spectaculars to sci-fi flicks, sentimental dramas, soap operas, detective films, and parapsychological fantasies. For each category there was a commission of advisers specializing in one of those themes. Lately, Metropolfilm had been focusing on big-budget war epics and on recycling sci-fi subjects of universal appeal, in line with what was being produced by rival studios abroad. The Brain had no time to lose, and nor any money to waste: he was looking for guaranteed profits and fat bank accounts, because he had numerous ex-wives to support, plus a swarm of mistresses who harassed him and who had themselves produced a sizeable number of offspring. The Brain regretted with all his heart that God had not created him sexless, or at least sexless enough not to have all those mouths to feed, because all those collateral losses drained him of energy, money, time, and lots of other things. Lately, he had barricaded himself inside his office at Metropolfilm, where he sat up until late at night watching the famous detective and love films of yesteryear. Yes, despite his harshness and his iron fist, the Brain was a secret sentimentalist. And also lately, he had started smoking marijuana mingled with tobacco to help him to forget the multiple troubles he was mixed up in. For the time being, nothing could touch him: the able mercenaries from State Security were on his side, because business was going well. But given that nothing is certain in this world, the Brain often thought about how the future might come crashing down on him like a typhoon and whirl him away, gut and all, even the gut being powerless to resist its blast. In the midst of such a mood of anxiety, which he suffered as a result of gradual intoxication with marijuana, barricaded in his office, the news of the three individuals suspected of being angels reached him. Believe it or not, tears began to trickle down the Brain's cheeks, although he was a man in his fifties. It was as if he had received the news he had been waiting for all his life. It was a sign meant for him, of that he was sure: it was a sign, albeit not necessarily a divine one. Was providence giving him a wink? Let us call it that, so as not to get involved in too many metaphysical convolutions. Providence sounds more neutral. The Brain was overjoyed that something that might change his life had shown up out of the blue. As soon as he discovered the news about the three young strangers, his managerial mind started spinning like a top and flung out the predictable result: yes, he had to invent a serial called *Angeliad*, which would tell the story of the three who had descended upon the Metropolis, as well as the tribulations of the authorities and all the speculations as to their arrival. He thought the idea was a stroke of genius, and so he stayed up all that night, barricaded in his office, smoking another five marijuana cigarettes. Then he began to have visions: in one vision, the three dressed him in a blue tunic like theirs, which had wings inside, or rather wings tamped like thick fur; in another, they carried him away on their backs high above the Metropolis, on a gliding night flight; in another still he merged with one of their bodies, sensing within himself, from head to toe, a fluid, honeyed light. Under the influence of the marijuana and his own needs and frustrations, the Brain was experiencing phantasmagoria, yes, that is the right word for it. But they were happy phantasmagoria, which had a personal charge to them. The serial would have to be conceived and elaborated in high-impact episodes; he himself wished to supervise the script and the filming. And perhaps his life would take a different turn. He wasn't sure, but it was possible. He would have to avoid corny complications. The script would have to be modern, but not ridiculous: that is, without women, wives or suchlike hindrances to the life of the average man; the angels would be angels and nothing more. The Brain delightedly pictured how the Metropolis itself would be encapsulated within one of those vast filming hangars: bathed in a bluish glow, with a starry sky above it, with its massive edifices swathed in colloidal mists after the rain, with swirls of smoke rising from the wood fires crackling in the hearths of the dreamy metropolitans. And happy, enchanted, his mind in the clouds, he fell asleep, his head lolling on his lacquered walnut desk. What the *Angeliad* would turn out to be in reality was already a different story, a completely different story.

A HUNTER OF SHADOWS AND HIS OBSESSIONS

In the sweet Metropolis, sorely tried by the recent quasi-angelic escapades, there dwelled a character strange enough to arouse the attention and interest of those who enjoy rummaging through the multiple layers of humanity: that character was the Hunter of Shadows. Obese, bearded, a great pipe-smoker and ice cream- and pie-eater. Naturally, he measured shadows, because it was at this that he excelled. He sought the shadows of people who were diminutive in stature, then the shadows of twins and of giants, the shadows of the blind and deaf, of the handicapped and the maimed. The shadows of ordinary people did not interest him. He had even got hold of the shadows of hermaphrodites: if anybody might wish to know what such shadows were like, well, they were smooth and clear. The Hunter of Shadows had even discovered the shadows of vampires, despite it being well known that vampires did not possess such a thing. And the shadows of the vampires were knobbly! The Hunter had found them because he was an expert, a professional. But now he was consumed by the thought of finding the shadows of the angels, if indeed the three strangers that had descended upon the Metropolis were angels. What the Hunter had discovered was definite: the strangers were neither androgynous nor hermaphroditic, but men. Being a Hunter of Shadows also meant, implicitly or explicitly, you had to be a bit of a sexologist, that is, one knowledgeable about genital anatomy, otherwise you would not be able to perceive the logic of the shadows. A thoroughbred and eccentric intellectual, the Hunter of Shadows was also something else: a philosopher of alterity. Not a classical or romantic one, but a derailed philosopher of alterity, what else? His home library, conserved in huge jars, contained only tomes of that kind, and the pages of the books in question were scented with myrrh, given that the Hunter of Shadows embalmed them that way, without really knowing why: his few acquaintances used to say that he had been an Egyptian priest in a former life, in other words an expert in mummification. The Hunter gave a strange smile when accused of having Egyptian origins: what he knew for sure was that he had got the idea into his head and acted accordingly, embalming his books. Now the Hunter of Shadows found himself in the position of having to gain a deeper understanding of the angelic question, so that he would be able to capture the angels' shadow effectively. True, he was not interested in capturing or possessing a triple, but rather a single shadow, just the shadow of one angel, any of the three. But what if the angels had no shadow? It was impossible for them not to have a shadow, be it only a halved shadow or a third of a shadow. For, they were ambassadors: that is, intermediaries between something and something else. Consequently, their shadow was necessary inclusively as a bridge between that something and that something else. The Hunter asked himself whether their potential shadows might be left- or right-handed: that is, whether their winged arms were more potent on the left or on the right. It was a stupid question, in fact, but he asked it nonetheless, without arriving at any answer. He did not want to be cunning or a fraud. He merely wanted to be the Hunter of Shadows, because shadows resembled daemons. At this point, the Hunter came to the question that had puzzled him all his life: the daemon. The three strangers had turned up in the Metropolis just when the Hunter had thought he had reached the end of the tunnel with his speculations on alterity, but in fact all along he had not even started the journey, he had not even taken the first step, which is to say, he realized that all along he had been in a kind of zero area, from which the ramifications of his thinking and understanding risked becoming a jungle. For the Hunter, angels in general were not models, but airy outlines and halos. Hence the impossibility of his speculations as to the discovery of an angelic shadow. The Hunter had been late in understanding one thing: angels were warlike, rather than flaccid mollusks. Consequently, their shadow would have to be substantial and impetuous, even if some angels, as the Hunter had read somewhere, flew on their backs, fluttering their wings upwards so as not to show their faces. The Hunter would have liked to measure the shadow of an angel in combat: at least one of God's anonymous angels had wrestled with a man and almost been defeated by that man, which was no mean feat. Perhaps God Himself had wanted that man almost to defeat the angel. What a masterful thing if would be if he were to succeed in capturing the shadow of a wrestling angel! But the times for such specimens were long gone: the three strangers sojourning in the Metropolis were peaceful and mute. It was unclear how harmonious they might be, but that they had proven to be at peace with themselves without their having to speak. As for their chastity, that was plain to see: merely from seeing them paraded on television like high-class villains the Hunter had been able to conclude that their bodies were non-corporeal, despite appearances. He had divined and sensed it precisely because he himself was obese, that is, overly corporeal and fleshy. And he had straightaway intuited the form of the three strangers' non-corporeality: it was elongated, like a dragonfly's. You didn't need to wear panoramic spectacles to be able to see that much, nor even to look through a magnifying glass or a microscope, or to take an X-ray. It was sufficient to be attentive to the strangers' veiled movements, to their smoothly broken fluttering. Their tied-back hair functioned as a fish or reptile tail and provided an accompaniment to their non-corporeality. The Hunter pictured what must be the angels' armor and white pennant: the armor would have to be made of platinum, definitely platinum. Neither silver nor gold. The Hunter of Shadows was not obsessed with the salvation of the soul; it was not for this reason that he wanted to capture the shadow of an angel. But if the angels were profoundly non-corporeal and the Hunter nonetheless managed to capture their shadow, then wouldn't what he had stolen be a kind of consummate soul in fact? That was what hypnotized him, arousing his criminal, but soteriological ambitions. I know it sounds pretentious, but even angels in themselves are pretentious, the same as humans. Especially given that the latter are rumored to be supra- or super-angelic! They are the over-angelhood, as a celebrated mystic once put it. Or over-angelic. The Hunter of Shadows would have got on well with the Linguist of the Metropolis, the man who had invented the formula NUMSISFANGLINDTRIN. But they didn't know each other, although they were twins, as it were, in their new obsession. Ultimately, angels exist only if people believe in them; if they don't believe in them, then logically they don't exist, said the obese Hunter to himself. On this point, the Hunter would have liked to eat some pies, but his plate was empty. I can't think on an empty stomach, our special character said to himself: the mind limps if the body hasn't been fed. Although there were no more pies, the Hunter did find the leftovers of some ice cream in his rather bare refrigerator. It was at least something. It's tricky classifying living creatures: some are immortal, like angels and have a minimal body, others are mortal and have plenty of body and soul, like humans, others have only a body, like animals, and others still are just blades of grass. It's never occurred to me even in my wildest dreams to hunt the shadows of blades of grass, the Hunter said to himself, making a *mea culpa*. But what if angels have an ethereal shadow? Oh, sighed our obese pie-fancier grumpily, then I'll really be in a jam! I ought to have become a shadow-tamer! Ah, *materia prima, materia prima*!

What a leap forward I would have been able to make for the benefit of over-angelhood if only I had had the *materia prima* to hand! Ecstasy, pure ecstasy! Sugar-rich utopias, we might say, if we were able to put ourselves in the sophisticated mind-set of the Hunter. But since we cannot, given that every character is relatively self-contained, then let us see what happened next. The Hunter had an inkling that the three strangers were not only angels, but guardian angels, although things weren't very clear on that score; in any event, he sensed that the challenge couldn't be greater: to capture not only an angel's shadow, but a guardian angel's shadow was his supreme desire. But what is a supreme desire? Do human beings still have the right to yearn like that? The answer was negative, as was only correct, but the Hunter or Shadows got it into his head to be a sophist and to vanquish the difficult question of human fulfillment and non-fulfillment. In the end, the body of an angel, ethereal as it was, resembled the body of a dead man, concentrated in the twenty-eight grams of soul. But let us return to the guardian angel; the Hunter had a presentiment that the strangers might be guides, if not counselors or protectors. And above all, yes, above all, he did not know why or how, he sensed that one of the three that had descended upon the Metropolis might even be his own guardian angel. Even though he was none other than the Hunter of Shadows and a philosopher of alterity, or precisely for that reason. But our labyrinthine character also knew something else: namely, he knew that each human has not only a supposedly nacreous guardian angel, but also a black angel. Heavenly friends and subterranean friends: what if the strangers were of the latter category? Then the Hunter would definitely have to capture their shadow and study it carefully. A dark, somber shadow would have completely transformed his collection of captive shadows. As the theologians of old said, even the Antichrist has an angel. But what if the three strangers together formed a single, as it were three-headed, guardian angel? Hmm, then things would get really complicated. The Hunter also knew one other thing: angels were not immune to suffering; angels too cried when they felt pain or when they witness evil's circus acts. The tears of angels? The Hunter of shadows tugged his beard and exhaled: what if he had become a hunter of tears instead of shadows? A teardrop collector. Difficult work. He recalled a line written by a tortured poet who had died of syphilis: *A misshapen soul in an angel's body*. But the problem was the following: did the angel have a mandate from God to be an intermediary between Him and humans or did he not? Was he an itinerant entity, a pilgrim? What if the guardian angel only revealed himself in the moment of death? As busy as a bee. Palliating. The Hunter of Shadows ruminated on this unusual verb: to palliate, as he had never used it before. Perhaps it would be better to find my own shadow and have done with it: I think I'm going off the rails, the Hunter of Shadows mumbled into his semi-patriarchal beard. It would be the only explanation as to why I'm so desperate to find protectors, shields, guides. In fact I'm a mercenary, my own mercenary in the substance of my alterity, as I have looked at every facet of the question, but I have not thought about the one thing crucial to the condition of angelhood: I have not talked about love. *Man cannot be his own angel*, concluded the obese gentleman, the lover of pies, ice cream and fine tobacco.

BRIEF RECAPITULATION AND ASSESSMENT

The reader will certainly recall that a short swarthy chap named Wee Devilkin had been sent to scour the Metropolis and bring back news of the supposed angels. The Devil-in-chief himself had sent him on this scouring and newsgathering mission so that a report might be drawn up for the Netherworld. And so, zealous and affable, Wee Devilkin set out, but not before deciding upon the most appropriate attire for the job. He hit on it in a fraction of a second: he would be one of the capital's postmen, with a navy blue tunic and velvet peaked cap, and, most importantly, a huge mailbag full of letters and telegrams. Let us be clear and let nobody be deceived: these were letters that had never reached their destination, for various reasons, including censorship, and which Wee Devilkin, thanks to his special talent, had salvaged from the mists of time. First of all, the new postman made a recapitulation: he visited in subtle form, that is, in ethereal and recondite wise, those who had debated the angelic question before the reader discovered that the Devil-in-chief was highly interested in the said question. And so Wee Devilkin plunged into the mind of the President of the Homeland, who had been hitting the bottle ever since the situation destabilized, in despair at not receiving any revelation from the Nation's Political Corps. Then the likeable apprentice of the Devil-in-chief took care to slip inside the minds of the three captains and nine lieutenants from the Ministry of the Interior, who had been investigating the newcomers, but none of them was experiencing any pangs of conscience or disquietude (let us be permitted the use of this word, one that the captains and lieutenants were no doubt unfamiliar with) or any chili peppers inserted in the nether regions. Nor did he overlook the medical specialists from the Department of Experimental Laboratories: here, Wee Devilkin made note of the data regarding the unnatural elongation of the three strangers' brains, the convolution of their DNA, and the things that distinguished them from each other individually, although the differences in question were insignificant: the lack of wisdom teeth in the first, the lack of a kidney in the second, and the strange mole beneath the eye of the third. But it was harder for the crafty apprentice to enter the minds of the crowds that had been swayed by slogans such as Give Us Back Our Angels! and We Want Our Native Angels! Failing in this and in order not to neglect that part of his mission, Wee Devilkin did something different:

he entered the brain of the Slum Philosopher, who wrote demagogic texts for the *People's Gazette* and sniggered at finding what he found in that brain obsessed by a single thing, namely, inner wings. He caught the Chief of Police as he was inspecting the rubber truncheon depository: he was convinced that he would soon be called upon to use them, raining blows upon Metropolitans eager for angels. In the slums at the edge of the capital, the churchgoing old women with their granny spectacles were dreaming of cherubim and seraphim and not even their everyday chores could stem the nocturnal tide. El Leader Maximo, i.e. the President of the Nationalist Party, regaling himself with his wonted glass of brandy, was imagining himself being acclaimed by his compatriots in a stadium where he played the forerunner to the three angels; at the same time, however, El Leader Maximo imagined himself making curt, imperious gestures, whereby he decided the fate of his rebellious fellow citizens, imprisoning them in the Zoo. It was unclear why the said citizens were rebellious, but it may be supposed that they were rebels pure and simple and they had incurred the wrath of El Leader Maximo. As for the head of the Caravan company, he continued to search for a unique angelic advertising slogan, and, being ingenious, he finally hit on it: Communicate. It's easy. An angel, a man. The future sounds good. Wee Devilkin not only chortled, but ended up roaring with laughter: the academicians of the Metropolis in the Commission for Investigation of the Authenticity of the Three Strangers, that is, the mathematicians and physicists, had found a compromise solution: they had lumped together black holes and white holes and come up with grey holes, which were thought to be angelically productive. But none of them was brave enough to launch this conclusion on to the market. As for the Midget, the boss of the toy shop chain, she was fast asleep, perched on top of a mountain of plastic toys depicting identical angels with rustling metal wings. The Patriarch and his advisers, each meditating in his ascetic cell, were each wracked by the same obsession: did self-contained angels exist or not? At the Spitted Tavern, the swarm of boozers were waiting for the big one, id est, the angelic choirs, which they could already hear, as they downed their autochthonous liquor, which is to say, rum. Locked up in the capital's hospice, the theologian nickname All-Knowing refused to say a word, declaring that the angels had forbidden him to do so, while in another room far from the mental hospital, the other theologian, All-Understanding, was wracking his brains as to why he had to live in such tragic times. The celebrated parfumeur, the Uncle, was obsessed only with how to obtain an angel's cuticle, to enable him to conclude the chemical game of concocting a divine lady's perfume. As for the Linguist, he was close to losing his mind completely: for the time being, he was searching for the name of the angelic language, wavering between angelusine, angelusvian and angelese. Master Chocolax was choosing the most appropriate tinfoil in which to wrap the brown matter from God on High, that is, Angelus Chocolate: the tinfoil would have to be purple with flecks of silver. Signore Metrocirkus was already designing the new poster for the Flying Circus, regardless of whether or not he would be able to hire one of the three angels. The Pontifex Maximus and his cardinals had abandoned praying that the individuals with the blue tunics would turn out not to be angels. Enveloped in marijuana smoke, the Brain from Metropolfilm was waiting for the new flyers' crusade that would propel him into the film industry of the soul and spirit, Angelwood. The Hunter of Shadows was languishing in a reverie full of butterfly nets, having augmented his provisions of pies, ice cream, and pipe tobacco. And that was about all. But nonetheless, somewhere not far away, much nearer than one might think, other significant characters were waiting to make their entrance. But as their rôles will not become our raw material just yet, let us relegate them for the time being to invisibility, inaudibility and intangibility. Consequently, having made this thorough recapitulation and reckoning of the metropolitan hominids, Wee Devilkin the postman returned to his master. The Devil-in-chief welcomed him cordially and waggishly: tell me, errant pageboy, how do things stand? Are they any better or any worse? Highness, began the swarthy apprentice, neither the one nor the other: everybody is meditating at full steam, or else smoking at full blast, because the whole lot of them are puzzled. What I mean to say is that they're meditating their arses off. Let the nitwits and the dunderheads meditate all they like, if they've got nothing better to do. We can hardly stop them. What do you say, Wee Devilkin? Why don't we go into a different line of business, branch out? Oh no, Highness, not at all! Here's the only place that is healthy and sound. There's nowhere like here. But, tell me, page, did you see the three, did you touch them, to be able to make up your own mind? That I didn't do, Highness! answered the doughtiest of apprentices. It was the only place I wasn't able to reach. Well, why was that, you foolish weakling? Because I was scared they might really be angels, said Wee Devilkin slowly. The Devil-in-chief was left open-mouthed for a moment, and then he burst into laughter and whipped out his hairy but handsome tail. He clapped his hands: you're a devil of a one, apprentice! Maybe you should have turned yourself into an angel! Not a bit of it, Highness, my place is here, Your Lordship! The Devil-in-chief stopped laughing. He fell silent and presently said: all right, young lad, now let's see to our own affairs, until such time as it will be decided what is with the three individuals. And here he gave his whip-like tail a heavenward flick. Enough! Now to work!

SPEECHES OF SEDUCTION

Things could not be left as they stood, since the times demanded not only a workable dialectic of demand and supply, but also strategies of manipulation to match. El Leader Maximo knew all this, because his adviser had been coaching him all night long, teaching him how to give pro-angelic speeches to seduce the nation. And so, after all the Commissions had had their own sweet way with the supposed angels, El Leader Maximo decided to appear before the Metropolitan people once again, on the For a Brave New Homeland (or Ef-bee-en-aitch) channel. He had to get in his own proclamation to the nation before any of the other parties had a chance. He imbibed a few substantial tots of his customary French brandy, garbed himself in his customary crowd-baiting white suit, and set off to offer his voice and brain to the inhabitants of the Metropolis. Brothers, he began, the future does not sound good, and for this reason it is fitting that we communicate precisely, clearly, and without exaggerated subtleties. We are the next generation, as it's fashionable to say nowadays, but we mustn't imagine that we can get everything we want. Man to man, I tell you that hard times are in store for us, and only the angels will be able to save us from them. That's why we need to experiment on ourselves and live the moment. Why we need to be together for better and for worse, since the key to the world and to life lies within us. The strong essence lies within us and only together will we succeed, only together will we be powerful. The energy lies within us. We have to remove the stains and the dirt from ourselves, to cleanse ourselves inside and out, because what is active on the inside is also visible on the outside. Because we're worth it. Because it's vital. Because we need a taskforce and because we think freely. Brothers, did you know that there are even guardian angels of car parks, angelic train, bus and tram conductors, and angelic drivers? Their world is exactly like ours: that's why we have to believe that angels exist in themselves and in general, even if the president of our Sacred Homeland (here El Leader Maximo gave a sarcastic bow) denies such a reality. True, I haven't seen the angels for myself yet, because I have been preparing myself to meet them in a state of purity and perfection. But I say to you with my hand on my heart that the angels are not strangers, they are like us and in our likeness, but they have been sent by God and they have within them much light to impart. In order to see them, we need to be disciplined and orderly. Because angels are archetypes: take note of this word, brothers, bear it in mind for evermore and it will be your guide. What does it mean? It means that angels have existed always, like atoms. They are my brothers and they are your brothers; although it would be more correct to say that they are rather like cousins. And that they give you an electric shock when touch them. Not just anybody can touch them, even if almost anybody can see them. And I should also make clear to you something vital: angels are neither men nor women, although they are sooner men. But let me get back to the three strangers who have descended upon our Metropolis. The country needs them and their energy, the people need their protection, and that's why, brothers, I say unto you that we must band together and demand our three angels from the government. Let the Government and the President reveal the truth and stop stuffing our ears with lies. Let them give us back our angels, for they are our angels. El Leader Maximo's speech had as usual been watched by the most unlikely people: the President had watched it from the armchair where he did his political rumination, and likewise the Chief of Police and his staff, similarly the members of Government. And so the President realized that he would have to give a speech of his own to counteract the populism of the owner of Ef-bee-en-aitch, the French-brandy-bibber and cigar-smoker: to counteract his intellectual-seeming populism, which was couched in that slangy idiom that drove him up the wall. El Leader Maximo's insolence was always like a bad itch for the presidency. The head of state put on his ordinary-man outfit and summoned the official television station to his villa in Metropolis. He needed to deliver a Proclamation to the nation, and to the capital and its citizens in particular. And this is how he began his speech, pulling a preoccupied face: My dear fellow citizens, please accept my cordial greetings as ever. I bring you the same news as previously: upon our Metropolis have descended three citizens believed by some to be angels. We do not know whether they are angels, but whether they be or not, dear fellow citizens and compatriots, the descent of the three guests has been a patriotic test for all citizens and a challenge. We have had to be vigilant! The Army and State Secret Services have been keeping their eyes open, likewise the Government and Presidency. So that our Mother, the Homeland, may find salvation and the Nation may prosper! But now the time has come for a Proclamation to the nation, in order to put a stop to the reckless words of the demagogues and prevent them from finding fanatical believers, especially when despicable politicians are trying to take advantage of the goodness and kindness of our people. And so this is what I have to say: a man cannot wrestle an angel, because the angel will always win and that is the way it ought to be. Atheists will not agree with what I have to say (here, the President was skillfully playing the rôle of the traditional believer), because they do not recognize angels except as notions. But the three strangers who have arrived in our Metropolis are not at all notions. To be more precise, they are more than just notions, as they are made of flesh and blood. None of the nation's Official Commissions has reached any definite conclusion. But what I have to tell you is something else: it no longer even matters whether the three strangers be angels or not, because it is sufficient that we believe they be angels and that we be proud of them. I repeat, even if they be not angels: he who has ears to hear, let him hear. The corrupt demagogues who give speeches to befuddle the ignorant ought to pay more attention to what they say and to keep their words in check: better mute than a fool or a liar. Dear citizens, the Nation's Political Corps, of which I am the head, has decided by a majority of votes that the three strangers should be allowed freedom of movement in our country and our Metropolis. They are free to go wherever they wish. Of course, they will not be left to their own devices, lest they come to any harm, rather they shall be accompanied by bodyguards for any eventuality. But they will be returned to the populace and to the city to which they revealed themselves and for whose sake they have come. And if they have a purpose, then it will become apparent in the near future. May God help our Sacred Homeland! The presidential speech came down like a bludgeon on the heads of the citizenry and the other politicians: it had been brilliant. The President had found the ideal political solution (without having consulted anybody—the idea had just come to him suddenly): even if they were not angels, people would pretend and believe that the strangers were angels. A stroke of genius! His staff was enchanted, excited; everybody knew that there would be a banquet. The invitations were made over the telephone and in haste, because there was no time for written invitations or the usual protocol. Moreover, everybody wanted to have a banquet, after all the stress and patriotic tests the whole nation had been enduring. Of course, after the President's speech, the leaders of all the other parties were desperate to have their say on the official television station, but their lamentable, improvised proclamations got across nothing but a couple of slogans: Let us dream together with the angels of the prosperity and health of the Homeland (the Workers' and Doctors' Party); Let us enjoy life with the angels (the Simple Man's Party); Let us build the City of the Future with the angels (the Small Tradesmen's Party); Let us be angels to the utmost (the Humanist Party). And so on, or rather that was about all.

A MAGISTERIAL BANQUET WITH SPIRITUAL DRAWBACKS

It was a masterstroke, remarked the presidential staff. But the president's adversaries also said the same thing. With reference to the speech, obviously. A concise, brilliant speech, a textbook speech, or even more so. The banquet, although hastily put together, abounded in that dish adored by the President and El Leader Maximo (in this respect they both were similar, although that was to the liking of neither): seafood. Huge platters of mustard-colored oysters, trays of prawns and crabs, lobsters, mussels, octopuses fried in exotic sauces, cuttlefish served with chili, garlands of calamari, all of which was displayed sumptuously, among ten-litre bottles of champagne that could hardly wait to be uncorked. The President had decided that champagne would be the only beverage available. But what had the presidential speech been getting at? What was at stake in it and which way did it tend, that speech to the taste of every social stratum of the Metropolis and perhaps even the whole of the Homeland? The guests had no idea: besides the leaders of the political parties, they included a large number of the characters already mentioned in the pages of this risky exposé on the subject of angels. To be more precise, all of them were there, except the Devil-in-chief and the bohemians from the Spitted Tavern. And I almost forget: all of them, except the Slum Philosopher and the masses. In fact, nor had the Hunter of Shadows turned up at the banquet, not having been invited. Predictably, such people had no business attending the party, given that they already dwelled in the space between different worlds and therefore had a somewhat better idea of the angels' status and the envy stirred up by the three strangers. As for the crowds, they might have been corralled into stadiums and fed in a manner that mimicked the feeding of the thousands once accomplished by Jesus. It was only now that all those who had been preoccupied with the angelic question, which had become a matter of state, saw each other for the first time: the three captains and the nine lieutenants, in uniform; the chief of Police, dressed casually; the medical experts from the Department of Experimental Laboratories, wearing their white lab coats; the boss of the advertising firm, wearing a spotted suit; the academicians of the Metropolis, in their official robes; the Midget from the toy company, wearing a star-patterned trouser suit; the Patriarch and his men, in ecclesiastical garb; All-Understanding, who had not yet lost his mind; the parfumeur, who arrived with a dozen small bottles of *eau de parfum* for any ladies that might be attending the banquet and who was keeping an interested eye on the Midget; the Linguist, who to everyone's amazement arrived wearing jeans and an old velvet jacket with scuffed elbows; the chocolatier, dressed from head to toe in brown satin; Signore Metrocirkus; and, of course, the Brain from Metropolfilm. All of them were ruminating on the essential sentence in the President's speech, a sentence that was like a boomerang or an uppercut, and which had shocked and pampered the ears of the nation: *it no longer even matters whether the three strangers be angels or not, because it is sufficient that we believe they be angels and that we be proud of them*. Consequently, it was no longer necessary, obligatory, imperative (put it however you like) that they be extra-hominids, it was enough that they be classified and presented as such. Did the pride of the nation depend on its angels, on messengers arriving from a so-called super-world? The guests at that aquatic banquet (since it was a banquet specializing in the aforementioned fruits of the ocean) asked themselves this question in their minds and fretted over the answer. Can you be proud of angels that are not angels? Can you make an absolute of the suspicion that some ordinary people might be angels? Can a nation believe in its angels (three in number) even if they are not in fact angels? These questions crackled and popped in the heads of every guest, from the chief of Police to Signore Metrocirkus. The only ones who did not ask themselves any such questions were the Patriarch and his retinue, as well as the theologian known as All-Understanding: for mysterious are the ways of the Lord, are they not? It is advisable never to try to unravel them. Nor was the Linguist interested in any radical truth any more, but only in the pseudopods of the truth: ultimately, that shabby-looking ultra-intellectual did not wish to succumb to the sin of asking the same rhetorical question as Pontius Pilate. On the other hand, El Leader Maximo was fidgeting inside his swishy politician's suit: he could not accept the defeat inflicted on him as a result of the vote-stealing presidential speech. El Leader Maximo was frothing at the mouth, for which reason he felt an urge to be insolent: he felt the need to act like a mad bull. And so, at one point he upset a platter of oysters and smashed his champagne glass. Nobody was surprised, however, least of all the President: they all agreed that El Leader Maximo had to lick his vanquished paws. Thus, El Leader Maximo's impertinence and urge to create a scandal were quite simply tolerated. But then something else happened: the President himself was suddenly set to thinking as a result of the words he had spoken on national television. Had he really uttered that crucial phrase: *it no longer even matters whether the three strangers be angels or not*? What did that *or not* mean? Are they or aren't they? In fact, what he was saying was that anything is possible and reversible at any time: you can turn a man into an angel, if you mentally and spiritually construct him as such. But what about his body? That was the thorniest question. The body will remain human no matter what, even if the soul be angelic. And so it was a trick like any other, given that the two could not be reconciled. The poor President already sensed that he was going to get a severe pain in his cranium, and so he decided to desist. In the end, *que sera, sera*, and *basta*! The champagne, by now having been consumed in industrial quantities, was beginning to take effect. The atmosphere was fraught with tart bubbles. El Leader Maximo had as if by a miracle calmed down, torpedoed by his defeat and the champagne that was no substitute for the virility of his favorite French cognac. And so the President, seconded by his advisers, got ready to give his little concluding speech. It was to be short and clear: The chief of Police and the other forces of law and order have been delegated to supervise a competition to select the angels' bodyguards tomorrow. One bodyguard per angel, he decided. One is enough for each. If they are angels, they won't need any protection, let it be clear. And then, bodyguards and all, we shall turn them loose to let the masses do with them what they will. Understood?

COMPETITION WITH A MOTLEY JURY AND A MULTITUDE OF BODYGUARDS

The competition to select the bodyguards, the number of positions being equal to the number of presumed angels, took place three days after the presidential banquet: the head of state was in a hurry to rid himself of the burden of the three intangible strangers, delivering them to the masses, as the Slum Philosopher had, if we remember rightly, demanded in his articles for the *People's Gazette*. Well, the wish of the plebeian philosopher in question was about to be fulfilled. The President had delegated one of his advisers to deal with the announcements for the competition and with putting together a competent jury. The jury was made up of the said adviser, nicknamed the Puma, because he looked just like the beast that was his namesake; one of the captains that had taken part in the initial interrogation of the strangers; All-Knowing the theologian (rather bizarrely); and, finally, the heart specialist from the Extraordinary Medical Commission set up to examine the angels. The competition was to be held at the Museum of Anthropology in the centre of the Metropolis, where there was a lecture theatre with seating for a thousand candidates. First of all, the applicants, some seven hundred and something in number, had to sit a written exam. And the question that the jury set for the written exam was as follows: what does it mean to be a bodyguard in this day and age? Give your arguments and counterarguments in no more than ten sentences so that the marking will go smoothly and will be able to be completed in half a day. And the answers were in keeping with the question, ranging from the aberrant to the comical and candid. Being a bodyguard means defending your homeland, being fierce, being a sentinel, keeping your eyes peeled, being loyal, working like clockwork, being mathematical, being sharp, being intransifent (the author of this neologism in fact meant to write intransigent), being a beast of prey, not being a dreamer, not being a sleepyhead, not being obedient, not being undisciplined, not being a lecher, not being weird, not being bloated, and so on: the list was enormous, as you might imagine. The jury selected around a hundred answers from the seven hundred, reducing the number of candidates drastically. In the oral test, they gave both their real names and their nicknames, believing that the nicknames were more likely to justify their being chosen as bodyguards to the famous strangers. And the nicknames sounded as follows: the Boxer, the Champion, the Artist, the Tiger, the Wizard, the Player, the Righteous One. There were not only men among the hundred candidates selected for the second test, but also a few women, self-dubbed or nicknamed by others as follows: Snow White, Cinderella, Sleeping Beauty, the Snow Queen, and so on. The jury sniggered into their beards or moustaches (depending on the case): who knows? Maybe those women were more capable defenders than the men, at least psychologically speaking, although some of them were well built and upholstered, athletes and amazons at the same time. The fact that they had acquired for themselves fairy-tale nicknames was daring and comical. There was also a puny little woman, who did not inspire confidence in any of them. Then the captain of the jury recognized her: it was the girl from the country who had sheltered the second presumed angel after he had landed in the medicaments factory. She had even specified in her application form that she wanted to be the bodyguard of the second angel, although nobody had paid any attention to that until she was finally recognized, her wish having been viewed as a female whim or a childish joke. From the very beginning, the jury noticed that the hundred candidates, be they men, be they women, did not have any professional pride and did not regard themselves as belonging to any warrior elite: most of them had applied in order to earn some money, being unemployed, or for religious reasons, given that they wished with all their hearts that the three strangers really were angels. Half of the applicants were atheists; half were religious fanatics. And so it was hard to choose. The jury itself did not have any particular criteria for evaluation and made it up as they went along. The three we finally select, explained the Puma, that is, the presidential adviser, won't conceal their faces, they won't wear balaclavas—I hope this is well understood? The candidates nodded. You won't necessarily be receptacles of any truth, the Puma went on. Because the truth might be anything. And you won't be shapers of any destiny, but merely its protectors. This rather obscure statement baffled the candidates. And at this point All-Knowing made the following glib but placatory interruption: What he means is that given that God might be busy elsewhere in the world it falls upon you to undertake the relatively sacred mission of protecting the bodies, souls and minds of our newly arrived guests here in the Metropolis. The other members of the jury were left open-mouthed in astonishment, as the explanation given by the theologian still in possession of his mental faculties (unlike All-Understanding) was confusing to say the least. What did he mean, for example, when he said that God might be busy somewhere else and why was the bodyguards' mission only relatively sacred? What I am getting at, said the sane theologian, clearing his throat, is that you both are and are not the hand of the people in the execution of God's commandments. But this explanation merely heightened the confusion. What I mean to say, said the All-Knowing, again clearing his throat, is that you are not supermen, even if you will be protecting and guarding angels or at least individuals who might be angels. But they are angels! blurted the girl from the country. Why are we acting like they might not be? Because, the theologian admonished her, the *corpus mysticum* is one alone and nobody and no thing may substitute for it. What the hell, exclaimed the captain, can't you put it more plainly? You're doing our heads in! Yes, muttered the theologian, ignoring the captain, you might on the other hand be specially adapted crusaders. The Puma looked at him askance and alarmed by the turn the theological discourse was taking, he made a discreet sign to the heart doctor, who quickly brought the All-Knowing a glass of water and asked him to sit down and allow the candidates to speak. But there was no stopping the theologian. Think of yourselves as apprentices doing military training, he explained to the bewildered candidates. But don't be robots! Don't risk being excommunicated! At this point, the Puma signaled to the men who had suddenly appeared from the wings and All-Knowing was gently lifted up and taken away, probably to the same place as All-Understanding. What was to be done? The competition must go on. And the general knowledge and other routine or merely random questions continued at their own rather idle pace, although everybody was in a hurry. Some of the candidates wanted the job only for a little while; others wanted it to be arranged around their own lives. The adjudicators could not wait to discharge their task in that strange and rather inadequate jury. After the oral test twenty individuals remained in the running, including the puny country girl, to the amazement of the other candidates, who were, predictably, well-built men, as well as to the amazement of the captain. They had had no choice: the girl had correctly answered the questions put to her during the oral test, and so there could be no discriminating against her. And here is where the impasse arose: given that the jury had no other criterion for choosing between the candidates, the solution of last resort was to bring the three strangers into the auditorium and allow them to choose their own future protectors (although some said that it would sooner be the angels who protected the bodyguards rather than the other way). And so the supposed angels were summoned and placed face to face with the twenty finalists, who were eagerly awaiting the verdict. As usual, the three strangers said not a word, but they immediately understood what it was they had to do. And so each of them chose somebody. The first opted for the Wizard: a middle-aged man, of ordinary height, with the face of an intellectual, given that he had thick-lensed spectacles, probably because of excessive reading; he was wearing jeans, like the three strangers, and he seemed niggardly with his words. The second chose the girl from the country who had sheltered him (but we all knew that that was what was going to happen, and ultimately even the captain knew it). And the third pointed at the lanky man who was nicknamed the Player: it seems that he was an inveterate roulette player and that he had lost everything he owned, even his wife, making insane bets. And so the competition came to an end, to the general dissatisfaction, excepting the three strangers and their newly invested bodyguards.

NOCTURNAL ANGELIAD IN THE NATIONAL STADIUM

Before the lofty guests could be delivered to the population, so that they might integrate themselves into everyday life in all its aspects (although nobody really knew what that would mean for real angels that had descended to earth, if that were what they were), the Government and the Presidency had proposed and provided a special gift: a nocturnal angel-themed show at the national stadium. Naturally, the three strangers would appear at the end of the show. The inhabitants of the Metropolis thronged to buy tickets, but there weren't enough seats, as may easily be imagined: the stadium only sat around thirty thousand. True, besides the official tickets, there were also tickets for standing room only, and so the number of spectators increased by around another five thousand. And if you also counted the forces of law and order on duty, then you might have said that the number of people gathered in the national stadium, including those in the official box, was around forty-five thousand, with men and women in roughly equal number, some of them flashy, others not. The show had been conceived by none other than Signore Metrocirkus in partnership with the Brain from Metropolfilm (both of them assigned to the task by the Puma, the President's well-known adviser), and so plenty of people were expecting a captivating blend of circus and cinema, a Molotov cocktail, a performance to short-circuit the minds of the spectators. Everybody was excited, although they were not hoping for any miracles. Remarkably, the show was up and running within a week, during which all those involved worked like dogs, day and night: actors, gymnasts, circus performers, performing animals, scriptwriters, stage designers, cameramen, lighting technicians, electricians, and so on. But behold, the day has come at last, or rather the evening of the so-called Metropolitan Angeliad has arrived, and so let us make our way to the national stadium to see what transpired there. The supreme host of the show was to be Signore Metrocirkus, even if the Brain or the Cigar from Metropolfilm also played an indispensable part in the proceedings. And so, against a backdrop of huge spotlights, which swept the stadium with violet beams, Signore Metrocirkus opened the show, introducing an act that combined acrobatics and performing animals. Ladies and gentlemen, the by now famous show brought to the stadium some hundred acrobats, lithe-bodied men and women, wearing wings made of fairy-lights, who invaded the stage setting up at dizzying speed blue trampolines emblazoned with green stars. Out of the blue, some other circus performers placed huge birdcages containing live flamingos and egrets around the trampolines, and hundreds of yellow and green parrots of the ordinary, that is, the dwarf, variety were released into the air and they flew madly above the stage and also the heads of the metropolitans, who were already applauding the newly begun show. Their cheers were to provide a constant backdrop to all the events that took place in the national stadium. Well, the acrobats swiftly built human pyramids and then made death-defying leaps between them, illumined by the fairy lights on their wings, fluttering through the air like miniature comets. The acrobatic flurry was accompanied by the flurry of the spectators and the flurry of the policemen guarding the stadium, keeping their eyes peeled lest anything untoward should happen: one of the usual sort of catastrophes, such as an earthquake, a flood, a massacre. To the sound of celestial music coming from who knows where (played on the harp, piano and saxophone), on the panels that watched over the endless rows of seats and the geographically or mathematically divided sections of the stadium were projected the faces of sculpted and celebrated angels, three in number, namely Gabriel, Michael and Raphael. The projected images were shaken and interrupted by blinding flashes. From the mouths of the three angels, equipped with firemen's hoses, gushed round bundles of violet confetti, which spread through the air, colliding with the parrots flying above the stadium. The first part of the show lasted about a quarter of an hour and then all of a sudden the acrobats vanished, likewise the bird cages with the flamingos and egrets, likewise, the parrots, summoned by an acoustic signal: all of them seeped into the ground, somewhere in the depths of the stadium, where the changing rooms were to be found. The empty stage was then invaded by dozens of circus performers perched on seven-foot stilts, who flapped airplane wings made of cloth, creating an agile, amusing ballet. But the surprise turned out to be something completely different: from the stadium's four watchtowers swooped swarms of glider pilots, all garbed in the same gleaming, incandescent costumes. It was clear: someone had conceived an unprecedented spectacle of sound and light. When the final glider pilots produced thirty-foot-long ribbons, which dangled behind their flying machines, the stadium was became, as it were, a volatile or at least levitational space. The crowd burst into wild applause. At the end of their performance, the glider pilots released swarms of lottery and tombola tickets, for the grand end-of-year draw. At least a thousand people were lucky enough to catch one of the tickets as they fluttered down, and they went on to try their luck in the draw, in which they might win a fashionable motorcar, a luxury flat or a lavish holiday on an exotic island far from the Sacred Homeland. The third number, which produced shock and amazement, was performed by thirty motorcyclists, to whose motor scooters were tied huge balloons and even miniature zeppelins: these burst almost noiselessly, making a tinkle if anything, while the motorcyclists, dressed in white leather outfits and white helmets, sped around the stadium's circular track. But the motorcyclists were merely the forerunners to a magnificent parade of giraffes dressed as ballerinas: the huge giraffes (ten in number) wore tutus and veils, as well as endlessly long scarves. These animals paraded in an orderly fashion. What was more, their brown and yellow hides had been painted black and white so that they would look like harlequins. The fourth number was a retinue of magicians, who made their entry with some huge, presumably magical boxes, to make the performance of a lifetime. And indeed, the boxes were not only huge, some five yards high and five yards wide, but covered in mirrors and tin foil. And the magicians' wands were seven feet long. The retinue of magicians also included some fish-women (mermaids, in other words) and glow-worm-women, so called because they had luminous skin and were round, with charming antennae on the top of their heads. Well, the women climbed inside the huge magical boxes and once the magicians had uttered the magic words, something resembling *Susmonticlavans* (nobody knew what that meant, but it was supposed that the sense was: He who lives between the worlds, you will emerge transformed!), from the boxes emerged blonde ghosts with endlessly long hair, floating androgynes, who rose into the air above the stadium, to a height of some seventy feet, inasmuch as they did not possess any apparent body, and if they did, then it must have been ethereal. Then the crowd began to shout, probably incited by the Slum Philosopher, who was definitely there among them: First class! First class! Bravo bravissimo! The stadium was already enveloped in all kinds of murmuring spectral lights, and so the time for the finale had come: all those who had taken part up to now entered the stage once more, which is to say, the acrobats with their fairy-light wings, the flamingos, egrets and parrots, the stilt-walkers and the glider pilots, the motorcyclists and the giraffes, while the magicians and their boxes remained where they were. Of course, the faces of the three famous angels, Gabriel, Michael and Raphael, continued to explode in flashing lights on the panels, and confetti continued to be blown into the air through the firemen's hoses. And then, yes, then the supreme moment arrived, in the middle of the stadium appeared the three strangers, dressed exactly the same as when they had arrived in the Metropolis, that is, in jeans and tunics, with the same blue cloaks and the same curly chestnut hair tied in a ponytail. They had the same elongated eyes, the same eyebrows, as if plucked and then painted, and the same slender throats. Behind each stood the bodyguard he had chosen, that is, the Wizard, the girl from the outskirts of the Metropolis, and the Roulette Player: however, they had been fitted out with costumes that consisted of shiny black tunics and trousers. At that supreme moment, the crowd once more burst into whoops of admiration, after which there began a kind of mumbled prayer of imploration and such a whirlwind of chaos was whipped up that the authorities decided to bring the show to a close at once, fearful lest the metropolitans be consumed in a mystical explosion. And so Signore Metrocirkus addressed the conductor who had had at last poked his head out of one of the watchtowers where the supposedly celestial orchestra was concealed and told him merely this: The show is over! Maestro! Start up a march! Oh, I think I've come across that line somewhere before, in some famous book! And the maestro, dazed by the uproar around him, by the screams and wails of the crowd, started up a military march, with drums and trumpets. You would have thought that the Apocalypse was about to descend upon the Metropolis from the firmament, to chastise its inhabitants for having gone crazy at the end of the grandiose spectacle provided to the capital by the Government and the President. The nocturnal Angeliad had come to a close.

OF HOW GOD DREAMS, ALTHOUGH THIS ISN'T NECESSARILY HEALTHY

Nobody knows and nobody will ever know how and why God dreams. All the more so if God is dead or has chosen for subjective reasons not to reveal Himself to anybody. And so, God should be left to His own devices. But by means of various wiles we may nonetheless enter the mind of God to have a look at what He is dreaming. And so we shall say only this, lest the reader grow overly suspicious: one night God dreamed of the three angels that had descended upon the Metropolis. And He dreamed of them as follows, which is to say, rather complicatedly. Ah, even God has human dreams, precisely because He is in the likeness of the creatures He has created, even without His having used His hands! So, God dreamed of a train carriage full of angels all crammed into compartments that were exactly first class. First of all He dreamed the three angels revealed to Abraham, and then Jacob's angel, the wounded wrestler, then the angel that closes the lion's mouth in the business with the prophet Daniel, then Gabriel, the messenger to the Virgin Mary, then lots of other angels, some more hands-on than others, including Jesus likened to an angel by Peter the Fisherman; and finally He dreamed of the angel that released Peter. It was only after that that He dreamed of the three strangers that had plummeted upon the Metropolis. Surprisingly, all of the angels crowded into the compartments had very small wings, which were transparent, like a dragonfly's; they were not even as long as an arm. For that reason, God's stupefaction was palpable. But let us now describe the angels dreamed of by the Omnipotent. The three angels that revealed themselves to Abraham had dirty feet and were tired. But they ate scones and beef and announced to the aged Sara that a child was on its way. And she laughed. Then the three angels that revealed themselves to Abraham were two: the third disappeared unexpectedly, nobody knows where or how. And the other two went off to see Lot in Sodom, who received them and fed them unleavened bread. And when the Sodomites came that they might know the angels, Lot did not allow them to know them, but offered them his daughters that they might know them instead. But the Sodomites did not wish to know his daughters, but rather the strangers. And then the angels blinded the Sodomites and took Lot, his wife and his daughters away with them. But in vain did they take them thence, because they then perished in their own way. Those angels did not have long hair and their wings were transparent and untouchable. God was amazed: wings cannot be untouchable because they are made of feathers, and feathers come from birds. Undoubtedly, it must have been one of those angels that prevented Abraham from sacrificing Isaac, but God was no longer very sure. He knew the voice of that subject of His, the angel that had prevented Abraham, but he could no longer remember his face, given that it blurred into the grey mass of all the other avian faces of the angels. The next angel was the one that wrestled with Jacob. This one wore chainmail and despite being garbed in this fashion he did not manage to throw Jacob, and so he struck him in the hip, thus transforming him into Israel. Perhaps this blow to the hip was uncalled for and rather underhand, but the angel blessed Jacob thereby and gave him a new name. Even if Jacob was left lame for life, it remained his wish until his dying day to discover the name of the angel he had wrestled. He never found out the name in question, but he often worshiped the wrestler in chainmail, God's emissary, who had put him to the test and then blessed him. Jacob sometimes even dreamed of the man in chainmail, with his gleaming iron skin. God was proud of His warrior angel, who had performed honorably in the wrestling match with the man. The third angel, the one that saved the prophet Daniel, proved to be an angel of flame: his mantle was red, his shoes had red claws, his mouth was scarlet and his eyes glowing flames. But his wings were small, as we have already made clear. His purpose was to sew up the lions' mouths with a thread of flame, which wasn't hard to do: the angel sewed up their mouths with coarse fishing yarn, imprisoning the beasts' fangs for all eternity. His fingernails were very sharp, for which reason God looked at him askance in the dream. Then God remembered the angel Gabriel, the messenger to the Virgin, the herald of His Son. For, this was no ordinary angel, and this is why he also revealed himself to Joseph in a dream. And he showed himself to him in order to give him the strength and to help him overcome his fear and doubt. He was a red-haired angel with ragged fingernails. Then God remembered Peter the Fisherman who likened Jesus to an angel: God laughed. Another two apostles had been hasty in giving a verdict on His Son: Matthew had likened Jesus to a philosopher, and Thomas had not likened him to anything. For the first time, however, only now, after so long, the Lord God pondered in astonishment what Peter the Fisherman had said. Then He remembered that the very same Peter was released from prison by an angel that unlocked the gates. And God realized for the first time that He had not sent the angel, but rather the angel was independent. But was there not something untoward there? Especially given that Peter the Fisherman had been mistaken for the very angel that had saved him! And finally, there came the turn of the three angels that had descended upon the Metropolis. And this was how God dreamed of them: with their blue tunics, their hair tied in ponytails, and almost mute, although they muttered softly. God, however, could make nothing of their muttering. If these are My angels, it means that I sent them. And so, why can I not understand what they are saying? And then God tried to perceive the small transparent wings that the three creatures did not seem to possess. At this point, the eye of God lost sight of the three strangers, because all of a sudden the Almighty found Himself confronted with that dream in which all the angels were crammed inside the compartments of a carriage, in a train that all but took flight: all the angels had small, dragonfly-like wings, wings that were transparent and not even as long as an arm. But now God was no longer astonished. Perhaps it was a carriage in the metro; perhaps it was the Orient Express, a troop train or even a *montagne russe* converted to suit the circumstances. But angels are companions, witnesses and custodians, to put it pretentiously: whom were they accompanying in that carriage, with its compartments stuffed to bursting? Because let it be clear, there were only angels there, and no trace of a human being. But God was not a theologian, and so let us leave angelic speculations up to the real theologians. Nevertheless, even if He was not a theologian, God could not help, even in His dream, but ponder abstractedly the structure and function of His very rare and very special envoys to the world. The main function of those flying pseudo-humans was to pray for the hominids and guide them in the path of righteousness. For such reasons, angels rarely knelt and mostly remained standing, like sentinels. They did not get varicose veins, however. Then God remembered Fanuel, a lesser-known angel, because he was the angel of repentance and nobody wanted him around. Fanuel mostly stood to attention. But Fanuel was not mentioned in the divine ledgers: he seemed to be a forgotten and rarely employed angel. And so even Our Lord God forgot him without remorse, because the Almighty could make and unmake angels without being accused of any misdemeanor. He was a kind of surgeon. In passing he also remembered Azrael, the angel of death; true, he was the angel of death in other worlds and with other gods, for which reason he had been abandoned without remorse. He had quite simply been left in the charge of a rarely mentioned angel. God was surprised, however, that he had not dreamed of the Tobias's angel, because that angel had at least done and spoken of many things. For, Raphael was clear in his speech and knew the paths, even if he manifested himself under the false name of Azarias. And Tobit, Tobias's father, had believed he was just a man and had blessed his son and the stranger by wishing that they might be accompanied by an angel, without knowing that the angel would be his own angel. Herein lies the unnaturalness and luminosity of that event. Then, on the journey, the angel had told Tobias to open the fish, to roast it, and to eat it, but to keep its heart, liver and gall bladder, given that they would be useful when it came to driving away evil spirits and healing the eyes. And do not worry about the Devil, the companion angel told Tobias. Which is what happened. Later, the angel was to terrify Tobit, revealing himself to him in all his splendor and saying: *I am Raphael, one of the seven holy angels, which present the prayers of the saints, and which go in and out before the glory of the Holy One. All these days I did appear unto you; but I did neither eat nor drink, but ye did see a vision.* Yes, this is exactly what he told them, that those people of olden times had seen a vision, rather than him, the angel. But in the end he showed himself to them as he really was. God had been satisfied with the words of Raphael: he had made a consummately angelic speech. Nevertheless, He had not dreamed of Raphael. But nor had He dreamed of the angel that had encouraged Jesus in the Garden of Gethsemane: he had not been a perfect angel and nor had he been a conqueror of worlds. He had not even been an angel covered in splendor: but nonetheless he had encouraged Jesus. God scratched His head. Maybe he needed binoculars or a magnifying glass. Then the Almighty turned his gaze back to the three strangers that had descended upon the Metropolis. Yes, they were probably angels fifty per cent, but invisible ones for the time being. Or maybe they weren't angels but merely the doppelgängers of angels. And then God suddenly became melancholy, because He did not know why He was God. But He was joyful at having dreamed of angels, even if some of them seemed to be handicapped.

THE LOGORRHOEA OF AN ALIENATED CENSOR RESULTING FROM THE PARTICLE NO

Angels oughtn't exist, it isn't allowed, it's forbidden. It's not on. Ah, Censor, with your curling lip and your grubby mouth, why are you afraid? Angels oughtn't exist. No. Nyet. Nein. Nu. Non. And the blue sky ought to be banned, because it makes the earth and everything in it look brown. There is no need for heavenly lands to exist, we don't need guardian angels, and nor do we need to spend time with them. We oughtn't imitate them. It's befitting that humans be humans and nothing more. Because the angels are acrobats and clowns. They don't have proper clothes, they speak in riddles, they're different from us. Herein lies the error: they're different; they're something else. The Censor was sitting and writing his speech, wearing a white nurse's uniform. They oughtn't be indulged, because that would bring madness into the world. Insanity. Disaster. Chaos. Anarchy. We don't need any plagues. The angels are plague-bearers. Because they don't exist. We just think they exist. Once upon a time there was a monk who went off into the wilderness by himself. He only held out for ten days, after which he went back to the monastery. But the other monks refused to open the gate to him. When the monk cried out to them that it was he, who had gone into the wilderness, those inside answered that he, the one who departed, was no longer a man, but an angel, and so he should open the gate himself or else fly over the wall. That's how the monk who had gone into the wilderness discovered that he was not an angel, but a man. And it's the same with us, the ones who remain here: we're just humans, and that's why we oughtn't be or believe we are angels. Nowadays, superstitions don't even fool a child, because everybody knows that angels are irresponsible. Even if there is a sect of angelics who believe the world was created solely by angels (rather than God), that doesn't mean that the current stratosphere consists of wings and feathers. Wings and feathers, even so, wings and feathers, a superannuated material, good only for pillows and duvets. They're not even good for that any more: duvets are made from paper and elastic nowadays. And since not even the heavens are strictly necessary, it may be deduced and affirmed that we don't even need birds. It is not fitting that we should be aerial (please take note, ladies and gentlemen, I said aerial and not Aryan!), but earthly, because this is our legitimate and official state. Consequently, let there be a resounding vote against angels, wings, feathers, birds! Though they may whisper it on street corners, winged souls have no business among us! We are thinking flesh and that is how we should remain. I believe in holy matter! The Censor looked in the mirror, dressed as he was in his white nurse's uniform. His favorite job, besides being a censor, was duty nurse at the hospital for the mentally alienated: it was he who turned the hose on those individuals who went berserk. There is something else we should make clear: the Censor couldn't stand rainbows; he had an allergy to them. Hence his wonted and vehement tirades against the heavens. Nor was he thrilled by the starry sky at night. But what irked him more than anything else was the chirping of the birds, because he suspected that the angels chirped just like them. And the mere thought of angelic choirs put him in such a bad mood that he would fantasize about strangling the birds in the yard. The music of the spheres was an intellectual fraud. There was no need of any Sanctus, Gloria or Hallelujah. When, at a fancy do at the hospital, somebody told him as a joke that some religious tracts claimed that Adamic man had been endowed with wings before the Fall, the Censor got blind drunk so furious was he. And then he puked the whole night. Even the idea of so-called angelic powers filled him with rage, hence his sullen repulsion towards the strange winged creatures, which he obstinately refused to accept. And when the angels' supposed warlike hypostasis came to his mind, his fury quadrupled: warrior angels quite simply made him fly off the handle. He thought of their breastplates, their broadswords, their armor, their helmets as sickly ingredients. He thought of the supposed winged beings as abortions. Because angels looked very much like abortions: wizened before their time, immaculate, transparent, even translucent. They were old maids, because the supposed angels were also effeminate as a rule! The Censor was a hygienist, a pest exterminator. That's what he had to be: the cleanser of all the fantasizing impurities from the minds of the inhabitants of the Metropolis and the Sacred Homeland. No heavens above! There was no need of any tenants in the so-called houses of Heaven! Let alone tenants with eyes all over their bodies! Because it was rumored that they had dozens of eyes implanted all over their skin. Why eyes and not fur or hair? Why weren't they covered in ears or noses? Could the reason be that God was rumored to have a single huge eye, the Supreme Eye? Stuff and nonsense. The days of the polyphemic Cyclopes was long gone. People weren't blind. There are only a handful of blind people here and there, and they were born like that. Consequently, the fact that angels were said to be encrusted with eyes was poppycock. It would be just as ludicrous to say that they were encrusted with countless ears or noses. I don't believe in beatitude, the Censor said to himself. If angels do exist, however, I'm convinced they must sleep: their eyes would have to get tired and bloodshot after a while. Then, too, their eyes might be subject to all kinds of ailments: conjunctivitis, cataracts, and so on. I wouldn't want to be like that kind of angel, the Censor muttered. I want to be a human being. But what if that isn't enough? Day and night I grow more embittered, disgusted, and determined. Those were the Censor's last words before he gracefully, symbolically lost it: which is to say, before he was put away in the mental hospital, of his own free will and unconstrained. Naturally: as permanent nurse and care worker, equipped with the water hose for the guests inside. Down with the angels!

NEWS FROM CYBERLANDIA

It's hard for anybody to believe that the cyborgs, those entities fabricated from metal, plastic and other fine or even insidious materials, could have found out about the three angels. But nevertheless, this is what happened, however astonishing and paradoxical it might be. Because in Cyberlandia, the said cyborgs or androids, although they are in a latent, i.e. unfinished state, already had premonitory memories and were endowed with the prophesying capacity of high-performance robots. From within their visual tunnel, which was so elastic that it could contain the whole world inside a peppercorn, a number of cyborgs, a dozen or so, even if they were not yet fully fabricated, had already prophesied the descent of the three angels to Metropolis. Although robots, the androids felt an intense jealousy towards the supposed angels and the spontaneous celebrity they had gained among the denizens of Metropolis: this was because the cyborgs yearned to be the only specimens that would fascinate and obsess the natives of not only Metropolis but the entire world. Through their electronic ports and even their metal flesh, the androids aspired to be perfect mirrors of the human world, which for various reasons had grown so vulnerable, pallid and bloodless lately. Their empire, formerly named Xanadu, had been renamed, rather predictably, Cyberlandia: by means of this name, among other things, the robots aimed to colonize all the hominid zones until complete superposition was achieved. But now, the descent of the three angels to Metropolis had annoyingly messed up their plans of invasion and conquest. In fact, the reader should be aware of the following thing: we're not talking here about finished, complete cyborgs, but about the memory of incomplete androids, which, having attained technical perfection, would have been able to become the new conquistadors of Metropolis and ultimately the planet. And so let us penetrate this latent memory, a memory as yet unpolished, not having received the master jeweler's touch, and let us look at these thoughts of crushing the human world and imposing metallic, and in any event anti-angelic, domination. Let the reader (but not only the reader) picture this memory as a fragmentary and therefore imperfect electronic library. Within this somewhat volatile library, there existed a predictable obsession: why didn't the three angels have wings? And if they didn't have wings, then why shouldn't the cyborgs have perfect, albeit flightless, wings? They simply had to demand to have robot wings fabricated for them. But from whom were they to demand it? Oh, let not the reader wrack her brains, because not even we know from whom the cyborgs might have demanded wings. For which reason, given that we don't know, let us allow the cyborgs to fantasize and to construct their own wings so skillfully that they might even look like the famous flight mechanisms of the angels! Having passed through the phases of perturbation and astonishment, the androids bounced back with revolutionary fervor and in their prophetic memory there arose the construct of not ordinary pairs of wings, but a single huge wing that would overshadow Metropolis, without a creak, without a sound, except perhaps a velvety noise, the wing in question having been greased with the subtlest oils to stop it rusting. The as yet incomplete memory of the cyborgs was rather bulimic in this respect: the wing was not just gigantic and greased, like a whale's back, but was much more than that. It was a gigantic double wing. Above the first wing a second wing had accreted, and if things did not stop there, a third wing would accrete and so on, until the single gigantic wing would come to resemble a jungle of polished metal, a massive, solid bush, like a baobab. How funny it would be if a playful child blew soap bubbles above such a wing! Or if the child decorated it with colored balloons! But let us pick up the thread of our story, which we had broken off at the construction of the single wing. Hmm, what was that wing when all is said and done? Naturally, it was an object: a luxury object, one might say, even a bifurcated object. Given that, if the wing in question was to have accretions, other objects might emerge from those swellings and appendages. Not other wings, but other objects. What were the advantages and limits of such a single wing? The immediate and greatest advantage was that, given we are talking about a single wing, all the cyborgs were monolithically amassed, flying or not flying depending on the actual mobility of the single wing. The limit of this extreme situation was that none of the androids would have its own personality, as they would be lumped together against their will under the guidance of a single wing. In any event, the site where the luxury object in question was to be constructed would have to be ineffable. The cyborgs did not yearn to be angels, but only to possess competent and perfect wings like the angels'. Super-angelic wings, to be more precise. But what if the three strangers that fell from the sky onto Metropolis were not angels after all? Such was the irritating or, contrariwise, flattering question that also found its way into the collective memory of the unfinished androids. In that case there would have been a need for a *Deus ex machina*, but where to come up with one? The three strangers had become seducers unwittingly; the cyborgs wished to be high-performance, deliberate seducers, and all the dominos would come crashing down if the three were not in fact angels. The robots' memory network had no cause to be jealous on that score. And so let us stop here, and let Cyberlandia remain within its own boundaries, that is, at a preventative distance from our story. Amen, worthy readers, amen!

A BAR OWNER WITH A FEBRILE IMAGINATION AND HIS DELECTABLE STRIPPERS

The owner of the Angelina reacted immediately on hearing the news about the three strangers: precisely because angels couldn't fail as an entertainment turn in a bar, he simply had to hire them. All the more so given that the theme of his bar was Angelina Jolie, the sexiest actress of the moment. The bar owner had made all his strippers inflate their lips with silicone, so that they would look like the real made-in-America Angelina. Mother Nature had endowed the girls with pneumatic busts, otherwise he wouldn't have hired them as strippers, and so the Boss had a collection of a dozen Angelina clones, who were just the thing for men in search of fantasies and willing to pay for human bunnies. It was almost perfect. When he saw on television all the hullaballoo about the strangers coming down to Metropolis, the Boss of the Angelina realized straight away that his strippers needed to change their image from relatively fallen women to angelesses. He got straight down to business, since nothing is out of bounds for a bar owner, even if one of the Apostles loudly asserted that he was on the horns of a dilemma: I wish to do good and I do evil (that's what Paul said in the Epistle to the Romans, let me jestingly make clear, lest the reader search the scriptures in vain trying to find the needle in the haystack). The Boss had been mentally suffocated in childhood by his mother, who read to him from the Bible, and particularly from the famous letters of Paul the Apostle, hence his knowledge of a number of the elegant pensées issued by the mind and mouth of the aforementioned electoral agent of the Son of God. Yes, the girls would have to transform themselves into angelesses, to bleach their hair blonde, to get themselves up in leotards covered in sumptuous feathers, and, bright and immaculate, their lips succulently lacquered, drive the men wild—the men who would pour into the Angelina in an avalanche. In fact it might even be a good idea to change the name of the bar. Maybe he should call it the Angelina Jolina. That sounded more godly, somehow sweeter, the Boss muttered to himself. Jolina Angelina Philistina, he thought, getting carried away. Angelina Pepsina Rougina or Jolina Divina Toxina. Ah, there were dozens of possibilities: but he would call it simply Angelina Jolina, so that people would know what it was all about. Let's not be hypocrites or Pharisees, but pragmatists. Then he got another brilliant idea: the stage for the strippers should have a huge angel with spreading wings. The Boss immediately ordered a costly glass angel with truly monstrous wings: from beneath those wings the strippers would emerge to do their priceless dance of lascivious temptation. When the glassblowers came to blow their blazing hot trumpets a disaster occurred: one of the girls had a nasty accident. Fluttering her delectable derriere among the glassblowers, she agitated one of the young apprentices so much that he dropped his tube and a few drops of molten glass dripped on the girl's shoulders, permanently disfiguring her. She squawked long and loud. Then, as if that misfortune were not enough, after the angel had been blown from glass and placed on the stage, somebody, it is not known who, flew down on a rope, like at the circus, landing on the angel's head, which fell off and broke. The Boss of the Angelina viewed all this occurrences as of bad augur and gave up on the now decapitated glass angel. He was reluctant to part with it, as it had been a terribly extravagant idea on his part to put a glass angel on stage. He knew that nobody else had a glass angel in Metropolis, let alone a huge one, and perhaps there was not one in the whole of the Holy Homeland: he had been most satisfied with the beauty of that translucent winged effigy, which was as glossy as if it had been coated in lacquer or even placenta. In the end, it could have been the Angelina's guardian angel. The Boss didn't sit twiddling his thumbs, but cast around until he came up with another idea: he had his barmen buy some soft clay, then the next day he shut himself up inside his premises and remained on the striptease stage until that evening, when he finally emerged, pale and haggard, but happy. When the barmen and strippers were let back inside what they now jocularly called "the sanctuary", they found there, in the middle, a kind of phantasmon, a phantom, an apparition, with winged arms and a helmeted head. The owner of the Angelina announced that he himself, with his own hands, had molded from clay a guardian angel and that thenceforth it would be the bar's mascot. The girls looked at him askance: had their boss lost his marbles? A glass angel was one thing, but one made of clay, molded by the boss himself, was just unnatural. But in the end all the staff got used to the clay ghost, and the girls weren't surprised at all when the Boss gave them the order to appear in their feathered body suits with feathers on their shoulders: even the one who had been injured had come to look on her burned skin as an angelic imprint. If the three strangers had been allowed to roam at will around the Metropolis, then the Boss would have taken them under his cassock, that is, he would have given them lodgings and shielded them from prying eyes. But for nothing in the world would he have demanded that they take any kind of part in one of the Angelina Jolina bar's nocturnal spectaculars. It wasn't fitting and nor would it have done any good. But regardless of whether the strangers were angels or not, their mere arrival had not left the Boss impassive. The Angelina Jolina had been transformed into a bar with a guardian angel. But some customers were wondering whether a huge crucifix would soon make its appearance in the bar. They were wrong: the Boss was content with the huge effigy of an angel, which he himself had molded, and he did not indulge in mystic or Christic reveries. He had proven to be a once only sculptor, and that had been enough, there was no longer any need for him to recall the epistles of Paul the Apostle or to fabricate a dummy God. And as for dreaming, it wasn't in his nature!

ON CLONE SPECULATORS AND THEIR DEFECTS

If a sheep, and then a pig, and then a monkey have been cloned then why not supposed angels? If they're not really angels, then so much the better, they'll be human clones and nothing more. This was more or less how the most famous genetics pioneer of the Metropolis and the Sacred Homeland was racking his brains. Rather predictably, he was known as the Cloner. And if there are angels, then through such a process of genetic and pleonastic mimesis, man might come closer to God. It was an extravagant philosophical and theological, if not heretical, speculation. But heresy nowadays is like air and water, that is, vital: so that we won't get bored and we won't die too prematurely, without having turned things upside down. The Cloner was sitting with a jug of cloudy wine in front of him: lucky that wine can be cloned legally, he said to himself bitingly. You don't need to be Jesus Christ at the wedding in Cana. Then he poured a few drops of milk in his wine: it was his ritual libation. What the Cloner craved was to get hold of the angels' aura, their devouring halo, that lofty gold. Not the wings, not the angelic bodies, not the delicate, nacreous faces, but strictly the halo, the brilliance with which God endowed the angels. Had he succeeded, it would have been as if he had battened onto the Most High and pinched His cheeks! The Cloner liked that self-consecrating image: the halo thief. He would have done it with lace gloves or butcher's gauntlets, or even a surgeon's or gynecologist's rubber gloves. Ultimately, somewhere in the wide world lab technicians had even produced mutants such as the trout-salmon and the wolf-fox. And in the secret headquarters of police forces all over the world it was rumored that strange humans were being manufactured: furry men, men without stomachs, soil-eating men, and so on. But nobody in this sacred world had attempted, inasmuch as it had not crossed anybody's mind, to clone an angel's halo! The Cloner was in fact convinced that even if the strangers weren't fully angelic, he, being a master craftsman, would still have managed to produce a copy of the supposed divine radiance of the so-called angels. Which is to say, that he would have been able to lay up some kind of post-alchemical rarefied gold. Not for nothing in his dreams did he double as a wing-user with a golden cap on the crown of his head! Always in those dreams there appeared open windows through which the Cloner espied the fringes of a sun as metallic and shiny as a mirror. Then he saw himself busy at an athanor in a room with lots of porcelain jars and test tubes, wiping his hands on his star-flecked cloak (it was always star-flecked). The Cloner dreamed himself floating above an ancient city, having flown swiftly out of the same windows, whither he then returned, weary, to the alchemist's chamber, after which he awoke once more to his normal human condition. There was something that he didn't like about those soothing dreams: he didn't like the fact that on awaking he felt nothing; he was completely drained. And so now the fact of attempting to clone nothing less than the haloes of the supposed angels gave him the impetus to be not only ingenious, but also impetuous. After all, by cloning, was he not thereby God's chosen one? How could one not be proud and risk anything, or rather everything, a life both human and non-human? For the Cloner there was also another maximum challenge, but which he had abandoned out of contextual delicacy: to clone himself. He had abandoned it out of genetic delicacy, one might say. On the other hand, he had no intention of abandoning the cloning of the angelic halo. He would not abandon it for anything at all, he had to do it, it was a way of convincing himself that he was not dead, that he had not yet died, or that he might never die. Ultimately, was not immortality the nebulous and amoral utopia of the third millennium? Yes, he was obsessed with post-humanity, although it would have been normal to be obsessed with pre-humanity. The Cloner did not dream of prostheses, stilts and other substitutes to lengthen human beings, but rather he reckoned that his only salvation lay in the cloning procedure. He was, this he knew and felt it even in his fingernails; he was a life-user. And now he wished to clone the angelic halo. On television he had already glimpsed something like hazy little horns on the three strangers' heads, but this had not worried him, although what he had seen were little horns rather than a disk or a salver stuck over the tops of the supposed angels' heads. The strangers couldn't be devils, but rather homunculi. This thought tortured the Cloner like a hot oven: if they were homunculi, then their descent upon the Metropolis would prove to be a fine old trick, and the Cloner would be able to play the enigmatic rôle of bookie. Might he not be able to cause a temporal loop within which the three strangers would be classed as angels by the authorities from the very start? Or might he not be able to come up with a mathematical formula whereby the strangers would correspond to that obligatory angelic equation, so that the authorities would no longer have any doubt? But did he, the Cloner, really believe that they, the three, were angels? Or was he forcing himself to believe it? What was the truth? He didn't know how to be Pontius Pilate: what is truth? He perhaps could have done with a hologram laboratory, whereby to produce the butterfly effect: he would have launched a tiny error, an approximation as to the divine nature of the three strangers, and from that approximation would have come a snowstorm-like chaos. After that the fears and expectations of the inhabitants of the Metropolis, the frustrations of the authorities up in the Fortress, and the snobbery of the leading intellectuals would have done the rest.

AN ANTI-LATINIST ASTROLOGIST

The Astrologist of the Metropolis had not sought any pseudonym for himself, not even one that would have provoked plenty of people: that of his forerunner, Nostradamus. That was a name with a blatant Latin sonority, as that unusual resident of the Metropolis realized. No, he wished to be called the Astrologist, full stop. This was because, for reasons unknown even to himself, he was an anti-Latinist, even if he found himself forced to consult books written in the language in question. He did not have his own television show, he did not write a column for any of the Metropolis dailies, but nonetheless he was famous as the most qualified practitioner of astrology in the city and the Sacred Homeland. He had a huge horologe at home, with the zodiacs of various cultural systems and their individual calendars, and also a musical clepsydra, which produced one and the same sound: the purling of water. In his Library were to be found not the originals, it is true (for it would have been costly to possess them and our man would have had to be a millionaire), but books he himself had made by hand, copying them from famous manuscripts. And so, in the said Library could be found *The Book of the Fixed Stars and Wonders of Heaven*, *The Book of Astrolatry with the Seven Sanctuaries for the Planets*, and *The Dream of the Sage*, the last of which established the accepted correspondences between heavenly and earthly creatures. Snatches of the *Corpus Hermeticum* could also probably be found in the Astrologist's Library, although this is far too complex a work to be mentioned here, and so we had better leave it in the care of the falling stars. From childhood the Astrologist had studied the six preferred beasts, that is, the Ram, the Bull, the Crab, the Lion, the Scorpion, and the Fish, with whose every vertebra (where the case) and manner of breathing he was familiar. Likewise, he himself had drawn hundreds of versions of the four zodiacal creatures, the Twins, the Bearer of the Scales, the Virgin, and the Water-carrier, before hitting on an image that might determine any destiny. Not least, he had often played with the two hybrids, the fish-tailed Goat and the Centaur, divining in those identities the composition most appropriate to modern times. In his workroom, on the longest wall, there hung a map with a minutely inscribed with a huge zodiac, as follows: Aries was the beast of sacrifice, with a golden fleece and curling horns, worshipping Mars. Taurus was an arched body corresponding to women obsessed with white quadrupeds and worshipped Venus. Gemini were linked to Apollo and Hercules, or the Dioscuri, they were naked, wore caps and sandals, and worshipped Mercury. Cancer, which was biting Hercules, had six legs and worshipped the Moon. Leo, once slain by Hercules, trampled serpents, was crowned with rays of light, and worshipped the Sun. Winged Virgo, girdled and crowned with wheat and carrying a caduceus, worshipped Mercury. The man carrying the Libra, who was sometimes androgynous, worshipped Venus. Scorpio, the stinger of the goddesses' favorites, had six legs and worshipped Mars. Sagittarius the centaur was exactly what he was and worshipped Jupiter. Bearded Capricorn worshipped none but Saturn. Aquarius, who poured out not water, but nectar, also worshipped Saturn. And the siren Pisces, who were masculine rather than feminine, worshipped Jupiter. Our one-hundred-per-cent devoted Astrologist made offerings of herbs and spices to the planets, convinced as he was that had he lived in the olden days he would have been a magician: on Sundays he made offerings of pepper to the Sun, on Mondays offerings of saffron to the Moon, on Tuesdays cinnamon to Mars, on Wednesdays allspice to Mercury, on Thursdays thyme to Jupiter, on Fridays basil to Venus, and on Saturdays cloves to Saturn. The reader might very well wonder, however, what was the point of these herbs and spices sprinkled not at all subtly among the planets and zodiacs. As the life of the Astrologist cannot be a matter of indifference to us, precisely because it plays a rôle in the present history, a meaning may naturally be found in the above. For, on learning of the arrival of the supposed angels in the Metropolis, he carefully examined the huge map in his workroom, hoping to find the star and the zodiac auspicious to virtual, if not necessary and real, angels. The tireless Astrologist turned over every facet of the zodiacs and planets, even juggling not only the familiar names of his beloved celestial instruments, but also their secret Arabic and Indian names. Saturn was Zuhal and Sanaiscara, cold, dry, sullen, dark. Jupiter was Mushtar and Hindbara, warm, moist, virtuous. Mars was Mirih and Mangala, inauspicious, violent, desirous of glory. The Sun was Sham and Surya, wise and lucky. Venus was Zuhara and Sukra, chill, opulent, indolent. Mercury was Utarid and Buddha, neutral, a diviner of truth. The Moon was Qamar and Suma, cold but auspicious. But what use is it to list all these names, qualities and defects? Well, there is at least one use: besides the seven planets, the Astrologist knew something that not many other people know, namely that hidden away in the heavenly tinfoil there is an eighth, invisible, fictive planet, whose form is that of a curled dragon, and the name of this planet is Jawzafar. Named the planet of the Dragon of lunar eclipses, it had never been identified in the firmament, but the astrologers had nonetheless managed to divine its heavenly garb, even if it was only a pseudo-planet. And so the Astrologist, albeit under his breath, asked himself whether this might not be the planet appropriate to the three angels, even if they were only quarter-angels, who had landed on the soil of the Sacred Homeland. Ultimately, every planet underwent an exile from time to time, entering an inauspicious or at least twisted zodiac. And so how would it have been if this pseudo-planet, Jawzafar, had had wings and not necessarily the form of a dragon, but only that of a lunar eclipse? How would it have been if he, the Astrologist, had managed to prove first to the Metropolis and then to the entire world that the zodiac could be adapted and interpreted not only according to day and night, but also according to the sacred or relatively sacred, but blatant, emissaries sent to a fractured world, a world torn into four pieces, a schizophrenic world? In his workroom the Astrologist had an astrolabe that he had bought from an antique shop and talismans by the dozen: the astrolabe he used often and even worked on its brass; but up until now he had never touched the talismans, given that there hadn't been any need. And so this was the moment when the talismans came to life, setting the Astrologist's workroom a-jingle, and even urging this celebrated resident of the Metropolis not to admit defeat, but to proceed to make a predictable demonstration: the angels or angel-men needed a converted or convertible planet, and that planet had to be Jawzafar. The Astrologist—oh, what a good thing that he hadn't chosen for himself the insipid moniker Nostradamus—stroked each spot on his gigantic stellar map and did not wonder that each character had four arms and two heads, to indicate the multiple powers of each planet: the Sun was androgynous and had two lions with intertwining tails around its neck, the Moon was bicephalous and had tattooed faces, Mars was a warrior bearing severed heads, Mercury was a scribe with two chins, Venus was a Siamese twin playing the harp, Saturn was a black king sliced down the middle and holding a book, Jupiter was a bipartite philosopher holding a fish in each hand. Why are the angels silent? The Astrologist was silent too, as if he were not taciturn enough already. The angels were silent because they knew too much and too intensely. The angels are silent or else they bear tidings, but even when they bear tidings they are silent:

they speak little, they are niggardly in their speech. So too the three who had arrived in the Metropolis. They were silent because they were listening to somebody else. Their silence was skillful and highly precise. Their silence never missed the mark. Their silence was a wager. The eighth planet, Jawzafar, must also be a silent or deaf-mute planet. At the court of the Sun King could be found princess Moon, counselor Jupiter, page Mercury, *guerillero* Mars, priest Saturn, and courtesan Venus. Ah, reader, you don't have to remember all these complicated names. They're nothing but breath-freshening mints. The Astrologist, Jawzafar. Utter them with care.

IS AN UNDERTAKER ALWAYS ALSO A THANATOLOGIST?

An angel was riding an angel with horseshoe bracelets. Neither had a sun hat or sunglasses. An angel was riding an angel shod with hair curlers. Where they were going nobody knew. The two angels did not fly and they had neither voice, nor wings, nor parchment above them, only a glass eye on their shaven or perhaps plucked chests. Then the pair met a third angel. It is never clear whether an undertaker is always also simultaneously a thanatologist, but what is for sure is that it is less likely for an undertaker also to be a poet. But there was one undertaker, an upstanding resident of Metropolis, who was precisely that, which is to say, a secret poet: he never set his verses down on paper, but recited them in his head, and then allowed them slowly to vanish, letting the words fade away. And so it was now, when the descent of the three strangers set him to thinking, first of all with the object of enhancing the prosperity and reputation of his funeral parlor. What was it called? Ah, the waggish reader can already imagine it: it was called *Carpe Diem*. Are angels our doubles? That was the question that caused the director of the funeral parlor sleepless nights. And if indeed angels are our doubles, then do they who appear immediately after our death or do they emerge from our mouths when we give up the ghost? Are angels mirrors? If God's madness was as huge and as intricate as is rumored in the scriptures, then angels can be nothing but His wiser, more mindful forms of madness. Then the undertaker thought of the function of trans-lucidity and the quality (or defect) of being trans-lucid. For, death in primarily something of that sort: a trans-lucid matter. Who does not die because he has lived? An insane question. Death at dawn or at twilight, but not death at noon, that being the most insufferable. The angel teaches us to love, but ought he not also teach us to die? To die a beautiful death, that is, an immaculate, pure, serene death. Hmm, not everybody dies that way. It's impossible and improbable, given that plenty of people agonize without having any choice in the matter. And it is not their angels that torture them so. If God first created the angels, then they must also be destined to be the last to disappear, when death ceases to exist, because death will have to die before them. One thing is sure: the angels never rest. The director of the funeral parlor all of a sudden felt as if he were levitating, floating on the clouds. But above all else he had to be realistic and pragmatic. The *Carpe Diem* firm needed a new look; it needed the angels. But they needn't be angels of death (everybody was sick of angels of death), that is, crepuscular angels, but rather the opposite, angels of life, of the sparkling variety. The secret poet pictured coffins with stylized wings, however macabre and risqué that image might be. The third angel was riding the two angels with bracelets on his ankles, and they were all wearing sun hats and sunglasses. They all had hair curlers in their long hair. But none of them was flying, because their glass eyes weighed too much and dangled like bunches of grapes. None of them was shaven. Bearded, with curled hair, with glass eyes, that is, blind from birth. The undertaker did not want to encourage necrophilia, however, even if he was meditating on coffins with angelic wings. But the dead body deserved to be buried, humanely or even inhumanely speaking, together with the insignia of its double, that is, the angel. The secret poet also thought of lacework made from goose feathers, to line the coffins and make them soft and paradisiacal. He thought of masks made of feathers to cover the faces of the deceased. Like at the carnival, except that this was to be their final carnival. A fluffy, airy requiem. In the event that the angels did not die. In the event that they were not borne off down the river. For, reason has killed everything. The secret poet smiled, while the undertaker frowned. If angels could not fly, the devil could fly almost anywhere. The director of the funeral parlor pictured angelically stylized coronets of flowers, but he discarded the image, finding it predictable and outmoded. That wasn't the kind of thing he required: what he wanted was to put forward a poetry, a lyricism, of death, or rather burial, inhumation, entombment, or whatever you wanted to call it. A poetry of funerals, to be more precise. But what if the angels were haughty in their angelicity? Categorically not, with a single exception, the secret poet told himself. But what I have in view is not fallen angels! But in that instant, the director of the funeral parlor was struck by a grave intuition: what if the three strangers were in fact fallen angels in the worse possible sense? Nobody had thought of that up until now! Fallen angels, that is, guilty, sinful angels, and hence mute, flightless angels. Because they were proud. The undertaker could not refrain from a little righteous shudder: alas, it wouldn't be at all healthy if the strangers were Luciferian! It would be more satisfying to everybody, including politicians, if they, the strangers, were or looked like birds: then things would be clear! But no, they didn't want to be or to look like typical angels. They had arrived in some other fashion. They looked different than usual, although not necessarily the opposite to the usual. Could they have fallen? Or rather, might they have fallen upwards? Receiving bodies like any other body, i.e. sexually differentiated, albeit not apt for pleasure, bodies coursing with living blood. Or had they fallen in the same way that everybody else falls: strictly downward. Where was the poetry of funerals? Let us get back to our pro- and counter-angelic discussion. The undertaker did not intend to wrack his brains trying to establish whether or not they were angels or what their mission might be, holy or otherwise. There was just one thing that he wanted to know: whether the strangers had fallen upward or downward, whether they had been sent or whether they had just come without being sent (or sent away) by somebody. On the answer to this depended the new look of the *Carpe Diem* funeral parlor, given that winged coffins by themselves wouldn't necessarily revolutionize the firm's advertising. And then an old prayer came into his mind (hmm): Angel, before thee I fall, my guardian, who is given unto me that I may rein in my sinful body and soul. Thee have I angered, thee have I driven away, thee I have slandered, and thee I have envied. How shalt thou seek me that thou might cleanse me? Woe unto my sins witting and unwitting, known and unknown! Phoo! Then, right then, the undertaker was touched by the boundless wing of inspiration: yes, naturally, of course, obviously, certainly, the wings of the coffin had to be acoustic, that is, equipped with recordings of short prayers like that one, recited by professional actors. In that way, the soul of the deceased would be genuinely guarded by entities, albeit pseudo-angelic ones. But that didn't matter; it didn't weigh so much as the dirt under your fingernails! All that mattered was the musicality of the coffins, not what they looked like: only their recitative musicality. There was no need for the music of the spheres. There was no need for angels of sugar. Angels of salt were also useful, and even more interesting. Angels of salt? The secret poet in the undertaker popped his head up yet again: the three angels were riding brooms of feathers. The bracelets on their ankles writhed like women. All three were wearing sunglasses. Their glass eyes were broken. None of them was shaved. None of them smelled of incense. All were bitter. As for death, where was death? Was death anywhere at all?

A MASTER OF CRYOGENICS AND HIS GLACIAL YEARNINGS

Angels are pure intellect, therefore their brains ought to be preserved in time, in order to be of use to humans in the future, when they will be more knowledgeable, prophesied the Metropolis's Master of Cryogenics. He was the director of the only eminently private and general institute that dealt with such matters and which had almost a hundred long steel crates, in which were frozen millionaires desirous of being brought back to life in a few decades. The sense organs are rhetorical in the case of the angels, the Master of Cryogenics further glossed, voraciously, like a *causeur* of the self. Cognition, reason and enlightenment are what count in any angelic question, decided the Cryogenic One, as he was privately nicknamed. Physiology and the humors are no longer of any import, but only the idea, because the angels are idea, made of pure ideas. Thus spoke the Cryogenic One to his staff at the Institute, who all had a background in the hard sciences: they were mathematicians, physicists, chemists, biologists, for the most part. Nor were experts in cybernetics and genetics lacking. And ideas are not prostitutes, as one philosopher long ago would have it, declared the Cryogenic One, continuing his inspired discourse, addressing employees who were all brain and reason. Ideas are not like prostitutes inasmuch as they could not possibly be anything of the kind: they function like a perfect, coherent, impassive brain. So too the angels: and it is only via them that we might reach the origins of the cosmos. The yearnings of the Cryogenic One were highly ambitious, for which reason the journalists of the Metropolis, all eyes and ears, used to try to storm the Glacial Institute, to scale its high walls. But it was not to be: for, the trenchant speeches of the Cryogenic One were addressed strictly to his underlings, for purposes of thorough professional initiation, and so the walls of the Institute remained just as high and as inaccessible to outsiders preoccupied with what was going on inside. Because they are made the way they are, the angels know no confusion and cannot be confused: they are equal to themselves, exactly like God. This was the turning point in the discourse of the Cryogenic One. They are neither toxic nor residual, I hope you understand, for which reason they do not experiment. It is wonderful that this is the way things stand! The angels are fundamentalist thinkers, even if such a position entails risks. They are pure cerebral energy, although they lack something essential: the human imagination. To compensate for this not necessarily culpable lack, scientists have come into the world. Naturally, it is not hard to understand that what I am now proposing is an angelophany: how to induce the resurrection of cryogenically frozen people, taking advantage of meticulous research conducted on a frozen angel. How to create the new, the second, the perfect Adam! This is the reason why our institute urgently requires the preservation of one of the bodies of the three strangers newly abiding in the Metropolis. At this point, the Cryogenic One's staff sighed, and it was no wonder: it was predictable that their director's ambitions should that way tend. Why had it not occurred to them from the very start? But as they say, when it comes to things visible and invisible, nobody can judge except the Almighty, and sometimes not even He. Maybe the other one, the Devil, might have had a word to say (but this is not the place to talk about him). Wrestling with the angel? The Cryogenic One suddenly asked. It means wrestling with ideas and the pure brain and it relates to the essentialized everyday, to life in the here and now. And our supreme freedom is to be able to wrestle the angel, to wrestle ideas. The staff gave their director a playful look: might wrestling with the angel transform this acerbic speech into a ski slope or figure-skating rink? Why do you think that angels are the only ones that have access to the face of God? Hmm, that is the question, words, words, words. Why is there only one supreme ladder by which the angels can ascend and descend? Ought we to invoke the angels precisely in their incorporeality? Then let us proceed accordingly: I call upon you to understand that which cannot be understood, to know that which we cannot know, to see that which we cannot see; do not separate yourselves from these hearts. The staff gave the Cryogenic One a funny look: what did the heart have to do with all the rest of it? It is not with the heart that you understand the man, but with the mind. Unless he is just a scarecrow. Our guardian angels, if they are all around, suffer due to the ones they guard. Did you know that sometimes it is the ass that sees angels, rather than humble man? Thus did the Cryogenic One convolutedly conclude. Nobody can swear that the three strangers were quite simply angels, let alone guardian angels. But dawn is breaking, and so let us end our discourse on ideas, shall we, reader? Let us draw the delirium to a close. Nothing is closer to the reason and the pure intellect than ice, than the supreme cold, which cause the flesh and the body to be forgotten almost for an eternity.

The brain of an angel perfectly conserved in a crate of ice. Then the second, the perfect, Adam would come, and resurrection would be a mere cooking recipe. The Cryogenic One was a visionary. But in vain. And I forgot to mention: the Cryogenic One was wearing overalls made of rubberized silk.

MERLIN MANUFACTURES ANGEL AVATARS FOR VITA ALIA

Naturally, God exists above all when you need Him, but when you are in need and He doesn't show up, then you can find somebody else much more pragmatic and closer to people. Who could it be? Who other than Merlin Stral! The said Merlin read as much as he could and guzzled information: he had been doing so for ten years, and now he was twenty-five and about to create an Empire: *Vita Alia*. Because he was fascinated with Noah's Ark, using ambition and self-hypnosis he had built *Vita Alia*, the most provocative alternative game on the Internet. He had black, unevenly trimmed hair, tied back in thin ponytails, and eyes equally black (let us be permitted not to create a detailed portrait of Merlin, but rather to leave his physical appearance shadowy). In his electronic Ark were to be found people of every race, sex and human type, plus animals from every continent, including fictional and fantastical beasts. One thing was missing: when Merlin found out about the descent of the three supposed angels to the Metropolis, he realized that the major lack in the *Vita Alia* system was angels. He felt his fingers itching as he pictured a section for angels. Merlin smoked like a chimney, but now he gracefully gave up the habit. He was the only resident of Metropolis who did not need to see the angels in the flesh and blood, given that he could concoct them from thin air: it was not a beating heart that Merlin required, but avatars. And avatars were his puppets in the electronic world. Merlin Stral drank a cup of strong coffee and twiddled the ring in his left eyebrow. God could no longer make angels nowadays, but Merlin could: a grave and merry Angeliad, this was what Merlin craved. A horde, a convoy of angels to suit the tastes of *Vita Alia* gamers. The number of maniacs was in the millions, not only in Metropolis and the Sacred Homeland, but all over the world. Because the idiom of communication was pidgin, Merlin had known from the beginning that he would need a language like a rainbow. The Metropolitans had immediately got used to the pidgin of *Vita Alia*, and they even felt initiated thanks to the idiom in question, because it was as if they had their own personal and collective jargon. Over the course of a few hundred days Merlin had built an entire empire. In fact it had been a wager with himself: naturally, his first aim had been to get rich, but then he had become fascinated with the world he had created and which he could use to manipulate other people. He was a high-performance manipulator. Nevertheless, something had been lacking up until then: the angels, the cursed or miraculous angels had slipped through his fingers. But Merlin was to have his revenge, because he was an inter-nautical wizard, a magician, or at least he yearned to be. He was to begin with the three angels, and then go on to create ramifications that would drive the *Vita Alia* gamers out of their minds. He wanted to make them permanently insane. As for the three angels, Merlin wasted no time thinking about it. Their name needed to be adapted to *Vita Alia*: they were to be called Mihal, Gabral and Rafal. And they would have the same surname as Mesmaea: and that surname was Cuttita. Mesmaea had not been an angeless to begin with, but queen of the Land of Mushrooms: Mesmaea cultivated hallucinogenic mushrooms and they were all she ate; she sold her mushrooms to nobody, and at the most accepted guests for a few days. Merlin had created Mesmaea Cuttita with the delight of a frolicsome demiurge. And now he felt the need to insert Mesmaea into the world of the three angels, who were to multiply exponentially. Mesmaea was to be the Bride. Perhaps Mesmaea would lay eggs and from those eggs would hatch distinctive hominids. And perhaps the eggs would lie in an Incubator for a time. Merlin did not ask himself pointless questions, because there would have been no point: why did Mesmaea in particular have to be the Bride to the three angels so that they could become a tribe, a caste, a people? In *Vita Alia*, anything was possible, which is why everything was permissible, including procreation with angels. In this way a new race was to be born. Merlin had eliminated from his vocabulary the verbs to fantasize and to invent, but he had kept the verb to concoct: he had eliminated the other two precisely so that he would have a free hand; not for nothing was his name Merlin. But now he was seriously thinking about adopting the name even in his identity papers and also, of course, changing his surname to the one he had concocted for himself: Stral. Merlin Stral. It was not for nothing that Mesmaea had been chosen as the angels' future companion: in the Land of Mushrooms she flew all the time, and not just anyhow, but without wings. She was able to fly thanks to the mushrooms she ate. Merlin intended to turn the new Angel Zone into an area especially for different types of flight: vertical, horizontal, fast, slow, rocket, butterfly, dragonfly, etc. As for Mesmaea, she was not to fly around for very much longer, as her magical rôle was now to procreate. Merlin didn't intend to turn her into some sort of Virgin Mary. Not a bit of it. Mesmaea had to be a real-virtual woman companion to the three angels: not a temptress, not a marsupial, not a witch. Quite simply a woman who was to give birth to a new race, produced by coupling with Mihal, Gabral and Rafal. For this, there was no need for a caste of Viscounts, or Sacerdotes, or Morpheics, which were a dime a dozen in *Vita Alia*. On the other hand, the new race, once created, would have to avoid the Death Dealers, that is, the gamers who operated within the system merely to eliminate the other players. Merlin did not want to come up with just any circus act, but rather a show, a performance that would allow him to be a full demiurge once again. Above all, the idea of a new human race fascinated him: and the new race was to be called *mangel*. The young Mr. Stral had already come up with the clothing for the new race: long blue silk tunics with a scarf around the neck. The shoulders of the mangels would be tattooed with blue wings from birth, likewise their chests and backs. And their eyes would be made up in blue. As for Mesmaea, she had to be their only Bride. The new race would have to avoid, as I have already said (and I repeat), the Death Dealers: the most dangerous of these was Lilih Angustias, a brunette with hair plaited in the African style, who was a liquidator in the old-fashioned gangster style. Merlin knew one thing for sure: human creatures had to imagine not as much as they could, but as much as they wished and as much as they didn't wish. Wherefore Merlin's aim was to make all the other castes, that is, the Viscounts, the Sacerdotes and the Morpheics, purchase and yearn for as many mangels as possible. Not to liquidate them, but to purchase them as guardian mangels. The most difficult part would be with the Morpheics, given that they, as somnolent mutants, were continually shifting and didn't have any fixed identity, but rather they were made up of two, three and even four avatars stuck together or hybridized with each other. There was also another caste, the Jokers, but there were not very many of them; the Jokers loved to play, and so Merlin's Mangeliad couldn't fail to delight them. There were also master-slave relationships; they weren't brutal, but just as jolly. Strangely or not, the future mangels would fall under neither the master nor the slave category. Merlin knew something else too: after the angels and Mesmaea mated and created the new race, in order to ramify the caste of mangels, he, the *demiurgus redivivus*, would have likewise to create the Alteri. These were avatars closer to the real thing than the first-rank avatars. They were, you might say, secondary and less histrionic avatars. Merlin intended the ordinary mangels to have huge eyebrows that would hang over their eyes like wings. And a moustache to match. As for their environment, Merlin pictured spiral dwellings, huge, twisting tubes, covered in tinfoil. And palm trees, lots of palm trees, white sand, and the sea, concentrated in a crystal fountain. Of course, the mangels would constantly have to avoid the Death Dealers and especially Lilih Angustias, who was also an undertaker and who held elaborate funerals for her victims. Lilih also own an avatar bodies company: here she recycled the bodies of the avatars she liquidated and sold them back to *Vita Alia* gamers. Usually, the recycling was carried out via human, Egyptian bodies, with animal heads on their shoulders. Merlin also desired to create an Archipelago for the mangels that Mesmaea Cuttita would give birth to, to which end he had already purchased various islands, invented by somebody or other, which he forcibly merged in inter-nautical space. The islands were to be stripped of their natives, all kinds of avatars, and repopulated with mangels. Also required were the so-called Taxi Drivers: these were marsupial avatars, hosts that agreed to gestate incomplete avatars or ones in the process of construction. To achieve the arborescence of the mangels that Merlin Stral wagered on, Mesmaea as queen bee would have to have a hundred Taxi Drivers at her disposal. Merlin also had another idea of near genius, but he abandoned it for supreme theoretical reasons: it crossed his mind to create a Church of Mangels. In the end he abandoned speculation in that direction, leaving it up to any virtual theologians who might be interested, after the race of mangels came into being and enhanced *Vita Alia*. On the other hand, he thought long and hard about whether he should equip the mangels with standard parachutes. Standard parachutes for mangels whose flight was defective. Hmm, it was not an idea to be discarded, given that there would probably be a number of rejects among the mangels and, as the Spartans of old used to say, if we don't do away with the rejects, then let's at least find them helpful prostheses. Merlin didn't want to have a mangel ghetto, but rather an expanding hatchery. It was essential to isolate the new race in the beginning, and after that would come the invasion and colonization, if the mangels proved to be at least three-quarters as perfect as the avatars in *Vita Alia*. Merlin's wager was with the world, with God, with computers, and with himself. What jobs and trades would the mangels ply once they reached maturity and, above all, once they achieved power? Even an idiot could have told you: they would sell books and music. It was the only more or less human occupation Merlin could imagine for them. As for Mesmaea, once she had been used up as birth-giver to the new race, the twenty-five-year-old demiurge knew that she would be in fatal danger of being liquidated by Lilih the exterminator, the Death Dealer. Unless rescuers appeared on the horizon: who else other than Anir Magnifico and Narkom Zarthus! But more about them later, as there is no rush. The rescuers can always wait, as they have good reason to do so.

THE PEOPLE AND THE ANGELS, OR, ONCE MORE ON HOW EVERYDAY LIFE UNFOLDS IN A METROPOLIS

Come, now, with me, reader, and let us see how the citizens of the Metropolis reacted to all the events that took place in the national stadium and those broadcast on national television. Let us see what they have to say and what the neighbor washing the dishes in her kitchen, the conductor on the tram, the ice cream vendor, the hairdresser, the lottery ticket seller, the estate agent, the milkman (if such a job still exists nowadays), the cleaning woman at the cinema, the steamroller driver at work on the highways of the Sacred Homeland, the horticulturalist at the Botanical Gardens, the chief accountant at the Ministry of Water, the copyist at the Registry of the Urban Population, the president's bodyguard, the trainee psychiatrist at the Private Hospice for the Nouveaux Riches, the owner of the metropolitan football team, the postman of a working-class district, and others think about it all. People, people, look at all the people! Let us take them one by one. The neighbor washing dishes in her kitchen, who might be any of the neighbors that are grateful when some gilded but faraway event graces their lives, was enchanted by the nocturnal Angeliad. Most of all she liked the giraffes, as she had often imagined herself in the jungle among the wild animals. The angels were also ultimately a kind of wild animal; even if they were human, they weren't entirely so. The neighbor thought of their long hair tied in ponytails, for example: they were definitely like a wild animal's. Remembering that the three guests were to be given the freedom of Metropolis, the neighbor said to herself that it would not be a bad thing if she were to touch at least one of them with her hand: either she would be instantly blessed, or she would find out that the angels were exactly like everybody else. The tram conductor, well, he began his day with a piece of bad luck: a black cat crossed his path early in the morning, causing him to trip and twist his ankle, but not severely enough to prevent him from arriving at work and the tram he had served for many years. He washed the windows rather apathetically, he exchanged some light-hearted banter with the tram driver, and then his working day commenced. Well, yes, said the tram conductor to himself: if you're an angel it doesn't mean that you don't have to buy a ticket when you board the tram. Except that angels don't travel by tram, he added. Their wings are their tram: true, the angels that have come here from elsewhere don't have wings, and so, at a pinch, they might travel by tram. But they would definitely travel without a ticket and I would have to give them a fine. At this point the tram conductor imagined fishing a receipt from his bag, filling it in, fining the angels, and swearing at them for good measure. The ice cream vendor had a cold and what was more he wasn't in the mood for chitchat. If those blokes from last night were angels, he said to himself, they wouldn't eat anything, but they might like to taste a little ice cream. But what flavor? Chocolate would be too tempting for them, vanilla too ordinary, and as for tutti-frutti, well, I don't think so. What flavor of ice cream would angels eat? The ice cream vendor scratched his head. The truth is, he said to himself, only humans eat ice cream. Angels never eat it: otherwise they'd damage their vocal cords. Maybe that's why they're mute. What a laugh! The hairdresser was arranging her sprays for different hair types on the shelf, then her scissors, combs, driers and gels, waiting for her customers from metropolitan high society to arrive. Her customers all had dry, fragile hair. If only they had healthy, yellow, wavy angel hair, what daring hairstyles I could create! Masterpieces, nothing less! Palaces, jungles, cakes. If the angels from last night let me give them a little trim, if I could get my hands on a tuft of their hair, if, only if, I might be able to discover the secret of the perfect wig for all the high-society ladies of Metropolis! I ought to become a wig maker, the duchess of wigs, oh, and then all those ladies would be nothing but shrews good only for throwing in the garbage! The lottery ticket seller was in a good mood: it may well be that somebody won those angels on the lottery, without word getting out. That's why they turned up so suddenly, without any prior announcement! They're winning angels and they bring good luck. Why hasn't anybody with half a brain thought of that? That's why they don't talk, why they're mute, why you don't get a peep out of them, why they're not surprised at anything. Because they know what they've got to do. But what the hell is it that they've got to do? The estate agent couldn't make head or tail of the nocturnal Angeliad. Those angels are pointless, because they don't know what it means to own your own home. They don't have anywhere to live. Who the hell sent them here to muddy the waters? And why did they have to land slap-bang in the middle of our Metropolis? They can't have a single penny, not even to buy a one-room flat. But let us leave the estate agent to his own thoughts, because it's obvious that he lives in a world whose single compass is property deals. After the nocturnal spectacular the milkman had been left with one question stuck in his mind: mightn't those angels, milky as they were, which is to say, milky-skinned, be able to produce a divine cheese for the people? Then the citizens would be able to tuck into angelic products, like people taking communion in church! The milkman kept turning it over in his mind, trying to find ways to get rich and urgent solutions to fill his pockets that would also be to the delectation of the nation. Not bread and circuses, but angels and circus! The cleaning woman at the cinema didn't have any idea at all: her mind was completely blank. She was busy mopping the floor. I don't have a clue why all those people gathered there in the stadium with all those animals; I don't have a clue why clever people say they're angels; I don't have a clue why they had to make such a hullabaloo here; I don't have a clue. The steamroller driver at work on the highways of the Sacred Homeland was trying to find the best way of flattening high-performance motorway asphalt. How lucky those angels are, how lucky! They don't need roads, they travel through the air, they don't need asphalt, they don't have put up with the smell of tar all day long, how good to be an angel rather than a human! If you gave them a steamroller, they wouldn't know what to do with it, at least I can be thankful for that much. The horticulturalist at the Botanical Gardens was watering the tropical plants in the hothouse, sprinkling earth and sand brought from afar. We could do with some angels here at the Botanical Gardens. They would be like sacred, well-behaved monkeys, who could give us all kinds of tips. I would let them swing from the banana trees in hammocks and get up to whatever they wanted in the palm trees; I'd let them flit around the greenhouses and hothouses to their hearts' content. Provided they could put up with the heat and humidity. Because that's one thing we don't really know about angels: whether they can put up with conditions like those. I don't know what tips I would ask from them, but I could do with some angels around here. The chief accountant at the Ministry of Water was carefully totting up the figures for the current month: such and such a quantity of water consumed per capita, such and such money, such and such losses, such and such outstanding bills. Then, suddenly, in the middle of a calculation, he remembered the Angeliad. What a huge waste on the part of the authorities! At a time when water was running short in this world, the authorities were busy with nonsense like that! Angels—who had ever heard the like? Angels! Pooh! All that counts is water and the air we breathe, nothing more, nothing less. Water, water, and thrice water! The copyist at the Registry of the Urban Population was bored to death: those angels from last night might at least amuse me a little if they turned up here. Come on, if that's what you really are, then show yourselves, angels! Come here and visit me, the undersigned! I'm bored to death and I've got no zest for life. I don't even know what I'd do if the wee angels did come: should I register them as part of the population or not? The president's bodyguard, who was a muscle-bound mountain of a man, had an unclean thought buzzing around in his head: what if the President needed an angel more than a bodyguard? What if I'm surplus to requirements? What if those angels are real? That would mean my job as a bodyguard was nothing but a joke. Mr. President, I wish to tender my resignation: this was what was going round in the gorilla's mind, although he didn't say a word. The trainee psychiatrist at the Private Hospice for the Nouveaux Riches (PHNR) was wondering whether the citizens of Metropolis who believed that the three strangers were angels might all need to be admitted to the Hospice or at least prescribed sedatives for a while. That didn't mean that the angels didn't have the right to exist, of course: but electric shocks might still be just the ticket in such a situation of collective delirium. Not to mention in situations of individual delirium. The authorities themselves ought to undergo a course of electric shock therapy, to get rid of the hornets' nests buzzing in their heads. Hmm. The owner of the metropolitan football team was deep in thought, resting his chin on his hand: I've believed in angels since I was a child, but I never imagined they would show themselves to me. Not just to me, but to everybody. Maybe for that reason the three strangers aren't angels after all. But rather something else, the devil knows what. But I admit that I could do with such specimens in my line of business: I'd hire them to get up to all kinds of tricks on the pitch, to trip the other players up and make the ball go astray. But I'd need something to lure them with: angels don't need women, or money, or booze. Nobody knows what it is they want. The postman in the Metropolis's most working-class district, walking with his head bowed, carrying his huge mail bag on his back, and wearing his threadbare cap, was wondering what he would have to do if the angels received a letter, or if the angels sent letters to the inhabitants of the Metropolis or his district. I'm a bit like a relative of theirs, because angels are postmen, too. Messengers, that is. At least I learned that much in church. Some people are God's messengers, some are people's messengers. Honorable reader, I could naturally present to you many other categories of metropolitan, but I shall stop here, as it's enough already.

THE ESTABLISHMENT OF A QUARANTINE ZONE, PLUS THE GLOSSES OF A LION TAMER AND AN OLD CLOWN

The President, the Government, El Leader Maximo, the television channels, and the press had all realized that they would have to release the three guests, who could neither be held hostage, nor as exhibits in some museum of advanced zoology, nor as privy counselors on theological matters, nor as anything else. The supposed angels had to be released onto the streets, among the ordinary metropolitans. But before that could happen, there needed to be a quarantine period and a quarantine zone, which was hastily established. The zone in question was thought up by one of the President's highfaluting acolytes, and this is why it looked never clever, nor paradigmatic, nor normal. It was a huge tent that would have been more appropriate for dressage events or circus clownery: a lead-lined tent disinfected with camphor, as if the three guests might be infected with viruses unknown to Earth. The medical commission had kicked up something of a fuss, demanding that three adult-sized disinfection incubators also be installed, in which the three might be examined under a magnifying glass as they slept, so that their suspected viruses would have time to perish. The strange thing was that even the three guests' clothes had been confiscated to this end, so that they could be X-rayed and then placed inside a steam oven. Placed on what looked like catapults, the three young male bodies were sterilized using camphor and then left to dry. It looked more like an exotic circus act than anything else. All that was lacking were acrobats and tightrope walkers and conjurers to entertain people, as if the guests that had descended upon the Metropolis were beasts to be venerated and abused at the same time. Predictably, none of the three complained about what was happening to them. In the incubators, their bodies had contorted at one point, as if somebody were spitting flames at them, but that was all. A famous Lion Tamer from the Metropolis, watching the quarantine ritual on television, immediately announced that some amulets wouldn't come amiss, if the citizens of the Metropolis were prepared to wear something like that. What kind of amulets? Anti-angelic ones, obviously. In the end, hadn't it been the crusaders who had in ancient times banned the citizens of Rome from watching the circus shows so dear to them? Crusaders who had not, however, given up clowns. Wherefore the famous lion tamer asked himself the burning question: what if the trio that had plunged down into the Metropolis were clowns in disguise? This was a nuance that nobody had come up with thitherto, for which reason it was swiftly rejected: although the metropolitans had a taste for saltimbanques and food counters, bibelots and other trifles, they had nonetheless battened onto the idea of angels, as if they were just waiting for holy relics or miracle-working unguents to fall from the sky. The three vagabonds, even if they weren't necessarily angels, could not possibly be charlatans. In any event, the quarantine zone, as it had been designed, looked more like a circus for sophisticated masquerades, including medical ones, in which the guests played the part of cripples. Anyway, not even in so humiliating a situation did the three complain, given that they were, after all, mute. But the heavenly and earthly pantomimes were, all the same, over the top. People wanted talk, not amputated tongues. In the days of old, such an apparition would have been a portent of imminent plague and would have been accompanied by sword swallowers and puppet shows. Likewise, in those distant times, the question would have arisen as to whether a huge, triumphal bearded woman might not be able to seduce the three quasi-angelic specimens. In the crazy quarantine zone an Old Clown was keeping watch from a distance: for him, the difference between the metropolitans and the guests fallen from the heavens was one of race. The Old Clown knew that the times for fiery sermons had passed and he also knew that the new world was poisoned with supervisory commissions, selection boards, meetings, complaints, petitions. All that was missing for a commission for letting off firecrackers to top it all. The Old Clown played dice, backgammon and dominoes at home on his own: he played by himself because he didn't have any interlocutors to match him. He had transcended the feeling of accusatory anger; he had also transcended human pettiness and the sterility of dialogue and monologue. When he was really bored he would blow soap bubbles for hours on end or weave butterfly nets, and then, wearing cellophane gloves, he would untangle the wings from the mesh and let the butterflies go free. His laughter was wry only because of old age, and the angels, or the supposed angels, aroused his curiosity for the first time in a very long while. He viewed their quarantine as a spectacle of sophisticated torture, invisible to the eyes of the many, and he knew all too well the reason for it: the guests were seen as monsters that embodied fear of the world, fear of God, fear of everything. In his youth, the Old Clown himself had been seen as a kind of diminutive, merry monster, hence his need for thick, strident make-up as a means of self-defense. The only thing that surprised him about the supposed angels was that their faces weren't made up: he would have expected their eyes to be made up in violet tones, for example, as if they had hypnotic bags under their eyes. He would have expected the angels to be kept in a boxing ring, without knowing why he felt that way, although it was probably due to the fact that the Sacred Homeland and its high-ups engaged in a frothy sort of political pimping, blatantly publicizing it at every opportunity. He had by then witnessed the countless public debates about the unproven and non-flying angels; the string pulling that went on behind the scenes was meticulous! But what interested him about the question of the celestial guests' arrival and descent upon the Metropolis was something completely different: namely, the quasi-angels' potential connection with death. Had they once and far away, not here and now, been angels of death, angels of a gently and sweetly announced death, attended by neither the Apocalypse, nor mischief, nor tricks, nor even a carnival? Were they or not? Or were they, hmm—nobody had thought of this before—merely the fantasies of some unknown person, who had caused them to turn up in the Metropolis out of the blue? Were they or were they not fatal precisely because of their muteness, their unpretentious and discreet way of being? For, not being androgynous, the three strangers had proven to be of the male sex, thankfully for the misogynists who would otherwise died of pique! The quarantine lasted for just one day, and so we can't say it was disinfestation in the classic sense, but rather a slapdash affair. The authorities wanted at all costs to get shot of the burden of the faux angels, as they were thus decreed stubbornly and emphatically, conclusively and not necessarily spectacularly. Of course, some politicians still said officially or off the record that the guests ought to be employed in the crucial sectors of the Sacred Homeland, that is, to attract souls eager for the sacrosanct, these being gullible or confused voters. The populace wanted miracles, they wanted angels: if these were not angels, then angels had to be concocted, in politics it was not the will of the Lord that counted, but the will of the dizzied electorate. The citizen that wanted angels should be given angels by the kilo, as it wasn't possible by the ton. By the milligram was too little, but by the kilo was doable. And so the quarantine didn't achieve anything much, as it wasn't a textbook disinfection, it didn't protect the citizens from the plague, and the visitors that had fallen from the sky weren't treated with any medicaments. The quarantine had been a sham, designed to impress, and even the Metropolis's garbage collectors knew it. The guests could now be delivered to the people, for the people to do with them what they willed. As the quarantine ends here, so too shall the chapter on it come to a close, but not before we make a ninety-degree turn back to the character mentioned above. Perhaps the Old Clown (and not the Lion Tamer) ought to have had a special place in this book, but his thoughts came to manifest themselves visibly only as a result of the quarantine period imposed by the authorities of the Metropolis. Consequently, why should we grant him a leading rôle, if he himself, judicious character that he is, does not wish it, but would rather remain in the shadow? Every author wishes to respect the desires of her characters, and so I too can only bow to the wishes of those about whom I write and whom I cause to speak. But let's see what happens next.

ANIMALS SPEAK, SO WHY SHOULD WE BE STRUCK DUMB WITH AMAZEMENT AT IT?

Humans are one thing, but what about animals? What did they have to say about the three visitors from the sky? And which animals might make a suitable pronouncement about such unusual, nay uninvited, guests? In a Metropolis, be it even the capital of the Sacred Homeland, there dwell ordinary animals such as dogs, cats, rats, mice, hamsters and perhaps even parrots and humming birds, maybe even tortoises, but that's about all. If, let's say, there were to be found in the Metropolis monkeys or tiger cubs, other than at the circus, living in gardens or special rooms in grand villas, then such beasts were the purchases of extravagant millionaires for whom price was no object and who would buy anything just to prove that nothing was beyond their means, no matter how abnormal. And so let us confine ourselves to animals more familiar, animals that we know for certain are to be found in any metropolis, both those that have been visited by angels and those that haven't had the pleasure of such visitants. Although animals do not possess human speech, they nevertheless have a language of their own, and so let us see what is to be done, in other words let us transcribe and transform the animal idiom into a human equivalent and see what it sounds like in the matter we are about to recount. And so: can animals such as dogs, cats, rats, mice, and parrots (we'll be dealing with them in particular) make glosses in the margins of the arrival of the three men with ponytails and blue tunics? We may say that the dogs' perception of it was profoundly canine: nevertheless, without resorting to classic barking, the dogs were nothing more than furry sages, sage enough to credit even the supposedly angelic arrival. If angels really exist, said one of these loquacious dogs, then we too ought to have an angel of dogs. Maybe one exists already, interposed another canine specimen. And if he does not exist, then he ought to be invented, at least for the times we're living in. Or maybe he existed in the past and got sick of being just an angel of dogs. He definitely wouldn't have wings, but he would have a tail and a muzzle. And his tail might be sufficient for a trial flight. Even if angels are long-distance pilots of their own bodies, we dogs have never had such daydreams, put in another individual. You liar! chided the first talking dog: we all have daydreams about flying. You mean to say, a Siamese cat interrupted the canine colloquy, angels might be travelling postmen, who bring letters from heaven. But we cats don't credit such ridiculous claims. We have nine lives and we can use them however we like, and so angels wouldn't be able to alter our destinies. Maybe if we were orphans, but as we're not, the rôle of the angels can't be historical, but only rhetorical. Therefore, the feline mission is to achieve exploits in which the angels would be nothing but soap bubbles. If you want to burst them, then burst them, if not, then don't. In any event, it's always been known that cats are cleverer than dogs. With their inimitable intuition cats will perhaps one day replace angels, and not just anyhow, but by fluttering their tails. And another thing hard to deny: cats always know how to tell stories more tangled than dogs do, including stories about angels. I've never heard any stories told by cats, interposed an old dog, because cats don't know how to tell real stories, but only retarded inventions. Only the god of cats could measure the intelligence of cats: in our case, we wouldn't be content with angels, but only with a fitting god. And then, if we are to believe in something, we might as well believe in mermaids as soon as angels. Look here, interrupted a rat with long whiskers: neither dogs nor cats know how to conduct a serious and responsible discussion about angels. For angels, my dears, are reminders of the rockets that crashed after being expelled from the lonely planets where they had arrived by mistake. That's tommyrot, said the Siamese cat who had loftily spoken earlier. It's a cacophony, protested one of the dogs present at that colloquy of beasts debating the existence or non-existence of angels. I could talk to you in riddles for a long time, continued the rat with the long whiskers. I could twist your brains in knots, but there's no point. Only those who have their own angels can talk about angels; let those who don't be on their way or shut up. To have an angel in us means to have a light that never goes out. You don't necessarily need wings or be able to fly to be an angel. You don't necessarily need long hair. That's why it would be better if we didn't talk nonsense, if we didn't get carried away. Let's be dogs, cats, rats, and let's carry a light in our hearts and heads. That's rather a simplistic theory, said the Siamese cat. He who believes in angels is capable of seeing them anyhow, anywhere, anytime. He who doesn't believe will never see them, not even in the afterlife, added the old dog. I foresee we're going to get into an argument about it, said the rat with the long whiskers. No sooner had he spoken than a mouse turned up among the orators. Angels are what they are, it squeaked: that is, murine creatures. Because angels are in the image and likeness of those that see them, just as humans are in the image and likeness of God. But if someone imagines that angels have no enemies, then he is mistaken. I wisely assert that the enemies of the angels are the cats, inasmuch as they can sniff them out from a mile away. Dogs can do that too, but cats are experts, they're amazons, and they surpass the canine race when it comes to the sense of smell. It's a rather simplistic theory, repeated the aforementioned Siamese cat: mice have exactly the same tedious discourse. The same snore-inducing discourse, added the rat with the long whiskers. Don't speak ill of the dead or of angels! Oh, no, exclaimed the mouse, you've got me all wrong: what I meant was that angels are part of a murky constellation, and so willy-nilly they have lots of enemies, precisely because they're unaware of them. But between them and us there is a link: we're all animals! For the third time I say that it's a rather simplistic theory, repeated the Siamese cat emphatically. Angels would only be animals if they had four legs, she pointed out. But they do have four legs, said the mouse timidly: two normal legs and two arms with wings, even if the wings are not always visible. As in the present case. In the present case, said the old dog, what counts are the wings that can't be seen, and not the wings that don't exist. Inasmuch as we cannot say that they don't exist just because they're not visible. Agreed, said the rat with the long whiskers. Exactly, added the Siamese cat. Agreed, exactly, just like in the present case, four legs, a simplistic theory, even if the wings aren't always visible, interposed a stray parrot who happened to be nearby. I learn words quickly. Four legs, dog, cat, rat, mouse, I'm a parrot and I don't believe in angels. But I might one day.

PART TWO

OF TINY TOTS AND DREAMS

After concise meditation in the Metropolis Fortress, the authorities therefore set the three guests free, and they, one ordinary afternoon, found themselves alone on the street, deposited in one of the Metropolis's outlying districts. It was not very clear why the strangers had been left not in the centre of the capital, but on the outskirts, as if they were criminals intentionally abandoned in such a place. It was a district of standard buildings, simple, poor-looking structures surrounded by weeds and overflowing rubbish skips, home to beasts of every variety: dogs, cats, rats. Such animals did not frighten the three strangers, however, and they did not seem at all daunted at having been left to their own devices. No sooner had they come to their senses than they found themselves face to face with two little children: a girl with a blue dress and lopsided pigtails, as if one had been cut short by mistake, and a boy with freckles. Both were holding teddy bears

"Who are you?" the children asked, but the three guests just shrugged.

Then the tots began to talk sign language to them: first they clenched their fists, then they opened their palms, then they folded their thumbs inside all four fingers, then they showed their fingers, first three, then two, then they twisted their hands as if they were imitating an animal's head, then they showed their thumb and their little finger, waggling them, and so on. In all they made twenty-six signs. It seems they knew by heart the sign language of all the deaf-mutes in the world. The three guests made no reply to their signs, but for the first time since their arrival they forced themselves to speak and answered without the slightest hoarseness:

"We are what we are. Not even we know very clearly."

"Can you not know what you are?" answered the children.

"Naturally," answered the three in unison. "Usually, you know who you are, but it sometimes happens that you don't know."

"And if we don't know exactly who and what we are, then other people ought to try to find out how things stand."

"Don't try to trick us," said the children. "Don't run away from us, even if you don't know who you are."

"Because not even we know who we are."

"Is that so?" said the three strangers, amazed. "Have we all lost our memories?"

"Our memories?" said the tots. "What's memory? All we know is that we are a little girl and a little boy."

"That's sufficient," smiled the three. "It's enough to know just that. As for memory, it's a broken toy."

"We have broken toys at the orphanage too," said the little girl.

"Broken dolls," added the little boy.

"But we are not broken dolls," said the three. "As we said already, we don't know what we are. But we have an inkling of what we might be."

"Have you ever looked in the mirror?" asked the little girl.

The three shrugged, because they couldn't remember having done anything like that. Then, they looked at the girl's lopsided hair. It was as if somebody had played a prank on her.

"You ought to have looked in the mirror to find out what you're like," said the little boy. "That would have been the sensible thing to do."

The three smiled.

"Sensible? That's an unusual word. Better we don't use it."

"Are you ill?" asked the little boy.

"We don't know that either," replied the three. "We think we are healthy. There's no reason for us to be ill."

"Maybe you should come to our orphanage," said the little girl, and gave them a wink. "We're the only ones who live there, with a lady and a bow-wow. And sometimes the postman."

"Do you think we could get our memories back at the orphanage and find out who we are?"

"We don't understand all the things you say," said the tots all of a sudden. "We're little children; you're grownups."

"That's right," the three said, nodding.

"At the orphanage you can't die," blurted the tots by way of explanation.

"Is something like that really possible?" asked the three.

"That's what we think," said the little children.

"What are your names?" asked the three grownups.

The little girl and the little boy looked at each other and shrugged.

"We don't know," they said. "Because of the broken toys. Memory, that is. We don't know. You've just taught us what memory is."

"Don't be sad," said the three strangers.

"We're not," replied the little children. "We're used to it like this."

"But do you dream?" asked the three.

"Sometimes, quite often, almost every night," said the little children.

"Have you ever dreamed of us?"

"Never," said the little girl.

"I've never dreamed of you either," added the little boy. "But I feel strange talking to you."

"Me too," said the little girl. "I feel really strange. As if I were talking to thin air."

The three laughed out loud.

"We're not made of thin air."

"Naturally," said the freckled boy confidently. "You're grownups, after all."

"Do you dream?" asked the little girl. "Or is it a grownup secret?"

"It's not really in our nature to sleep or to dream," said the three strangers. "They say that nobody knows where dreams come from, even if almost everybody knows where sleep comes from."

"At the orphanage they say that dreams don't come from anywhere," said the little boy.

"That's not very plausible," answered the three, contradicting themselves. "Dreams always come from somewhere. They are born, come to light and die somewhere."

"But why do they die?" wondered the little girl. "They might live a whole lifetime."

"That's not possible," said the three. "Everything perishes in the end. Even dreams."

"I don't think I believe that," said the little boy. "Whoever is alive dreams, and whoever dreams is alive."

"Look at this, we're dealing with a philosopher of dreams," said the three, smiling.

"I'm not a philosopher," said the little boy.

"And I'm a little girl," pointed out the little girl, rather sulkily.

"Maybe dreams are born only at the orphanage," added the little boy.

"What language are you speaking?" the three suddenly asked.

"Our language," said the tots. "We only want to grow up if we'll be able to dream all the time."

"That's not very hard," replied the strangers. "All you have to do is to wish it with all your heart."

"Does that mean we'll be able to dream all our lives?" asked the tots.

"You'll be able to dream up until when you die," answered the three.

"But what if we never die?"

"Then naturally you'll go on dreaming forever," answered the three strangers.

Then silence fell. The little children were due back at the orphanage, but nobody was expecting the three strangers anywhere. They were completely free.

"Where should we head to?" they asked the tots.

"Wherever you like, it's all the same," said the little girl.

"Whether you go right or whether you go left, it's all the same," added the little boy. "You'll end up somewhere, whichever of the three points of the compass you follow."

"Aren't there four points of the compass," said the three in surprise.

"I know just three," explained the little boy. "North, south and east."

"That means there's nothing in the west," said the three.

"West? I've never heard of that direction," said the little girl.

The three strangers were already used to such oddities. But the tots weren't surprised any more either.

"I cut her hair with the garden shears," the little boy told the three strangers, pointing with his finger at the little girl.

"That's what we suspected," said the strangers, smiling.

"We would have liked to have a cup of tea with you," said the children all of a sudden.

"So would we," replied the three, "but it's too late, even if we would have liked to drink a cup of tea and tell riddles."

"The truth is we're good at riddles," said the little children. "At the orphanage we speak only in riddles."

"Dusk has fallen, and so now we have to part," the three said to the tots and tousled their hair. "Don't be sad."

"We're not sad," answered the little children, smiling. "Adieu."

THE ART OF DIVINATION AT EVENTIDE

The fortune-teller had grown bored of all the similar-looking hands she had seen in her life: she had grown old reading palms and seeing the same lines, creases, breaks, intersections, and so on. Humans differ from one another only rarely: in her life she had encountered calm hands, agitated hands, eccentric hands, ordinary hands, she had encountered every conceivable kind. And now she was set on reading the palms of the three supposed angels. She was not skilled in reading the flight of birds: ornithomancy, as that art was known, was practiced only in Antiquity. Obviously, if the strangers had been able to fly and if they had had wings, then it would have been a different matter. But as they did not, all that remained was to read their palms. Although her hair was white, the fortune-teller still wore it long and curled. She knew exactly where the three strangers, having been released by the authorities of Metropolis, were going to appear. And so she waited for them among the buildings surrounded by weeds and rubbish skips and after the newcomers finished speaking to the two tots from the orphanage the fortune-teller crossed their path. By her ear she wore a yellow flower pinned to her hair, tangled in her white curls. First of all she looked at the ring-watch on her left index finger—it was almost eight in the evening—and then she opened her mouth and spoke at length to the three, knowing that they would answer her.

"I have come to read your palms. Not to tell you what the future holds, but only to see whether your hands are different to other people's. That's because I am bored of ordinary hands, which I have been reading a whole lifetime."

"Not only have we never met a fortune teller before, but for sure we have never met and shall never again meet a bored fortune teller," they said and smiled rather mysteriously.

Then they added:

"Hail and well met, white-haired fortune teller."

"Hail to you," said the old woman, twisting her long hair around her little finger. "I feel rather strange standing here in front of you."

"We have felt strange since the day we were born," said the three, rather amused.

"Because you were born different," said the fortune-teller sagely. "Everybody knows or at least suspects that you are different, that you are something different."

"Things aren't quite so complicated," replied the three. "Here we are talking to you, but up until now we have spoken to nobody except two little children from the orphanage."

"Hmm, yes," said the old fortune-teller with a smile, "I espied the two little children from the orphanage in one of my dreams. As for you, I knew that you would not remain mute forever, that your tongues would be untied, even if you won't necessarily tell the story of your lives. What is more, I was sure that you spoke the language of Metropolis, our native tongue."

"The language of Metropolis?" asked the three, shaking their ponytails as if they were manes. "It's a language like any other, anybody can speak it; it's not hard to learn."

"Everybody knows that you were not born in the Metropolis," said the fortune-teller, amused. "You came from somewhere else, although I don't know where, but nor am I dead set on finding out."

"It is very polite of you," replied the three, "not to try to wheedle it out of us. You're the first person not to want to find out whence we came. But in any case, even if we wanted to reveal such a detail, I don't think we would be able."

"If we could know exactly who we were in every instant, I don't think it would be wholly a good thing," said the old fortune-teller.

"That's right," replied the three. "There are too many things in this world that cannot be understood."

"Don't you think we are conversing *too coldly*?" asked the fortune-teller.

"What does *too coldly* mean?" asked the strangers in surprise.

"It means aloofly. *Too coldly* is the opposite and the inversion of *too hotly*."

"It would have been amusing to be able to speak *hotly*," said the three. "It would have been like travelling from one side to the other, without getting anywhere."

"Oh, no," said the old fortune-teller, "you always get somewhere. Some people might take you for madmen!"

"We're all madmen around here," said the three, laughing. "It's utterly normal to be."

"We're all madmen around here is the same as 'They're all mad around here'. I just say what I think," added the old fortune-teller. "What is the resemblance between an angel and a man?"

"They look the same, but they're not the same. The difference is in what they say and how they walk."

"How about that," said the old woman, amazed. "And so, it's not time that sets them apart."

"What do you mean by time?"

"Immortality, although it sounds wild and pretentious to use such words," tittered the old woman.

"Time has never been at odds with us," said the three with a laugh. "Because time has always minded its own business and not poked its nose in where it's not wanted."

"You talk like All-Knowing," said the curly-haired fortune-teller. "Are you what you seem to be?"

"We are what it seems to others that we are. But we might just as well be that which it does not seem to others that we are."

"You are playing with me," said the old woman.

"We are playing because there is nothing wrong in that and because you permit it," said the angels in a singsong voice.

"You speak like you were mentally defective," said the fortune-teller. "I look at you, you're young men, and I'm an old woman. And here we are talking like retards. Strange."

"It's not at all strange," said the strangers, "precisely because you are the third person to have untied our tongues. The first two were the tots. Up until then we were silent, but the time has come for us to talk, even if our words are still unclear."

"If your words have a beginning, then they have to have an end," said the fortune teller, tactfully.

"It may well be. The same as our journey," replied the three.

"Why do you always speak all three of you at the same time?" asked the fortune-teller abruptly.

"We don't know why, but we feel the need to. It's as if a single voice issued from the three of us."

"You're like the three musketeers," laughed the fortune-teller.

"It may well be, although we don't know what musketeers are."

"It's of no great importance," said the woman with long white hair gaily. "Old fortune tellers have the right to do that sort of thing to the people whose fortune they are telling."

"We are a little tired," confessed the strangers abruptly.

"It's natural that you are, after all the committees and commissions that have been investigating you. You ought to sleep for a whole week straight."

"It would have been good if we had not been made of flesh and blood. We're human too."

"That's one way of putting it," tittered the fortune-teller. "You're not made of bone china after all! Be careful you don't get chipped if something happens to you!"

"What might happen to us?"

"I don't know, I was talking at random and tossing a coin, that's why I'm a fortune teller," laughed the old woman with long curly hair. "And now I would like to read your left palms, as is fitting that I should do to three supposed angels."

The reader will no doubt remember that the strangers were dressed in jeans and tunics and on top wore a cloak that was blue, azure even. That they had long, curly chestnut hair tied in a ponytail. That they had elongated eyes and eyebrows that looked as if they had been plucked and then painted. And that their necks were long, like a flamingo's. Well, their jeans had become scuffed, their tunics were rumpled, and their cloaks were fraying, but all the rest, the hair, the eyes, the eyebrows, the necks, had remained the same. The first had no wisdom teeth; the third lacked a kidney; and the second had a mole under one eye: these were the only things wherein they differed, and otherwise they were as alike as three drops of water. The old fortune teller grasped the palm of the stranger without wisdom teeth: his Jupiter mount was prominent and at the same time inconspicuous, that is, the feature in question was ambitious and humble, something impossible. The vertical and horizontal lines did not etch the mount. Then, his Saturn mount was small and underdeveloped: that indicated acute melancholy. The rosette at the wrist had a single thin, frail line: for the first stranger life did not have many changes in store. His head line was broken. And his heart line was as if bloated. The longhaired woman then grasped the left palm of the stranger without a kidney: his Venus mount was crumpled, lacking any network of lines. On the other hand, his Mercury mount was supreme, imposingly visible: this stranger's intellect surpassed all bounds. And the two Mars mounts were blatant, marked by power and patience. The rosette at the wrist was triple, with concentric rings. The heart line was faded, barely visible. But the line of fate was as thick as a rat's tail. Finally, the fortune-teller grasped the left palm of the final stranger, the one with the mole beneath one eye: his solar mount was glossy and engorged with blood, and his lunar mount betrayed a unique extra-sensoriality, albeit undermined by a tendency toward illusion. The marriage line was erased, and the line of bodily wellbeing was normal. The rosette at the wrist had two rings like miniature life buoys. Usually, this indicated divine protection, but was that really how things stood? The old woman babbled for a little while, she was a professional fortune-teller, as her grandmother and great-grandmother had been before her, and so she did not allow herself to speculate idly. With poppy ink, on the skin and flesh of the strangers she traced all the lines and mounts existent and operative on a human palm. At her waist the fortune-teller always carried a pot of poppy ink. After she told them everything there was to be divined in their left palms, she paused to catch her breath.

"I don't want to start with the beginning or end with the ending: I've no idea what the future will bring or how you will meet your death, or where or when."

"We're not interested in such things in the slightest," pointed out the strangers. "Death depends only on itself."

"Strange words, although not at all pointed," said the old fortune-teller. "I consign you to the Lord's care," she then added, somewhat sulkily.

"Strange words, indeed," replied the strangers. "Fortune teller, remember us only when time will have patience with you."

"Hmm, yes," said the woman with long curly hair, from the corner of her mouth. "Hmm, yes. I'll do just that."

Then they parted, and the woman made her way between the buildings and vanished. At one point, her pot of poppy ink fell from her waistband. "Oh," she said to herself, "I knew that was going to happen."

BODYGUARDS, CROWDS AND NIGHT ON EARTH

We all know that the strangers who plummeted down on the Metropolis each had a bodyguard: there had been a competition to select them, at which more than seven hundred candidates had turned up, the winners being the Wizard, an intellectual specializing in reading, hence his thick-lensed spectacles and shabby jeans—he was to be the bodyguard of the first stranger and had also been chosen because he was parsimonious with his words, which made him highly suitable; then there was the girl from the country who had briefly lodged the second illustrious guest, she too being taciturn and retiring; and as for the third guest, his bodyguard was to be the so-called Roulette Player, who had lost his home, wife and who knows what else as a result of his insane bets, for which reason he kept a stubborn silence. As the strangers had been released by the authorities and left on the street, the key question was as follows: where were their bodyguards? Why were they not with those they were supposed to be guarding? Where had they wandered off? Well, those bodyguards, who were as bizarre as their charges, had not been informed as to the hour when the angels were to be released. Some unknown person had intended that the official guardians selected for that task should not accompany the strangers on their first night of total freedom. Was there somebody who wished that something in particular would happen to the strange wingless guests? Were the three strangers perhaps blameworthy for the fact that they did not have wings? Or because they had not said a word to the authorities? Or because they both were and were not angels? Hmph, too many questions and too few answers: it would be more appropriate if we refrained from speculation, attitudinizing, exaggeration, hyperbole when it comes to a given lifestyle and from creating inappropriate logical connections. And so we shall say merely this: the bodyguards had been informed a few hours late, not very many hours, however, as this would have been too blatant, they had been informed of the possibility that the three strangers might be wandering around the Metropolis. The bodyguards had an inkling that the guests would not be dumped in the centre of town, but somewhere on the outskirts, as if it were intended that the acclaimed and much yearned for angelic specimens incarnated by the three should mingle with the crowds. And there was no better place to mingle with the nocturnal crowds than the most wretched, the most poorly lit, the most weed-infested district of Metropolis, which was also the district most frequented by stray animals and tramps, and so the bodyguards, although affected by their misfortune, knew exactly where to go if they were to bump into their famous charges. The strangers had just finished talking to the old fortune-teller, who, whether accidentally or not, was about to drop and break her pot of poppy ink. But this was also to be the penultimate time when words issued from the strangers' mouths, given that after the quasi-hallucinatory dialogue with the tots and the fortune teller, the guests were thereafter to lapse into muteness once more and for a very long period, without it being very clear why. Apart from the bodyguards, a darkling, silent crowd was to make itself felt in the vicinity of the three: harsh, swarthy faces and, contrariwise, gentle, luminous faces, faces with skin of every color and every kind of mouth, the majority of which were closed. The reader will recall the motley crowd that not long ago marched to the main square of the Metropolis, chanting We Want Angels, or rather, Do We Want Angels? Simple country women, teachers, engineers, rockers, cripples, swarming among the stalls selling bibelots, sunglasses, booze, key rings, flowers, a fluttering host of colored balloons, confetti. A carnivalesque crowd. One thing had been crucial at the time: the word angel could mean whatever was most convenient. The Slum Philosopher, with his bird's nest hair and eternal pipe, in the midst of that crowd, had explained in simple terms that the wings were inward, even if the little old women were still dreaming of textbook seraphim and cherubim, and that we all have wings in fact. At that the flock of sheep bleated lustily, and then, because in the meanwhile it would not be quelled, the police had turned the water cannons and tear gas on them, frightened lest the sudden arrival of the strangers unleash a mini-revolution. Where were the angel badges, flags and t-shirts craved by the agitated crowd? Nowhere—at least for the time being. But nor did the crowd desire such things any more: thanks to the television and the newspapers everybody knew that the angels had been examined by a host of commissions, which had pestered them and all but tacitly lynched them, harrying and wearying them. And so the residents of the overgrown, flaking, fire-blackened, dilapidated buildings did not want anything in particular, except that the angels should dwell amongst them, to live alongside them, to be alive there at the periphery of the Metropolis. On their first night of freedom the strangers were not hassled and nobody vociferated around them: the crowd lined up in silence to touch them and to get a better look at them. And here the bodyguards intervened—it was about time for them to make their appearance and to bring a little order to the proceedings—and they marshaled the silent, nocturnal and ultimately well-behaved crowd. That night the hominids were desirous of the company of none but the starry sky and the silent, wingless guests with their strange tunics, with their equally unusual ponytails, with their elongated eyes and flamingo-like necks (very few people knew what a flamingo was, despite the Angeliad that had been held in the national stadium and which had featured the said birds). Thousands of people had already gathered, and the bodyguards estimated that the ceremony of touching and seeing would have gone on for very many hours, perhaps even the whole night. The bodyguards were prepared to defy the crowd and to protest, but the three strangers gave them a discreet signal with their eyes, to be precise, they closed and opened their eyes three times and then the bodyguards understood that the ritual was to continue through the night and would come to a close in the morning. That was the decision. The three guests sat down one next to the other, shoulder to shoulder, although the two at the edges were slightly to the front, like in a semicircle. They allowed each inhabitant of the Metropolis to touch their faces, hands, shoulders: things had to unfold in this way inasmuch as people would thereby be able to convince themselves of whatever they wished to find out or not to find out. Were the three one-hundred-per-cent angels? Naturally not. But were they at least three-quarters angels? Hmm, that was a completely different kettle of fish, hard to say, hard to chew over, hard to affirm or deny. They were something or other, that was for sure, but what exactly they were God alone knew. And perhaps not even the Devil knew (and what might Wee Devilkin and his boss be up to now?). Nobody knew for sure. Perhaps they were angels after all. And so all that the simple and the complicated folk could do was take part in the aforementioned ceremony in the hope of finding some kind of answer. It was only when they touched the strangers' shoulders that they understood that wings couldn't grow there, because wings weren't like arms or legs. That a man with wings would have to be a bird at the same time, at least in dreams, if not elsewhere. That feathers were flying skins released from the burdens of life. But those tongue-tied hominids knew equally well that none of them could have lived with wings and feathers alone. That it was ultimately a curse rather than a blessing. That to be an angel was an ordeal. The bodyguards kept their silence too:

the Wizard reviewed in his mind books that onerously dealt with the angelic question (and there were a host of such books; he could not even count them), the girl from the country did not take her eyes off her favorite angel, and the Roulette Player displayed the smile of one initiated into the winding paths of perdition. As for the three strangers, they impassively waited for each inhabitant of the periphery to touch their faces, hands, shoulders, as I have already said. The ritual unfolded in unwonted silence, through the cloudless night, until morning: thousands of people managed to have concrete access to the three putative angels. But it was enough already. The crowds were endless, they had reached the tens of thousands and would have kept on growing had the bodyguards not rightly broken off the ceremony. Enough! said the Roulette Player, the most decisive of the bodyguards: that's enough, now let everybody go home. The guests need to rest, said the girl from the country. *Satura*, exclaimed the Wizard in a well-known dead language, we can't risk any hurly-burly. Wherefore the queue of those still waiting became alluvial and finally burst. There was to be no more touching and seeing the strangers. Nevertheless, plenty of things were yet to happen, as anyone might easily guess.

WHO HEALS WHOM OR NOT, AND WHERE, WHEN, HOW

The Slum Philosopher had thitherto kept his silence, but he was among that crowd, and so his turn to perform a memorable deed came at last. It would be better, said he, cautiously: it would be better if we took our guests to the homes of the sick, to see whether they might be able to cure their misfortunes and disappointments. That way, we could be able to check whether the guests are really angels, said somebody in the crowd, which was by then retracting like an old weary octopus, back to the weed infested buildings. That's not something that needs to be checked at all, the Slum Philosopher admonished the importunate speaker: of course they are angels. Therefore, let us take them to the sick and let us not think twice about it. No sooner said than done, because nobody made any protest, not even those implicated in that major charitable action: neither the angels, nor the sick. And so they led the three guests through all kinds of impoverished apartments, where there languished all kinds of invalids: the crippled (those missing an arm or a leg), the blind, the deaf, the mute, those suffering with skin diseases, somnambulists, cancer victims, and so on. The reader should not imagine that the periphery of the Metropolis was swarming with the infirm. There were a few hundred, three hundred to be precise, no more, no less, and so the figure is no exaggeration. Naturally, the sick had not been marshaled and sorted according to their affliction, and so the peregrination of the three strangers with ponytails was at random, and they were accompanied by an ad hoc commando, made up of the neighborhood's busybodies, and guided by the Slum Philosopher. These were patresfamilias and kids, that is, grown-ups and youngsters, some ten in number, and the name of their group came about spontaneously, as if it were self-evident: The Nameless. The bodyguards were just as curious as to what would happen, and even more so the sick. For, one thing will never perish in this real world of ours, no matter how pure or how sinful it might be: curiosity. We shall not describe here every meeting between the angels or semi-angels and the approximately three hundred invalids, but we shall give a summary of what happened, just so nobody will get bored. It wasn't possible to heal the limbless, as might be imagined: regardless of whether they were angels or not, you can't replace a missing body part unless you lop the same part off somebody else. Consequently, the strangers had no way of healing those who were missing an arm or leg or those who were missing an eye (the empty socket being covered by a black pirate's patch) or an ear (there were indeed one or two cases of this kind, although how those people had been deprived of their ears was lost in the mists of time), since they would have had to amputated somebody else's arm or leg, torn out somebody else's eye, cut off somebody else's ear. This is why it might be said that if some poor wretch from the periphery hoped that the maimed might be made whole, he was cruelly deceiving himself. There was no chance of anything like that. There was another fiasco when it came to the blind: the strangers contained a special light, as everybody had observed, even the nit-picking, malicious authorities, but in vain did they lay their elongated hands on the eyes of the sightless, in vain did they stand there, their six hands laid one on top of the other, like hands severed and laid out to dry, in vain, and to no avail, as the blind remained blind. Another failure occurred with the people with skin ailments: the hands of the gentlemen in blue tunics were unable to work any miracles, no matter how hard they tried to transmit energy to the ailing skin of the patients. Their skin, or rather skins, quite simply refused to be healed. Those skins were entities unto themselves and so ill that nothing could be done with them. They were dead skins, in fact. The strangers themselves shrugged their shoulders helplessly, despite the fact that The Nameless and even the bodyguards encouraged them with words, whispers and shouts. The Slum Philosopher alone remained silent, he said not a word, but merely watched. He watched and was silent. It was clear, however, that his belief in angels had not died, despite the fiascos he had witnessed. But the time has come to speak of their successes, their triumphs, their victories, given that such things come about when you are least expecting, when you're just about to give up, when you think that everything is pointless, that death is more like life than it is our final condition. And then, just when you think you are defeated and everyday life has rejected you, something flowers and grows and bursts forth and conquers the world. Maybe not forever more, but it conquers it for a while and brings it to its knees. And so it was with the ceremony of healing gently demanded of the three strangers and performed upon the sick at the periphery of the Metropolis. While in the specific case of the limbless, blind and skin disease sufferers the angels failed, because it wasn't possible any other way, in the case of the other infirmities they managed to achieve some degree of healing, to the wild excitement of the dwellers among the weeds, and above all to the delight of the Slum Philosopher and the bodyguards. Let us take it slowly and by category. Firstly, the deaf and the dumb: hmm, hard as it is to believe, this time the strangers' hands, laid over the sick ears and mouths, achieved a strange focus, as if capturing acoustic energies from the air and earth at the same time, as well as from water and fire. The six hands lured the sounds emitted by the four elements, or rather they lured remnants of unused and unknown sounds, which they gathered together, cleansed them of impurities (it is too complicated to explain here how they did so, and so the reader is asked to rein in her curiosity) and then transmitted them into the deaf and the dumb. This whole healing process did not take place all at once, which is to say, abruptly, quickly, but with patience and skill: the new sounds were captured as if in a butterfly net. Naturally, it was something unusual, and so we won't pretend to have seen the like every day. Naturally, it was a kind of miracle, but only a kind of miracle, not a complete, blatant, nacreous miracle. And for the third time, naturally, the deaf and the dumb did not begin to hear all of a sudden or to hold forth like orators. For, although the act of healing was obviously a triumph, it was to be slippery and rather unpolished: those who had been deaf only heard certain sounds, namely they heard only the vowels of words, but not the consonants, and so the language they perceived was liquid, flowing, a piano-language. As for those who had been dumb, what issued from their mouths was solely composed of consonants! As a result, the language they spoke was harsh, military-sounding, and unintelligible, as a language without consonants is tolerable and permissible, but one without vowels sounds like the tongue has been cut out of a tongue. In the end, what mattered was the fact of healing: and the deaf and the dumb had been healed, as to that there was proof. That the languages they heard and spoke were only part normal and classifiable as human, well, that was a footnote to the events and the ritual of healing. That having been said, let us continue with our story. When it came to the cancer sufferers, it was almost impossible: nor were they completely healed and not all of them, but only to some of them came the success that everybody was expecting. The supposed angels gathered in a circle around the person with the fatal disease, until they sensed he was levitating, a few inches above the floor, oh, sorry, I made a mistake, a few inches above his bed, since the patients were in bed, of course! Although all of them levitated a little way, only half proved to have been healed to any extent after the angelic ceremony, when they were examined a week later. Probably the half who weren't healed were immune to the idea of levitation or to the belief in angelic saviors. Or maybe the strangers failed because they weren't concentrating hard enough. Maybe they were exhausted by then and it was a mistake to make them perform like long-distance runners, as they weren't in a marathon. Any of these explanations might be valid or rejected with a snarl, and a shake of the head just in case never goes amiss in the house of somebody from Metropolis. With the somnambulists, on the other hand, it was a famous and glowing victory: it is not known exactly what the supposed angels did, but the somnambulists were cured instantly, in a halo of light that lit up instantly around their foreheads, as if they had been connected to the electrical mains. The next night, none of them travelled over the rooftops, at risk of losing their balance and falling, none of them roamed the periphery with their eyes closed, but all slept soundly thenceforth. Some of their neighbors regretted it, however: in the end it was picturesque and amusing to have somnambulists in the neighborhood, it was like having nocturnal hominids at your disposal! Or rather it was like having amateur acrobats to entertain you, walking a tightrope without a safety net, ready to fall to their deaths at any moment. And that was no small thing! What should be concluded from all these cures and non-cures is that the strangers had, for the most part, managed to do what was suggested to them. The Slum Philosopher was satisfied, and so were The Nameless (there were four kids in the group who applauded the cures like they were at the circus), likewise the bodyguards, although their faces betrayed a certain amount of concern: they were guarding angels, but even angels get tired, don't they? Even angels might start panting from exhaustion, their tongues hanging out, and even angels might get sick. But we won't allow them to get sick, since we need the angels to be on top form.

CONCERNING NAME DAYS, BAPTISMS AND WHAT COMES AFTER

Following the fragmentary triumph in the matter of spontaneous therapy applied to the sick of every variety, the Slum Philosopher meditated concisely: perhaps the angels are not complete angels, but they will become whole angels, if the necessary conditions be created for them; consequently, the periphery needs to be isolated from the Metropolis and even the former Empire, and so a secession needs to be established and proclaimed. Ultimately, the Metropolitan authorities had rejected the three strangers as angels, it had denied them this status, and so if the periphery alone had proven capable of perceiving the greater or lesser sanctity that had descended upon the Sacred Homeland, then why not break away from it and above all from the Metropolis? Autonomy, that's what we need, concluded the Slum Philosopher, smoking his battered pipe. We don't need a capital and maybe not even an Honorable Homeland. The Nameless reacted positively to the Philosopher's proposal. As for the angels, as one might easily suspect, they said not a word, because they had fallen dumb and dumb they would remain for quite a while to come. And then the Slum Philosopher, seconded by The Nameless, called the people onto the streets so that—no matter how surprising it might seem—they could vote for or against the secession: the vote was to be held by means of a show of hands. In about an hour the news had travelled like the wind, and the crowds had gathered in the former fruit and vegetable market, now denuded of stalls and booths and transformed into almost a stadium, albeit without benches. And the vote was unanimous: against the Metropolis and in favor of the secession. Let them be our angels and ours alone, roared the crowd. We're not going to let anybody examine them any more. They're going to stay right here, to sanctify the place. The angels of the periphery. The Slum Philosopher was satisfied, inasmuch as things had taken their natural course, although there was one thing that made him uneasy: the periphery would have to be renamed, that much was obvious even to a nitwit, and, hmm, rather tricky, the periphery would have to be ruled by a Governor, a Mayor, or a Minister, or a President, or whatever name you cared to give such an individual invested with authority. *En fin*, the periphery needed a leader: and the Slum Philosopher realized that he would have to take on the task. *Angelus Angeli Angelorum*, as one might say. The angel of the angel of the angels? When he put to the crowd the need for a leader, they reacted as if he had pressed God's button: you're the man for the job, in the end it was you who came up with the idea of the secession. Down with the Metropolis! Down with corrupt politicians! Down with everything. Down, down, but how far down, wondered the Slum Philosopher. After a given point he would have to teach people to shout: Up! How far up? But there was plenty of time until then. What had to be done first was to find a suitable name for the secession zone, for the periphery that aspired to become a town in its own right. The City of Angels? No, no, protested the first bodyguard, the one nicknamed the Wizard: they've got something like that beyond Europe and the former Empire, in America. Los Angeles, as we all know, although Spanish isn't current in the Metropolis or in the Sacred Homeland, although it is rumored that it is the language of angels. So, Los Angeles is out of the question. We're not conquistadors or colonialists or invaders. But nor is the Castle of Angels suitable: firstly because there isn't any castle in the periphery, and then because the Castle of Angels already exists in the Rome of the Pontifex Maximus, added the Wizard. The Slum Philosopher vaguely recalled the massive statues of the two Saints Michael perched on the so-called Castle built on the ruins of the mausoleum of a famous Latin emperor. And he also recalled photographs of the bridge that led to that Castle of Angels, which bridge was bursting with angels, making you sick of angelism, angelity, angelophany, angeloidism, and so on. Angeloidism? he asked himself doubtfully. How on earth did that word come into my head? Can angels split a person's mind in two? Can angels unleash a schizoid episode? Of course they can, said the Wizard, who had overheard his thoughts: don't be so surprised. If you came up with the proposal for the secession from the Metropolis and a new name for the periphery, then you have to finish the job and stop confusing people. The Slum Philosopher gave an embarrassed cough: what I want to do isn't at all easy. Stop complaining! said the third bodyguard, the one nicknamed the Roulette Player. Do what you have to do already. But don't waver now and don't play the prude. The Nameless said nothing, but listened to this strategic rather than raucous debate: in fact, the kids would not even have had the right to say anything, as they were minors. I say let's be grown-up and responsible, put in the girl from the country, whose mission was to be the second bodyguard. If we break away from the Metropolis, they'll lay siege to us. We need to be aware of that. And because the thing has already been decided, let us get on with finding a new name, without dilly-dallying, so that afterwards we can deal with things that will be harder to achieve: our daily bread. They all fell silent for a minute. Then the Roulette Player proposed the new name: let it be Angels' Shanty, because it's not a town in the proper sense, nor is it a region, or a country, or an empire, it's just an outlying district. Angels' Shanty? repeated the Slum Philosopher, The Nameless and the other two bodyguards in unison? A shanty is a sort of abandoned tavern, a derelict house, or something of the sort, but never mind. And because they had all said it in unison, they realized that this was the new name. And so it remained Angels' Shanty. The second order of business was to isolate the new town geographically from the rest of the Metropolis, and this essential move was achieved by means of a boundary of sandbags, as there was sand aplenty in the former periphery (we'll call it that so as not to detract from the new name): the line of sandbags was in fact to instate Mile Zero, and that name, also decreed by the Slum Philosopher, was to irritate those on the other side of the border no end. Why Mile Zero? What do you mean, Mile Zero? This is what: the world was to begin all over again. Was it a second Genesis? Naturally. While the crowds were working on that border, the Slum Philosopher was appointed Governor, the commando of The Nameless was established as his secretariat, and it was decided that the bodyguards might very well play the rôle of advisers. Everybody was in agreement: nobody asked the angels about anything, knowing already that they would in any case make no sign, give neither their approval nor disapproval. The first thing the Slum Philosopher and Governor (we'll call him mostly the Governor from now on, to avoid confusion) decided to do was to issue certificates of residence in Angels' Shanty, to prevent infiltration by vagabonds and unwelcome imposters among those chosen to acknowledge the messengers from Above. To this end he had the old Metropolis printing press at his disposal, which was located within the former periphery, and so along with the Wizard and the patresfamilias of The Nameless, the Governor issued tens of thousands of such certificates, this first series to be followed by a second, based on a census of the new population. For, it wouldn't go amiss to know how many people there were in the new town of Angels' Shanty. Of course, by such certificates the Governor did not in any way wish to suggest that the inhabitants were Aryans or that by virtue of that fact they would automatically go to heaven, but this idea somehow insinuated itself among the first recipients of the much-coveted certificates. Those responsible for distributing the certificates in a more or less orderly fashion were the Roulette Player and the kids among the group of The Nameless. As for the girl from the country, we all suspect the same thing, readers and characters alike: she did not let her angel, the second angel, out of her sight, and so she could not be pressed into organizing the printing and distribution of the certificates. But there was another thing she could be used for: when the Governor promulgated his second law, the law of chastity and abstinence, the girl from the country found a perfect place in the propagation of this convenient legislation. The inhabitants were thenceforth to be pure: no parties, no drunkards, no fun and games. No coupling, either official or unofficial. No sex. It was only in this way that they could prove to the Metropolis that the secession had an example-setting mission, that nothing was left to chance. Nobody swore an oath of chastity, but they all realized that Angels' Shanty was to become a kind of dormitory with two separate sections, one for women and children, the other for the menfolk. It was very surprising that nobody protested. It seems that the law of chastity was in any case on everybody's lips, that they had all, in principle, thought of something like that. This is why the girl from the country became a kind of abbess of the law: she did not keep watch over the enforcement of abstinence, because she couldn't have done so, but she moved among the inhabitants with her semi-martyred countenance, accompanied by the second angel, so that everybody would understand that, although she loved that young gentleman who had descended in the guise of an angel, never, but never would she sin with him or any other man. It had been a *coup de foudre*, as the Frenchies say, but even so, she, like the second angel, were to remain chaste *pour toujours*. And all the others were to do likewise. A third law that was obvious even to a nitwit was connected with the food supply, and it was also the girl from the country who dealt with this: as there weren't any great reserves in Angels' Shanty, given that the former periphery had been impoverished, the inhabitants' basic diet was to consist of bread and potato soup, perhaps with a few potato pies or baked potatoes with a bean filling. And that was about all. Other raw materials for the stomach weren't really available. Sometimes, a marmalade pie might be permitted, because there was plenty of that filling in the huge barrels in the basements of the weed-infested buildings. To drink: water, and in case of severe thirst, the amber-colored rotgut specific to the place, since the majority of the periphery-dwellers distilled the stuff with ease and it wouldn't run out even during a siege lasting months, in the event that an attack came from the Metropolis-dwellers. But canteens needed to be set up to ensure orderly feeding of the masses. The last law passed during the short period since his election as Governor was connected to compulsory pedestrianization: traffic was banned, to prevent any Metropolitan spies or other undesirables infiltrating the town. As there was no subway in the area, but only trams, these were abandoned, so that they would stop circulating in the direction of Metropolis, and within the town they were no longer needed. And so all the inhabitants of Angels' Shanty had to walk, the only exception permitted being makeshift rickshaws for the elderly and infirm, as long as they were pulled by relatives, the journey was to hospital, and they could not travel unaided. In any case, in ordinary cases of illness, the angels would be employed, as their therapeutic powers had already been proven. Not only were the trams abandoned in their depots, but also the few motorcars in the area. At first, these old-fashioned, shabby motorcars were left in the street, but then, in order to avoid any *malentendu*, they were given numbers and parked in the tram depot. That's enough about the elected representatives of Angels' Shanty for the time being. Let's have a look at what the mood was like in the by then less famous Metropolis.

GENERAL HYSTERIA: METROPOLIS ON ALERT

It is not hard to guess the reaction of the neighbors of Angels' Shanty, in what had once been the resplendent Metropolis: general hysteria gripped the authorities in the Fortress and panic gripped the populace, causing a stampede. The Chief of Police put out a call for the arrest of the three angels, the Governor, The Nameless, the bodyguards, and the entire population of the former periphery that now styled itself Angels' Shanty. But all these things were predictable, as the girl from the country had already explained. We all recall that the former empire had frayed like a yellowing doily: well, now it was at risk of fraying to bits, thanks to the secession promulgated by Angels' Shanty. The President issued an emergency decree, in which he accused the periphery-dwellers of illegal separatism and aberrant, stateless behavior, and gave a televised speech which began and ended with the words Dear compatriots, the Sacred Homeland is in danger! Even if the supposed angels were neither spies nor terrorists nor extra-terrestrials, there was something noxious smoldering in them, and so the President declared them *personae non gratae* and took into account the possibility of their expulsion once they were recaptured. The Minister of the Interior quickly resigned, and his post was to remain vacant for the foreseeable future, as nobody wanted to take on such a responsibility in times of upheaval and serious danger. The Chief of Police sent telegrams to all his superiors, in particular the President, arguing that live bullets would have been more appropriate when the populace took to the streets to acclaim the strangers, as rubber truncheons and tear gas had only dampened spirits temporarily. And now the uprising had burgeoned into full-blown war! El Leader Maximo constantly appeared on the Ef-bee-en-aitch channel, with the same paternalist discourse: My sheep, my flock, I swear on my soul, as he announced an altered crusade, which could not help but take an equidistant turn when it came to God. Nobody could make much sense of his unsupervised speeches, since El Leader Maximo had sacked his canny PR man. The drunks from the Spitted Tavern, which is to say, the ten leading speakers, did something surprising, however: they declared themselves tea-total for life and quickly crossed the border, leaping like saltimbanques over the sandbags, given that their tavern was on the periphery and the dipsos, as we already know, were themselves periphery-dwellers and bohemians. Their decision was acclaimed by the population of Angels' Shanty, which immediately adopted the newcomers: here, the former drunkards integrated perfectly, so much so that you could no longer tell them apart from any of the other periphery-dwellers. The ingenious Linguist of the Metropolis also tried to cross the border, convinced that he would be able to spell out the supposed language of the angels (he, like many other Metropolitans, had by then found out about the strangers' conversations with the tots and the old fortune teller), but as he was a linguist, rather than a professional frontier man, he was easily captured, like a weary snail, arrested and taken away to be questioned by the authorities, even though they knew there was not a lot they could do to him. The Cryogenist, the Undertaker and the Old Clown would also have been tempted to cross the border illegally, but something told them that it would be pointless and that they wouldn't be able to adapt to the atmosphere of the periphery and the excessive exaltation that was now the order of the day in Angels' Shanty. And so the Cryogenist abandoned his dearest dream: to freeze an angel as a way of discovering the secret of immortality. With the permission of the border guards on the Metropolis side, the Astrologer took up residence in a watchtower, from where he could scan the heavens above the Metropolis and above Angels' Shanty simultaneously: his prestige was sufficient for him to be permitted to do this without him getting mixed up in the matter of the siege and probably the war that was to follow. The Censor began to appear more and more often on Speakers' Corner to harangue the curious with his eternal obsession: Angels ought not to exist! We don't need angels! But people no longer paid him any mind; he was like an old, forgotten rat. Many of the other characters we mentioned in the first part of the story minded their own business: the chocolatier the Midget from the toy company, the nez-parfumeur, the owner of Metropolfilm, the cyborgs, et al. Signore Metrocirkus, who had not made contact with the strangers even at the spectacular held in the national stadium, where he was the ringmaster, tried to cross the border disguised as an angel, using ropes and his former acrobats, but failed; the border guards captured him by means of aerial detectors and sent him straight to the cells. The Cloner also intended to cross the border, but he broke his left leg making a botched leap over the sandbags: the border guards had a hard time dragging him back, what with the periphery-dwellers trying to pull him into their zone. Unfortunately for the Cloner, there was a delay in hospitalizing him, he contracted gangrene, and was deprived of the affected leg, which was quite simply amputated by doctors enraged at his having dared to aspire to cross into the separatists' zone. After this unfortunate experience, the Cloner developed a new obsession: to create a new left leg for himself by cloning his right leg. For the entrepreneurial boss of the advertising firm, everything that was happening in Angels' Shanty was fascinating and had the potential to be used in a commercial, and so his industry prospered. On the advice of his secretary-in-chief, known as the Inkwell, the Patriarch, with his catchphrase *Kyrie eleison*, protested when he found out that the chief of Police wanted to destroy the artificial border with a platoon of huge bulldozers to pulverize the sandbags: what if the three strangers were subtle entities? What if they were angels after all? The border must be removed peacefully, without victims, and the authorities had no other choice than to find a feasible solution. The Pontifex Maximus also sent an urgent missive: the insurgents must not be massacred, mass murder was undesirable, the eyes of the whole world were fixed on the Sacred Homeland, and the name Angels' Shanty, which the separatists had adopted, was viewed with approval in certain parts of the Earth. In addition, the Pontifex Maximus sent his cardinals back to the Metropolis, so that they might keep abreast of events, and it seems that they too attempted to cross the border, but in vain, as the forces of law and order captured them. Well, well, whom else might we invoke, whom else might we mention? Have we perchance left anybody out? Ho-ho-ho: the Devil-in-chief, with a freshly opened bottle of Veuve Clicquot, was chuckling away. Wee Devilkin, he cried tipsily to his favorite page, the hominids are going to hell in a handcart what with all their nonsense and their madness! Too much cleverness gets you into trouble, answered Wee Devilkin. What are my muses up to? the Devil-in-chief then asked. What muses? said Wee Devilkin, pretending not to understand. The angels, you dunderhead, they're my muses, aren't they! They're doing quite well, answered Wee Devilkin. They've started talking and healing. *Merci*, muttered His Highness, I thought they were dumb. In the end we're even, we've reached a draw: they don't have wings, but nor do I have a tail or horns, contrary to rumor. And what does Mr. Big have to say about them? Mr. Big doesn't say a word, he just dreams, explained Wee Devilkin, with reference to God. I've never dreamed, or rather I cannot remember ever having dreamed, confessed His Highness. Dear reader, forgive my being so complicated, but I have been saving two characters for the end of this tumultuous chapter, namely the Shadow

Hunter and Merlin Stral. The first managed to cross the border, enveloped in a specially manufactured sand-colored shadow, so that not even the periphery-dwellers of Angels' Shanty could detect him. After he disrobed himself of the shadow and washed, in order to return to his usual appearance, the Shadow Hunter, who, as we know all too well, was a philosopher of alterity, presented himself to the not very surprised Governor and said merely this: I am your Double. After that, he was known as the Double, and the Governor immediately appointed him his chief adviser, recognizing him by the pipe they both had in common. As for Merlin, ah, yes, the peerless creator of the *Vita Alia* system, he did not intend to cross the border, as the moment had not yet arrived. But it would arrive in due course, and then some. For the time being, Merlin Stral kept watch, inasmuch as his story, and that of Mesmaea Cuttita and saviors Anir Magnifico and Narkom Zarthus, is far too complicated to unravel for the time being. The Metropolitan troops had amassed at the border, wearing camouflage, but they did not have a bellicose allure. Not yet.

ON THE OMPHALOS AND OTHER WHIRLWIND SPECULATIONS

In order to prepare the Metropolitan populace for the confrontation which, in one way or another, was about to commence, the authorities programmed a long series of televised proclamations to the nation, plus a number of patriotic spectaculars, mobilizing a host of the capital's celebrities—writers, actors, artists, journalists—to speak to the common people in a language they would understand, telling them that a civil war might just break out, a micro civil war, as it were, and thus the need for televised intervention. Prudence and vigilance were required, however, since the eyes of the whole world would be watching the Sacred Homeland and nobody wanted any fatalities. But the talking heads did not talk very convincingly, rather they were constrained by the circumstances, for which reason their speeches were snore-inducing and gristly. The same thing happened on the Metropolis's various radio stations, and so the Governor and his Double did not waste much time in deliberation, but decreed that Angels' Shanty did not need mass media over the airwaves. Those peripherals that possessed television and radio sets dumped them in the street. To replace them, the Governor and his chief adviser founded a special newspaper, named *Jester*, which dealt in squibs and parodies at the expense of the measures being taken by the haughty capital, which was at risk of being dethroned by the highly puzzling ideatic movements of the erstwhile outlying district, which, lo and behold, had now become a town in its own right, and an angelomorphic one at that. The members of the new area government were to write for *Jester*, as well as anybody else who had anything genuine and suitable to say to the new citizens, as *Jester* was intended to be a forum focusing on the problems of the periphery. In a way, the newspaper in question was an evanescent version of *The People's Gazette*, where the Slum Philosopher used to write a highly popular column. But now, both he and his Double, who, I reiterate, was a philosopher of alterity, were to focus on drawing up statutes or even a constitution for Angels' Shanty, so that the new town or city might achieve at least heavenly, if not earthly, legality. This was also necessary inasmuch as the Metropolitan authorities, having discovered that all television and radio sets had been eliminated from the so-called infected area, were flying over Angels' Shanty and dropping manifestos containing various slogans and announcements created in the heart of the Fortress, such as the following: Inhabitants of the Periphery—do not collaborate with the enemies of the Metropolis! May God help us defeat the Beast that has arrived in the Sacred Homeland in the guise of a deceiver! Fellow citizens, do not believe in the false angels that nobody has sent! Ladies and Gentlemen, do not lend your ears to secession and separatism! Do not rend the body of the country and the capital! Women and men, act according to your nature, that is, as reasoning people, and do not believe in bunkum! The flock of the Sacred Homeland is on the verge of being decimated by the wolves of envy and dissent: do not allow this sacrilege to happen! He who sins and knows not that he has sinned will pay the price, but he who sins and knows that he has sins will choose the path of truth and righteousness! Choose light, not darkness! And so on and so forth. The Governor and his Double were amused by such feeble and infantile manifestos, but in the end they would still have somehow to counteract the blather of the authorities across the border, and so they had a philosophical chat on the subject. We have to put a stop to this demagogy, said the former Shadow Hunter: it's not for nothing that I have a library at home in which the books are conserved in jars of myrrh, almost embalmed. You are truly my Double, said the former Slum Philosopher, now the Governor, amused: did you really intend to capture the shadow of one of the three angels? As they both lit their pipes, the Double confessed his only doubt: that the angels risked having only half a shadow, or, to be more precise, only a third of a shadow. But we're not talking about angels in general, replied the Governor, by now puffing away on his pipe, but about angels in particular. Precisely, said the Double: think of daemons. What about them? asked the Governor. They're my obsession lately, confessed the Double: daemons are not visible, whereas angels are, but their status is the same. The only difference lies in visibility and the form of this visibility. Our angels resemble dragonflies! the Governor joked. Maybe they are indeed dragonflies and not angels, replied his pipe-smoking philosophical companion. In any event, what interests me is the soul of the angels, admitted the Double. I don't really believe they have special souls, because they are nothing but soul, said the Governor: that much is obvious even to a barnyard hen, let alone a philosopher who has been recycled into an adviser. Have you ever heard of super-angelity? asked the Double. It is an expression like any other, said the Governor. But what if the strangers really are guardian angels? challenged the Double. It would be sufficient for only one of them to be, answered the Governor. And what if they are our guardian angels, or yours or mine? said the Double. I don't really think we ought to speculate on such matters: the three came for the sake of everybody here, and so they can only be the guardian angels of all of us, answered the Governor. In any event, they are not angels of darkness, he added, causing his Double to start. I would not be interested in finding a shadow of darkness, muttered the erstwhile hunter: my priorities have altered in the meantime, inasmuch as, behold, now I am your Double, your eyes and ears. That's right, said the Governor: and so let us proceed to words and deeds comprehensible to the many. I say that we ought to decree that Angels' Shanty be a kind of omphalos, a centre of the world, and that way, ne'er-do-wells and the military authorities in particular won't be tempted to use force against the periphery. Of course, to speak of an omphalos in the manner you propose will mean claiming that we are inextricably bound to the very cradle of European civilization (we all know where that is): wouldn't that be rather risky? Why would it be risky? Angels' Shanty is one bellybutton of the world, metaphorically speaking, even if we don't have a meteorite or sacred rock to prove it to the masses or to others. A new and very small Jerusalem? asked the Double ironically. Not a bit of it, said the Governor. I'm not looking for Christian symbols or makeshift inventions, but rather things much more distant in time and much easier to perceive. We don't need imitations, because what is happening here is genuinely new, and I for one believe in the uniqueness of this area and its inhabitants. I believe in it, and that is why I came here, why I crossed the border clandestinely, admitted the former Shadow Hunter. Then we're sticking with the idea of the omphalos? concluded the Governor. Let's put it more plainly, the way you expressed it at the beginning of our talk: let's call it the centre of the world, advised the Double. Or let's simply call it the Zone. Angels' Shanty was too sickly a term for a small town that had broken away from the Metropolis, and the term omphalos would have been too pretentious, except in the mouths of intellectuals such as the Governor and his Double. And so they opted for the simple term, the one that had been on everybody's lips when referring to the separatist area: the Zone. And so the Zone it was, yes, the Zone. It sounds awful; it even makes me shudder slightly. Even leaving aside other speculations that would burden its meanings and nuances. Very well then. Even if it will set plenty of people against us. Just so. I hope that nobody gets killed. And I too. Let's write the next issue of *Jester*. No sooner had they said that than something happened in the former fruit, vegetable and meat market, which had been turned into a public meeting place or stadium without seats for official assemblies of the Governor and his adjutants (*y compris* the said angels of the periphery) and the masses: a huge fountain sprang up out of the blue, and thenceforth it was to be the centre of the new town. It gushed from the bowels of the earth as if there were some clandestine ocean down there. And it didn't just gush, but it was an octopus with tentacles of potable water. It was perfect. Then, even before the two philosophers concluded their quasi-conceptual conversation (which we, being in a hurry, have rendered here in abbreviated form), something else happened: a larger than ordinary parrot with grey and red plumage appeared from who knows where and perched alternately on the left shoulder of the Governor and the right shoulder of his Double, alias the chief adviser. It's a sign that we should never part, laughed the two of them. And the parrot remained with them forever more. And what might "forever more" mean in a story such as this, may we be permitted to ask? It doesn't mean anything. Absolutely nothing. A parrot, even an outsized one, with grey and red plumage, is nothing out of the ordinary. Or maybe it is. But what was interesting was something else entirely: it was a silent, non-talking parrot. A mute one. Hmm. It ought to have uttered with that mimetic parrot beak at least a single word: Zone. But it didn't; it kept mum. And that was why it was an odd parrot.

WORDS ABOUT PLAGUE VICTIMS AND ABOUT THE MANNER OF THEIR INNOVATIVE PLAGUE

The fate of the many characters in this tale is to remain anonymous and hence to act in an alluvial fashion: sometimes, however, one or other such character may break through the net of anonymity and burst to the surface for a little, for a very short space, long enough to accomplish some ordinary or, contrariwise, extraordinary feat. Such is the case of the Puma, the presidential adviser, should anybody recall the name. For such was his nickname, the Puma, which was fitting, in that it pointed to the quickness of his intellect and the words that came from his mouth in his rôle of live-in adviser at the Metropolis Fortress. But the Puma was about to make a fool of himself: under pressure from the President and other grey eminences alarmed at the turn taken by events and at the birth of the Zone (yes, even the Metropolitan officials had found out about the shorter, simplified name for Angels' Shanty), the Puma made an appearance before hundreds of foreign journalists, at the most widely publicized press conference ever held in the Metropolis, and he called the separatist inhabitants of the periphery, he named them, yes, you will barely believe it, plague victims. He spoke of them as the plague victims of the new millennium. In its turn, the Zone was declared an area infested with the plague, the plague in question being rather unusual, given that we are employing useful metaphors after all: but this metaphor on the part of presidential adviser Puma caused serious offence. It was a gaffe, and gaffes are the delight of the press and the political class. What do you mean, a plague, are you sure about that? sourly asked none other than the special envoy of the Pontifex Maximus. I am as sure of it as I am sure that I am the presidential adviser and that I am at a press conference, replied the Puma. But this glib reply merely caused greater consternation. There hasn't been an outbreak of the plague for more than a century, Mr. Puma! a journalist admonished him. What are you trying to suggest? That people are dying in droves? Metaphors are meant to be suggestive and to explain things succinctly, but tenderly, replied the Puma: we are surrounded by symbols, after all. But symbols work only up to a given point, replied another journalist, and not always tenderly. And then you used the word Arian to criticize the inhabitants of the Metropolis's periphery: is such an accusation warranted? Aryans with a y, pointed out the Puma: we prefer to write and pronounce the word with a

y. Hmm, yes, I'm going to have to speak plainly, decided the presidential adviser, with a frown: the inhabitants of the periphery have officially grouped themselves into a destabilizing populace that claims it has a new centre of the world dominated by Aryans, and that centre is called Angels' Shanty or the Zone. In our opinion, that is, the opinion of the Metropolis's politicians, the separatists ought to be labeled as mentally unbalanced pariahs, but we prefer to use the metaphor of the plague in order to point to the fact that in their case it is not just a form of fatal illness, but an infectious malady, which therefore must be rigorously, even violently, isolated to stop it spreading. I declare before you that at this very moment our troops are massing by the sandbags insolently piled up by the rebels to separate themselves from the capital, and so our troops will from this moment be called intervention border guards, and they will be joined by fire brigades. Fire brigades? asked the journalists in unison. How so? A siege involves fires and other types of destruction, which is why the firemen are required, explained Mr. Puma. Then he abruptly declared that the press conference was at an end and withdrew back into the wings, having been called to order by some unknown person, perhaps even the President himself. Or the Patriarch. Plague victims? Aryans? Are you out of your mind? a voice was heard to say in the wings. Yes, I'm out of my mind, answered the Puma. The siege is now underway, he added. True, something harsh, something serious had to happen, given that increasing numbers of people were draining out of the Metropolis and into Angels' Shanty alias the Zone: associations of guides for those desirous to cross the border had even been set up, clandestinely, of course. Those desirous were not numerous, but sufficient in number to exasperate the Metropolitan authorities. But once the peripherals had been declared plague victims, then plenty of acts of violence, moderate for the time being, were given official sanction. Then something happened that peeved the capital's grey eminences: the Astrologer, sheltering in one of the border watchtowers, was caught sending a message to the rebels, and that message was not at all to officialdom's liking. As he had suspected merely from his examination of the stellar charts after the angels' arrival in the Metropolis, during one of his nights in the watchtower the Astrologer glimpsed a fleeting eclipse of the moon, which lasted no longer than a minute: but within that minute he managed to espy for a few seconds the eighth planet concealed between its sheets of tinfoil, ah, and he espied none other than the pseudo-planet Jawzafar, known as the planet of the Dragon of Lunar Eclipses, which had never before been identified in the heavens. And then he knew that this was the zodiacal planet of the three strangers, who could be none other than angels or at least akin to angels. Predictably, for that reason, his message to the Governor and his adjutants was frenzied: I want to be with you, alongside you, through thick and thin. I want to be your scribe and to record the story of the angels. Although the Astrologer's message was intercepted, and he was immediately evicted from the watchtower, under suspicion of adherence to the plague, and although he was therefore secretly kept under surveillance by the police (secretly given that the Astrologer was too famous to come to grief), the contents of his missive nonetheless reached the ears of the rebels. But the Governor and his Double sent back a rejection of this application to emigrate: We don't need any scribes (anonymous or famous), given that the story writes itself here. This sentence, addressed to the Astrologer, was published on the front page of *Jester*, alongside squibs aimed at Metropolis and the first plan of measures drawn up by the former philosophers in charge of the Zone. What we also know is that the Astrologer was offended by this answer, but he felt even greater vexation at the fact that he would not be present at the celebration of the birth of the eighth planet, despite having detected the special signs that foretokened it. What the Astrologer did not know was that a less sophisticated seer, an old woman with long white hair, had already spoken to the three angels and told them what she had to say, and that the strangers had answered accordingly. And so what need was there for an astrologer among the peripherals? An Astrologer cannot cure the plague, if plague it be, but merely tinker with it. The plague, if plague it be, needs raven-beaked gravediggers and smoking censers to combat the dreadful buboes. But in the case of the so-called omphalos (as the philosophers called it, not wanting to be preachers, but nonetheless having a vocation for it) there were no buboes, no dead, and no death throes. For the time being, the people were fulfilled and peaceful, albeit poor. The angels were not very visible as angels, but nor could they be anything else, even if they had no wings. That was all that mattered on the other side of the border with the Metropolis. The Governor and his Double had in any event decided not to allow emigration into the Zone, as they would very soon have to deal with the serious questions of food supplies, accommodation and other household affairs arising under the conditions of secession and relative rebellion. The

Metropolitans who wished to flee the capital would have to stay at home or flee somewhere else, if they were lucky enough to have somewhere else to go. But it was no longer possible to flee to the Zone, it was already overflowing with hominids, it was an anthill, and hard times, famine and devastation could arrive at any moment. And so for the third time let us say that the plague, if plague it be, needs victims and perhaps even martyrs, but nobody wishes to be those nowadays, not even if there be three angels at the ready. In any event, nobody had asked them, the strangers (what else should we call them?), anything for quite some time. Azure tunics, chestnut hair tied in a ponytail, elongated eyes, flamingo necks.

ON A NUMBER OF EVENTS IN THE ZONE

Immediately after they decreed that the borders be closed (this was a joke, obviously, given that they didn't have any peripheral troops to enforce it and nor did they have any intention of forming an army, defensive or offensive), the Governor and his Double straightaway knew, as if they had experienced a minor but highly pragmatic revelation, they knew that life in the Zone would have to unfold according to a pattern of its own, neither isolated from the rest of the world nor wholly like the ordinary world. It was no wonder that the story there wrote itself, without needing any special scribes, astrologers or whatnot: it was a coiled, tangled tale whose curlicues untwirled of themselves. Let us first of all see where the angels lived, since we seem almost to have forgotten them, and that won't do in a story that writes itself. In the Zone there were, as one would expect, a number of little churches for the folk of the periphery: as a headquarters for the three was chosen the church closest the former vegetable, fruit and meat market, which was now the place where the Governor and his adjutants held meetings for the masses. As the three angels had no requirements when it came to food and drink (although they had imbibed liquids when they were under arrest and being interrogated, they had done so merely out of politeness towards the warders and interrogators, rather than out of any strict physiological need) and therefore did not have any waste matter to eliminate, they were able to take up residence in the church, near the altar, where they could sit on the thrones, not needing to stretch out on a bed. The priests no longer officiated services in that church, instead using the other churches for the liturgy (usually they celebrated mass in the open air, next to the fountain). If the angels had nonetheless ever needed normal human rest, they would have had at their disposal the hammocks in which their bodyguards slept, these being situated on either side of the church: a tent on the right for the two men, the Wizard and the Roulette Player, and another tent on the right, for the girl from the country. The hammocks had not been bought from the shops, but sewn by the three bodyguards themselves, after they had consulted with each other on the matter of sleeping arrangements and other details, which, although unimportant to the angels, are vital to hominids if they are to live a decent life. As for washing, they went to the huge dormitory that had been opened by the new fountain and where the women and children slept separately from the men. All the inhabitants of the Zone had accepted willingly the law of abstinence. The dormitory was not big enough to shelter everybody, even though it was so large that it looked more like a circus big top, and so there were still citizens who, willy-nilly, slept in their own homes, but without it bothering anybody. The three strangers were kept busy: during the day they were taken to the bedsides of the sick, even if the patients were suffering from nothing more than a headache or hair loss, and they healed them as best they could, without anybody forcing them to do more than they were capable of. In any event, a picturesque phenomenon came into being shortly after the first collective healing session, a phenomenon that would have allowed the strangers to be discovered even if they had hidden down a mouse hole: for, around them glow-worms began to swarm, both night and day, regardless of whether they were in church or some other place. And those glow-worms could not be driven away; they clung like burrs to the three mutes in the azure tunics. Whence they came nobody knew; but the reason they clung to the three strangers everybody knew. The glow-worms did not just rustle, but also they sang, and the sound they made went like this: tzyoo-hyoo-lyoo! And so the guests could easily be identified thanks to the swarm of glow-worms and also this unusual sound. Other things happened, too: slender flamingos appeared on top of the street lamps, and then they descended to the public square, where they remained, feeding on beetles and other insects, but never the glow-worms. What song the birds sang was not at all clear, given the Metropolis and the Zone was not their usual habitat: they were not in proximity to any deltas or so much as a reedy lake, and here all they had was a fountain, weeds and buildings. All that was known was that the flamingos had nothing to do with the ones that had taken part in the spectacular in the national stadium, which had also included egrets. After a while, the flamingos—they were probably a flock that had landed to rest and failed to fly away again—stopped flying altogether and walked among the people of the Zone, as if it were their own territory. They lived in the space by the fountain, but without making contact with the people: they lived alongside them, but without colliding with them. At night, the flamingos huddled together and their reddish orange plumage gave off a glow, like a huge chandelier. The Governor, the Double and the other two men with whom they conversed from time to time, namely the Wizard and the Roulette Player, ironically nicknamed the flamingos the Garbage Collectors, which is what they were: elegant, subtle garbage collectors, which cleared the Zone of unwanted insects (with the exception of the glow-worms, which had a different mission) and even rodents. Yes, the story is writing itself, as the Governor was wont to begin his ritual twilight speech to the friends gathered around him, the aforementioned men and kids who made up The Nameless Ones. But sometimes the story needs to be helped to write itself, added the Governor's Double. And sometimes the story needs to be interrupted, to stop it getting boring, quipped the Wizard, drawing the protests of the others. And sometimes, the story adds to its open suitcase other stories that cross its path, said the Roulette Player, rather predictably. The girl from the country was not in the habit of sitting amongst all these wise men, since her fixation remained unchanged: the angel with the mole beneath his eye, whom she guarded like the eyes in her head, and when the Wizard and the Roulette Player were in conference with the Governor, the girl also took care of the other two emissaries from on high. Other unusual things worthy of mention: it started raining in the Zone every afternoon, usually for no longer than an hour, and never longer than an hour and a quarter. The inhabitants of the Zone did not need raincoats, macs or wellington boots, however, given that the rain did not wet them, but vanished on contact with their clothes, as if it were a dry rain, whose purpose was unknown. And at the sandbag border the rain came to an abrupt halt, as if sucked up by an invisible hose. The Metropolitans had bought lots of pairs of binoculars and from the nearest tall buildings they watched how the rain stopped at the edge of the Zone as if by command. The Metropolitans were also eager to watch the flamingos resident in the Zone and to hear the faint strains of the glow-worms. And there was another miraculous thing that had started to happen lately. After the rain, the lilac bushes, which had, it is true, grown in the Zone even before the secession, had begun to burgeon hugely, like a jungle, joining together to form a canopy, a pagoda-like corolla. There were plants or flowers other than the lilac in the Zone, but that stray lilac burgeoned and multiplied. I think we are heading towards a new Garden of Paradise, joked the Governor to his Double, closely examining the phenomenon. There is no joking about such matters, said the former Shadow Hunter: and a Garden of Paradise is not necessarily a Garden of Delights. Better we ready ourselves for war, as that is what is on the way. *À la guerre comme à la guerre*, said the Governor in his favorite language, the French of dictionaries of proverbs and sayings. There is an entire populace to defend here, chided the Double: we need strategies, stratagems and strategists. Let's be realistic, cautioned the Governor: the officials of the Metropolis can't afford to victimize the Zone, and they know it full well. The whole world is watching us, if only because we are the only people who still believe in the angels and their coming to earth in the here and now. How long do you think it will take before the Zone is dissolved? the former Shadow hunter curtly asked the former Slum Philosopher. I don't know: it depends on what the angels will do and what they want of us. For the time being we don't know and nor do they know what they want. I'm waiting for a definite sign from them. And what if the sign never comes? I believe in Chance, said the Governor. Nobody should die, and therefore nobody will die. At the most they'll die of old age or disease, as they have always done, but not otherwise. In Chance? said the Double in surprise. And there you were saying that you didn't want to be a preacher! God is not mute like His angels, and so He will say something, said the Governor. A word, a single word. Or else He will give a sign. But aren't His angels signs enough? asked the Double with ever the slightest hint of mockery. They are and they aren't, replied the former Slum Philosopher rather strangely. It would seem that the angels are sufficient unto themselves. I don't believe in coincidences, added the Double. I hope that you're not going to try a parody of Genesis? But the Governor made no reply. Perhaps this brief exchange should close a chapter in the life of the Zone, perhaps not. What ought to be added for the time being is the following: besides the glow-worms, the flamingos, the fountain, the giant lilac and the rest, three-legged cats and dogs had begun to be born in the Zone, the third leg being thicker and situated at the end of the body, but in the middle. The residents of the Zone were alarmed at first, but then they realized that it must be connected with the three angels. What that connection might be, nobody could say, but the connection was clear for all to see. In any event, as the girl from the country said, encouraging the peripherals with well aimed words from time to time: let us be angelically strong!

ON DEATH, RESURRECTION AND EMBALMMENT

As if the Governor had augured ill, the first dead bodies appeared in the Zone exactly because of the reasons expounded not long since: not so much from disease, as much as from old age. At first two old people died, and then, a few days later, a little girl. The little girl died in her sleep, nobody knew why, because she had not been ill. The angels were quickly summoned and brought to the scene, although it was suspected that they could not heal the dead by resurrecting them: only God could do that. Such a miracle was asked only in the case of the little girl, not the old people, whose death was natural. The strangers had tried to revive the little girl's body through mouth-to-mouth resuscitation, since their breath must have had something special, especially given that it came from mute angels who, after all, stored up their energies for curative and holy purposes. Angels are angels as much as they are able, but not even they can be more than that. They had proven to be healers, no question about that, but could their healing powers be sufficient to bring about the much-desired resuscitation? Perhaps the angels' mouths harbored some superhuman energy or a power worthy of super-angelicity: in any case, the little girl awakened from death, to the joy of her parents and the hominids of the Zone, but she awoke only for one day, since the next night she died once more, also in her sleep. Although the angels might have been summoned a second time to revive her, they were not called upon this time: everybody understood that in the case of a second resuscitation the little girl would in any case die for a third time, because there was a definite internal logic to it, or else because in the Zone death operated slightly differently than elsewhere. But how exactly did death operate and why are we asking this insane question only now? In the story that is now writing itself, beneath your very eyes (as a number of characters have already coolly pointed out), we have mentioned death before, but we have done so with reference to the Apocalypse and other related questions. But this time we do so in completely the other sense: for death in the cases of which we speak, those of the old people and above all the little girl from the Zone, was the beginning of a world. It was a death that opened up something new, which negated itself, but only at the margins of its thorny territory, revealing that rough and ready resurrection was possible, for a limited period, long enough for an hourglass to heap up time, roll it over and then reduce it to a fine dust. There follows a moment of ataraxia, then time gathers itself together again and starts to function by the book, like death. Yes, this was the unusual logic of the way they did things in the Zone. The two former philosophers understood this quite quickly, closely followed by the bodyguards: the Wizard understood it best of all, however, in that he had read enough books to fit nine cats' lives and he knew the whorls and hummocks of vanquished and vanquishing time. Of course, such an expression might sound pretentious in the given circumstances and might cause irritation or even neurosis. Given that we do not wish to offend anybody or to infuriate any non-adherent to such a theory of temporality and death, we shall end our little speculation here, without discarding it altogether. Let each perceive death and let him even die according to how best suits him or according to his desire. We do wonder, however, whether death had not somehow become transparent and hence the drawback of its being able to be annulled, but only for a short while, before reoccurring identically, without anger, but nor with any smile on its lips. Inasmuch as death is ultimately colorless, although not odorless. You cannot see its approach, but you can smell it very well, although nobody necessarily wishes to smell or see it. Its tangibility causes us all to suffer, because it is extreme and as a rule it occurs just once in our own lives, but more than once when we are routine onlookers. Well, in the Zone, death chased its own tail, biting this dorsal appendage in the case of the little girl, who had been revived just once. After that, the second and the third time, the resurrection would have become banal. Sometimes there is a need even for death in order to sanctify a place. If the taste of the three foreign angels was sour, then why should the taste of death be otherwise? Neither harsh, nor stringy, nor sickly, nor sweet, nor savory, but sour! Once the first deaths had occurred in the Zone it was necessary that a site for a cemetery be found in a hurry, and this was burdensome, because no such thing existed in the peripherals' territory, although it would have be normal for the place to have had at least a Paupers' Cemetery, as such amenities are to be found in any sensible capital. But in the present case, the two cemeteries, the central and the secondary cemetery, lay on the other side of the sandbag border, where the border guard forces were waiting to intervene, and so burial in a classic, traditional cemetery was impossible. And it was then that the Roulette Player and the girl from the country found an acceptable solution: in the church where the angels dwelled there was an unused crypt, which ran for the whole length of the church. It had probably been in use centuries ago, and in the Metropolis's history textbooks there was mention of a small ossuary, but now it was empty and disused. As the bodyguards were already disquieted by the first deaths in the Zone, since they were trying to prevent any outbreak of the plague, and fearing not only for the fate of their wards, but also that of the peripherals in general, they decided in joint agreement with the Governor and his Double to use the old crypt as a makeshift cemetery in such emergencies. There was still one impediment, namely how the deceased were to be buried in such a way as to prevent any health hazard: and at this point a laboratory technician came to their aid; this was how he introduced himself to The Nameless. The laboratory technician was a middle-aged man. The others weren't quite sure whether he really was a laboratory technician, but they brought him to the attention of the Zone authorities nonetheless. As doctors were few in Angels' Shanty, and they were not necessarily coroners, only one acolyte volunteered to help the laboratory technician to embalm the corpses, along with the two bodyguards, since this was the revolutionary method proposed by the technician: to teach the three basic corpse embalming, using paraffin, vinegar and tar. The materials in question were plentiful in the Zone; they did not have to be obtained via the black market. Nonetheless, it was a good job that there were not many deceases per square foot in the Zone! As for the first bodyguard, nicknamed the Wizard, he did not want to get involved in the project, but stood aloof, for reasons that are not relevant to our story. On the other hand, the girl from the country and the Roulette Player, assisted by the laboratory technician and the only doctor to volunteer his services, agreed to do what needed to be done. As anyone might imagine, the embalming was not perfect, but it proved to be the sole adequate solution for dealing with the remains of those who died in a area where there was no cemetery and no possibility of establishing one. After embalming, the corpses were wrapped in shrouds, which was the simplest thing for everybody concerned: ultimately, they were doing what they used to do in ancient times, since after all it was in a shroud that the Son of God had been laid in the tomb, although without being eviscerated and embalmed first (that would have been the last thing He needed!). Who knows, perhaps we used to be Egyptians and it is only now that we have regained our true identity, joked the Double to the Governor, remembering his playing cards at home, embalmed in jars of myrrh, as he cleaned his pipe and commenting on the latest events in the Zone. I wonder what Death would look like if it were mummified, replied the Governor. Not at all: it would look like a frozen brook, replied the Double. I wonder how many times the little girl could have been resurrected? the Governor suddenly asked. However many times death desired her, answered the Double. To be precise, however many times God wished her to die, added the Wizard, arriving unexpectedly. I don't agree with embalming, he then added. It is like death in a huge test tube and you shake it from time to time to disturb the sediment. Yes, that's what it's like.

SOMETIMES STATUES DON'T HAVE HEADS, BUT PEOPLE ALMOST ALWAYS DO

Many things were happening around the Zone, but nor were the Metropolitan authorities sitting idle up in the Fortress. One of the measures they took was to cut off the electricity throughout the periphery: of course, this might have been particularly hard-hitting, but it wasn't entirely. The Zone was not rigorously cordoned off, and so there were a number of cables still operational there, although most of the electrical connections had died. In any case, it wasn't much of a problem during the daytime, as there was still solar illumination, and so the lights hadn't been turned off, as it were, without our employing any metaphor, but rather speaking the plain truth. But at night it was something of a problem. And then, so that the Zone would not be plunged into pitch darkness, the angels gathered of their own free will next to the recently created artesian well, and they formed a tight circle, holding each other's hands. They stood like that, concentrating, more elongated than ever, until their hands began to shine, causing a kind of golden globe to emerge from between and among them, which lit up the night. Along with the plumage of the flamingos, which at dusk huddled up against each other to form a sort of huge chandelier, resting on the ground, that dual light was sufficient for the darkness not to be total. Nobody was at all surprised. Another measure taken by the Metropolitan authorities was to cut off the water supply, rather predictably. But the water problem was solved much more easily than the problem of illumination: the artesian well produced unlimited drinking water, and so nobody would die of thirst in the Zone or fall victim to skin disease as a result of not being able to wash. In the meanwhile, the Governor and his Double had preventatively decided to have a whip-round for jewelry, if such accessories existed in the peripheral territory, so that the Zone would be able to purchase food reserves in the event of a siege. The inhabitants donated slender chains with crucifixes, wedding rings and earrings, as they had no other jewels, and these were delivered to the traffickers at the sandbag border, who provided potatoes, flour and dried beans in exchange, that is, the ingredients required for a staple diet. The two former philosophers had themselves donated their pipes (they had no jewels, not even wedding rings, as neither of them were married), which were by then famous in the Metropolis and for which exorbitant prices had been offered, as if for amulets: the purchasers proved to be ladies from the capital's high society and members of the Metropolitan Police, cerebrally exited by the performance of the Governor and his Double. Even if their ephemeral existence might have caused plentiful irritation, the clandestine traffickers managed to dwell almost undisturbed at the frontier with the Zone, realizing that the black market had a purpose, but avoiding the authorities like the plague. Some of the border guards knew of their activities and tolerated them, more out of curiosity towards that strange, rebellious Zone. During all these events and occurrences, a not very dangerous earthquake struck the Metropolis: even so, a border watchtower collapsed, without claiming any lives, and in the centre of the capital a number of magnificent buildings were fissured. To the disappointment of officialdom, however, nothing was fissured in the Zone, and certainly nothing collapsed: probably the buildings were so dilapidated that there was no point in their collapsing. Or perhaps it was a case of some logic different than any known thitherto, a logic of non-collapse or non-falling, as it were. It was sufficient that the three foreign angels had fallen or tumbled or plummeted down onto the Metropolis, and now they were the patrons of the Zone: why would any buildings have fallen down, if such a thing served no purpose? Since everything that took place in the Zone had a moderate halo, but a halo nevertheless, The Nameless, the patresfamilias and kids, had one day come up with a cheerful suggestion: in the territory there were no monuments or statues, and so why not erect a statue to depict the important guests who had descended on the Sacred Homeland, and who were now the creature-fetishes of the peripheral space? Of course, the expression creature-fetishes is wholly ours, the author's and the reader's together, inasmuch as the patresfamilias had given voice to their wish in far simpler terms. The Governor and his Double immediately agreed to this, likewise the bodyguards; the angels remained mute as usual, and in the public square the population voted in favor of the statues. In charge of the monument were The Nameless, as it had been their idea. They thought about it a whole day, and finally decided that the statue should be made of wood: at first, they had wanted to make three statues of the angels, but in the end they decided on a single statue, which would be gigantic, a hundred feet high, so that it could be seen from everywhere in the Zone. The Governor and his Double remembered that somewhere, in a south-American country, there was a gigantic Son of God, which was exactly the same height, as well as being perched on a mountain top: consequently, the peripherals' statue risked being mimetic, a toy copy of the other statue. But that was no problem: an angel was not the Son of God and nor was the former an angel, and so there would be no competition. Rivalries exist only between humans and gods, not between statues, fortunately, as a logician would say. Rivalries exist between all the things that function on this earth, an intriguer would say. So as not to let any drop of rancor or frustration seep in, let us opt for the opinion of the logician. The Nameless got hold of the trunks of some mature oaks, although in the Zone thickets of lilac bushes were to be found more than any traditional species of tree. The trunks were bound one on top of the other with wire, like prosthetic legs, and then the ten started to carve them enthusiastically, without any set design, working from immediate and collective inspiration. They worked a day and a night, until they managed to bring to light a kind of chimerical creature: it was chimerical since it had no head, as was plain for all to see. Moreover, the wings were attached to the back, as if sewn on or as if bundled together like an unopened parachute. The Governor smiled, but his Double fell to thinking. If we were to dive down into the unconscious of our chosen population we might deduce, esteemed former philosopher, that this unconscious contains an inappropriate image of the angelic creatures: they are headless and have dodgy wings, said the Double. And if we were to dive down into our sophisticated unconscious, esteemed former philosopher, said the Governor: we might deduce, might we not, that this unconscious sets excessive store by a pretentious and at the same time superfluous hermeneutic. Why don't we leave the hominids of the Zone to feel as they wish and to give material form to their angelic phantasms as best they can, even if these be vaguely monstrous? No sooner said than done, wherefore the huge statue was erected next to the artesian well. And there it remained until the end of the Zone. Paradoxically, nobody was surprised at the headless angel with bunched up wings. Ultimately, even if it didn't have a head, it was very good that it had wings! And so the disputation of the wise men, not with the world, but with themselves, seemed to have reached a conclusion. As usual, the para-philosophical parrot spoke not a word.

ON HOW A SHIP OF FOOLS MIGHT BE BUILT, EVEN IF IT WERE NEVER TO SAIL

Plenty of highly curious people in Metropolis were wondering what the inhabitants of the Zone were up to, what they were busy with, if they were not seeing to spiritual matters, which was what it sounded like to judge by the law of chastity and abstinence that had been collectively passed. The question in point was not idle curiosity, but highly pertinent: the inhabitants of the Zone were getting up to all kinds of things, from cleaning to supplying food for the canteen that cooked for one and all. From keeping watch over the sandbag border to laundering clothes and admiring the gigantic statue of the angel. From visiting the three strangers lodging in the church to accompanying them on visits to the sick. From contemplating the flamingos to trimming the messy lilac bushes when they got out of hand and threatened to transform the territory into a jungle. Everyday life went about its minimal and maximal (depending on one's perspective) business, and the traffic lights of existence showed green or red as the mood struck them in either direction. As a result, everybody in the Zone was up to something; nobody was unemployed. Nevertheless, there was not yet any major undertaking with a practical-redemptive purpose that might involve all and sundry, body and soul. The first people to think of such a thing were not the two former philosophers, but the bodyguards, the by then famous bodyguards, whose wish was that both the population and the angels alike should be content. In fact, the idea we of which we are going to speak in the following originated with the Roulette Player, who imparted it to the Wizard, who in his turn, as part of a domino effect, recounted it to the girl from the country, who, apparently pleased with the idea, rushed to the Governor and his Double in order to make them party to it and so that they might put it into effect. The Nameless were also consulted, but optionally: they were to become the supervisors of the lofty action that was perhaps soon to come about, beneath our very eyes. And now let us ask ourselves the following rather rhetorical question: what could isolated inhabitants like them do, inhabitants vituperated by the rest of the world, regarded as heretics and rebels, but at the same time envied for their cheek, courage and madness? What could they do to satisfy the utopias and desires of hominids worldwide, so that their symbolic island of beatifiers and beatified would willingly renounce winding paths and follow one smooth, resourceful road? Hmm, what indeed could they do? Should they sacrifice themselves, feel sorry for themselves, start hallucinating? Not a bit of it: all they could do was to go on causing a scandal, unswervingly. At least once in our lives we have all come to a fork in the road and regretted not taking the one we didn't take. Well, the inhabitants of the Zone avoided any such confusing forks in the road of existence, leaving hysterical or historical (what a difference a couple vowels can make!) complications in the Lord's hands, and accepted to adapt to the circumstances, albeit guided by their superiors, who, although they had no experience in the area of miracles, at least had experience in the area of utopias. Ah, utopias again, we all know how bitter and vertiginous they are, but also how full of splendor and sweetness, precisely because, being unachievable from the outset, they become challenging through their mordent, strident, and unliveable content. To let the reader catch her breath, let us now concisely confess that the idea that occurred to the Roulette Player, which idea was then disseminated in single file to all the other decision-making bodies, was as follows: what if the inhabitants of the Zone were to build a huge wooden ship, a ship in which the entire population of the peripheral territory might fit! We refer here to the viable population, naturally, as the old and sick would be left behind. Oh and ah, but was not this primordial project a replica of Noah's Ark or, closer to the present day, a replica of the vessel named *The Titanic*, which had, alas, sunk, throwing the whole world into mourning? And where was the sea or ocean on which this ship of peripherals might float? Quite. Where? Next to the Metropolis there was no vast body of saltwater on which there might float wooden vessels conceived by the impassioned minds of a Zone that believed in angels and their descensus, without casting into doubt their authenticity. And if there were no nearby sea or ocean, could that ship have floated on the dusty ground or glided over mud or mire? But none of the necessary topographical ingredients were to be found in the vicinity of the Metropolis. And thus the two former philosophers found the flaw in the queer project. There was nothing wrong in the peripherals building such an albeit impractical structure together; it was useful that the peripherals work on lofty projects together, and so a ship, even one that would never float, would have been no obstacle in the path of redemption or salvation, quite the opposite: it would have made manifest the nacreous meaning of the Zone's sentiments, in such a way that its inhabitants would no longer be obstinately anathematized by all and sundry, by whomever had a tongue in his head. Passed, said the Governor and his Double in unison, even if it will inevitably be nicknamed the Ship of Fools (and how many such ships have been built down the ages!). But in essence, it will be a Ship of Anti-Fools! The parrot with the grey and red plumage jumped from the shoulder of the one to that of the other, like a jack-in-the-box. At least we won't die of fear and we won't be cowards, added the Roulette Player in a sprightly voice, given that the idea was one hundred per cent his. But mightn't they view this ship as a token of hostility by the Metropolis? asked the Wizard cautiously, darting his eyes towards the capital: they are waiting to see what new things we will come up with, and so let's at least shock them, since they'll find an excuse whatever we do, be it banal, be it bizarre. Maybe we ought to consult the angels, added the Governor: they'll know best whether such a ship will have any purpose among us here and now. And so the strangers in the azure tunics were consulted, but their muteness underwent no alteration: they smiled and that was all. That the proposed Ship of Fools was to be an adornment of the Zone, a considered risk, or a spectacular curiosity for the benefit of the binoculars beyond the sandbags was in no doubt. That nobody would board that ship, when it was finished, was self-evident. Where can you go, if you can't float, given that there is no liquid to buoy you? Nowhere. You remain where you are. But none of this had the slightest importance. Ultimately, what such a messianic project would leave behind would be the bitter-sweet taste of adventure, of transgressing boundaries, of the stormy desire to do something almost superhuman, precisely because we are humans like any others and at the same time different. Alterity, holy alterity, was what delimited courage, madness and faith from boredom, comfort and forgetting. The Zone's ship was to be a ship of virtues rather than vices, let it be clear! On that point, the former Slum Philosopher and the former Shadow Hunter were agreed, smiling meaningfully, waggishly and frolicsomely. The sun did not shine brighter than usual, and the stars did not light up the sky more dramatically than on any other night. Everything was as it should be and as it had been thitherto: but nonetheless it was different. This difference, one that was inward rather than outward, caused normality to give birth to the phosphorescent abnormality that gently marked or, contrariwise, stigmatized the lives of people. The Ship of Fools (although it was not at all meant for fools, as has been made clear above) was and would be a hallmark of the Zone and the peripheral territory, a vehicle full of souls, rather than bodies, without floating on any body of water, in that it might eventually float through the air, where almost all things become welcoming and created anew. Would the ship really float on the firmament? If we think about it, the term firmament suggests a heavenly vault of fixed stars, a crystalline sky, a firm heaven. The two former philosophers knew that: in the olden days, people thought the heavenly vault was made of crystal, firm and fixed. Could it be that the present-day Ship of Fools had to be built for such a sky? And what should the much-desired ship be made of? Of all kinds of wood, whatever was available in the Zone, including lilac branches. If such a vessel were ever launched on water, it would surely sink straight away, pointed out the Wizard. Undoubtedly, agreed the Roulette Player. We are all agreed on that point, there is no doubt about it, added the Governor. When what is the point of building the ship? asked the Double under his breath. We will build it so that it will never float, said the girl from the country: sometimes it is just such a ship that is needed. Ships like that confuse even God, said the Roulette Player. And then, to protect Himself, God dreams. Full stop.

A FULMINATORY PRESIDENTIAL STATEMENT FOLLOWED BY PATRIARCHAL WHISPERS

The construction of the ship of fools or anti-fools (it is no longer important which) was the drop that filled the cup of presidential and official wrath to overflowing in the Metropolis. Everybody on both sides of the sandbag border had realized that something had to give, that things couldn't go on like that, that the lethargy and waiting had to be set aside or, even more radically, eliminated (even the reader knew this was coming and must have been expecting it for some time). Ultimately, utopias can snap like a strand of hair or they can go on growing until they burst, having been pricked accidentally or deliberately by a wasp. But now the wasp in question had come to maturity, it had filled with fury and frustration, it had swollen like a virtual avalanche and could hardly wait to come tumbling down, to crash down on the guilty, to punish them. The scourge does not always come from God, but most of all from men, it would seem. Perhaps here we ought to discuss the matter of guilt, who is guilty and why, if indeed that was the case and the blame had not arisen somewhere else entirely. But perhaps its circularity had proven so striking that willy-nilly, at random, it provoked anybody that got in its way. What is truth, as Mr. Pontius Pilate would have said, a man by no means overlooked in the ledgers of history. Nevertheless, there is a presumption of innocence, as the jurists will point out, just as there is a killer instinct in every individual endowed with desires, appetites, cravings, temptations, and, ah, discontents, dissatisfactions, shortcomings. The rise and fall of utopias does not depend on their thinkers, but on the public enemies of collective fantasies elevated to the rank of intellectual oversight. As it were. Whoever wishes to carry out an autopsy of the fantastical will find there not only compensatory worlds, but also disfigured, sick worlds, or to put it better, worlds singled out as being sick and contagious because of their having degenerated from reality. Ultimately, what the fantastically minded are always accused of is that they are not plugged into life. Perhaps their plug socket has burnt out, perhaps it is just old and needs replacing, but what the hell, who knows? But aren't endless dreamers entitled to forget about the socket and leave it permanently broken as long as happiness accounts for only an infinitesimal percentage of the human condition? Perhaps ecstasy arises precisely because of permanent abandonment of the electric socket through which the cosmic circuit supplies its products stigmatized by the fable of the present; perhaps even agony and its attendant hallucinations are fuller of life than the meaning of overqualified reason. Finally, let us return to our story, the one that is writing itself, without famous scribes, but also without any startling slang. On the advice of all those around him, and not just adviser Puma, the President made ready for his last public appearance and his last speech before ordering the assault on the Zone. The Metropolitans had to be informed and spiritually assisted, likewise the international press. The Sacred Homeland was to take drastic measures to break the impasse and so that its self-image would emerge triumphant before the whole world. The presidential speech was to be accompanied by a brief sermon from the Patriarch to his flock, to both his faithful and his lost sheep. But why do we call them sheep? They might just as well be kids, rabbits, ducklings, kittens, puppies, etc. or the opposite sort of animals, those that warrant the name wild beast. Dear compatriots, began the President: greetings. Once again, he was wearing a traditional local shirt, so that the Metropolitans would feel at home among his words and his emphatic gestures, which were intended to be convincing. I repeat that we are people and that consequently we have the right to believe and at the same time the right to doubt. The angels are enigmas, as I said before on a different occasion. This is why I humbly repeat with my hand on my heart that I do not wish to know who sends the angels, because that somebody sometimes sends them with a purpose, but sometimes not. But the purpose might turn bad and might become a national problem, such as in the present case. Some strangers came to our beloved capital not long ago: or rather they fell from the sky, as most of the official reports have stated. We investigated them with the help of various commissions, which, however, certified the fact that the strangers in question were more likely not to be angels. For this reason, we thought it best to let the strangers go free in our Metropolis, with rights equal to those of any other citizen. But the freedom given to them has borne an evil fruit: for instead of bringing peace and serenity, the strangers, three in number, have caused discord and shortcomings and they have cut off the periphery from the rest of the capital, which has rebelliously proclaimed itself the Zone. We already know what happened after this opprobrious act of secession. First of all a clandestine and illegal artesian well came into being. Then some invasive birds of prey arrived, causing damage, their name being flamingos. Then the vegetation went on the blink and our capital was exposed to the risk of being overrun by a jungle. Then a dead little girl was resurrected, although death is inviolable by decree, and setting aside humaneness, we ought well to remember the fact. Then our traditions were set to nought by the barbarous reintroduction of embalming the same as in primitive antiquity. Then three-legged domestic animals started to be born, which entitled us to impose a law akin to martial law, namely, the law requiring that all quadrupeds have four legs. Then an aberrant headless statue was built. Then, in an act of supreme heresy and incommensurable recklessness, the inhabitants of the Zone started to build a completely useless ship, just to defy us. What was to be done as a result of all this chaos instigated by pseudo-philosophical voices? Our public order has been disrupted in a major and inadmissible way! Anarchy threatens to spread its multiple fog! In order to prevent national disaster, in which our international enemies might be politely and smilingly playing a hand, it is right that we take drastic measures, in which our loyal military forces will be involved. From this moment I declare war on the Zone. Let our Motherland prevail, now and forever more! Thus ended the long-awaited presidential speech. Perhaps there might have followed another speech, by a political opponent, El Leader Maximo, for example, but given that the latter had supported the so-called angels in his speeches, the Ef-bee-en-aitch channel had received a hefty fine and ended up bankrupt after the Zone declared its secession and autonomy, although El Leader Maximo's personal fortune was not necessarily diminished thereby. He still had a newspaper, but it didn't have a very wide circulation; and so, although he might have emanated some quasi-messianic speech, El Leader Maximo didn't have the opportunity to appear on the television screen, and his Jehovah-like voice could not even be heard on the radio. Steeped in his cognac, El Leader Maximo remained but a frustrated onlooker in the power struggle gripping the Metropolis, outside the Nation's Political Corps, his mouth brimming with curses, gazing glassy-eyed at the speckled jacket, white trousers and zebra-striped necktie hanging in the living room of his luxury flat. He had been left out of the "patriotic business", voila, and there was nothing to be done about it; all he could do was grind his teeth. And so now let us listen to the patriarchal speech of the aged leader of the legitimate priests of the Sacred Homeland, a speech whispered rather than spoken and highly concise, bewildered by the bane of the advent of the angels (all three of them!). A speech advised upon and negotiated by Mr. Inkwell, the honorable secretary-in-chief of the head of the church, who was trying to avoid any extremes, any stridency, allowing the Patriarch to appear in his favorite guise: that of beleaguered Job. What wouldn't be appropriate was a speech about annunciations, warriors and the publicans of life and death, nor a speech about sin, nor one about God. What was needed was a speech about contemptible and repugnant matter. The angels were not matter, but anti-matter, began the Patriarch, for this reason they oppose matter, even if they reveal themselves to matter from time to time. Perhaps matter seems true, but it is mendacious and errant, without ever being redeemed. The same as in his first speech, the head of the church uttered a certain phrase quite appropriate to the circumstances: Let us lave our spiritual eyes in anti-matter and thereby proceed along the path of our life on this earth, without our seeking definitive explanations, because there is no absurdity in perceiving angels, even if there are contradictions in our souls regarding them. Well, the word contradictions was what was to arouse interest in that tangled sentence, all the more so given that this time, the Patriarch had no intention of summarizing in his speech the famous Pseudo wise man, and his angst connected to the coming of the three strangers, although it had not been allayed, had not grown any worse, but rather remained stable. Let us ask ourselves what the spiritual eye is and what its advantages are, the Patriarch went on. The spiritual eye is an accolade of ideas occurring as a result of absolute contemplation. Definitive explanations as to anti-matter are not possible, and as for the absurd, that is something we can discuss only in absurd language, because it is not fitting to deal with it in any other way. But that which dwells inside us and outside us is above all spiritual contradictions: on them we feed, with them we are born, with them we live and we die. Consequently, I cannot say either what angels are exactly or what they are not, not even if I could reach out and touch them or see them with my own eyes. For, everything is contradictory in this world, not to mention in the next world. And so ended the, meticulously whispered speech of the Patriarch, who was ill at ease beneath his burden sooner than radiant at his mission at the beginning of the new millennium. Ah, I was about to forget: *Kyrie eleison*. Without doubt, the two sophisticated theologians, All-Knowing and All-Understanding, might have assisted the head of the native church with brio, but as they had both gone mad one after the other, there was nobody to issue various epistles to the population explaining the emissaries sent by the All-Seeing Lord

God. There was nobody to ask, for example, whether there existed not only the relics of saints, but also the relics of angels. Yes, angel relics, however inapposite such a thing might sound. The maximal eye sees as much as it can and however it can: if it closes, it sees between its eyelashes and draws the necessary conclusions, fringed by tiny hairs like miniature toothpicks, whatever they might be. One thing was for sure: Christendom, large and crowded in its faith, was not to receive with great fanfare tidings of the three strangers.

BEING, ANGEL, TIME, VOID, AND CO. IN CRISIS

Subversion exists in humans, but above all in Time, which makes humans what they are rather than what they might be or wish to be. Time sometimes unfurls in loops especially in the case of utopias: hence a certain excessive speed on the part of Time, as has been apparent in the second part of this story that is writing itself, unlike in the first part of the same story, which unfolded lazily, given that it was written by multiple hands and narrated by multiple, insatiable mouths. To help us understand that the second part had been unfolding in fast-forward, we ought to explain the manner in which temporal loops burst, i.e. swell and pop, and that what comes out of them is no longer Time in the proper sense, but residual time, nothing but crumbs. There was once a mustached physicist with messy hair who invented the theory of relativity (although it is rumored that his wife was the originator of the theory): perhaps this theory would be of use here and now, in this story about humans and angels, perhaps not. Relativity is useful to many things, but not when it comes to its own relativization, and so we had best leave it to one side, together with the gentleman with the messy hair, may he and his theory rest in peace. To return to the temporal loops that pop when they fill to bursting, revealing residual strips, in the case of destroyed utopias and fantasies left to die of hunger, we should also say that they twist within and around their own time until they manage to turn it into space, even if only for a few seconds. This startling idea deserves to be brought to light in the following. And when such a delusional space rises to the surface, even if only for a short time, we may say that the mission of the real world has been fulfilled, that mission being to cause an implosion to allow invisible worlds to explode and legitimize the ephemeral but essential overlap between the outward and the inward. Naturally, there are skeptics aplenty who would reject such a simultaneously cosmic and human project. The temporal loops can pop not only because they become too full, but also because somebody from the outside pricks them with a pin to make them burst unnaturally. Let us take, for example, the case of the angels, so that we may see how such a potential skeptic as to delusional worlds relates to them. As we know, there exists the angel-in-himself, who is dependent on nobody, not even himself, and this makes him impenetrable, inasmuch as he is self-validating. It may be objected that here all that is outside our human or non-human thought comes into play, given that the angel-in-himself exists and existed prior to everything and anything else. But then comes the thorny question: how might predestination be altered? Let us be reasonable: it might be altered if the angel-in-himself emerged from himself, by means of mirroring, let us say. But in the mirror in question would be visible only images that are something else, namely, that are the angel-for-himself. Within such a regimen of the specular, the decompression of the angel-in-himself is implied, if the angel-for-himself is a model that might become a project for transformation. Any noble but nit-picking mind might nonetheless ask: and where is time while all this is going on? Let us therefore answer: time intervenes and manifests itself precisely in the evolution from angel-in-himself to angel-for-himself, the solution being that these two entities influence each other, and the former is transformed into the latter. Oh dear, we are getting a headache already: what is to be done when besides the two aforementioned entities there is also an angel-in-himself-for-himself, i.e. God? There is nothing to be done, given that we don't have anything to do. As for looped time, its spiral is like a snail's, let us not deceive ourselves with such cheap metaphors, metaphors so worn that they are nothing but skin and bones; its spiral is sooner an escalator simultaneously ascending and descending, hence the peculiarity of the situation. In a story about angels, spiraling Time allows aberrations and impossibilities, negating precisely the commonplace, banal and everyday. The authorities that always control reality may protest, they may grow furious, they may annihilate the utopia, but they can never erase the memory of the utopia, its root, whose bulb is made up of multiple layers of worlds. Given that there always remain among us witnesses to the destroyed utopia, there always survive the fervent believers in the utopia on stilts, which believers confess, such is their rôle, they confess to the other worlds that throb and burn, even if they are unseen and only intuited. Here then is an apology for the Zone and even for the angels, although they are mute and wingless. And what about Time, which soon changes into Space, and the whirlpool that engulfs itself, and in swallowing itself vanishes only to reappear twofold or even threefold? Let us also say that the human condition was once angelic and perfect; the fall into Time was the ingredient that traumatized poor human flesh, coagulating it and burdening it beneath the times. For which reason it is sad and often absurd in this world, in which the flesh never ceases to prove incomplete, because its destiny draws it contagiously towards Death, Time has remained to measure not only the erstwhile severance from perfection, but also the flight from death or the Void's attempt to flee towards the whole. But it is not appropriate that we discuss deficiencies and defects in the microcosmic construct right now. Just as there is a gland of Death, although it has not been identified, it surely exists, so too there is a gland for the production of compensatory worlds, which gland operates precisely in order that human beings might forget about Death, although the latter cannot be annulled. And where does the enigma of the Angel come into this tangled web? Why and whence was he banished for long enough to make our souls spark with expectation? Perhaps we would require a fleet of ships to seek the Angel on all the seas and oceans of fantasy. Or else we should give up such imaginings, since they are in any case too vain to prevent the gland of Death from having its way. Our greed for other, impossible worlds is connected to precisely this: let us eat, let us guzzle voraciously all that is not humanly possible, since given that it is not humanly permissible, why then should it not be non-humanly permissible? But the Angel—at least in this respect there is a consensus—was, is, will always be non-human. He has no way of dying, because Death is not his datum. Super-angelicity was intangible from this point of view. Consequently, we have arrived at the end of this enlightening divagation: the three strangers, regardless of whether they were angels-in-themselves or angels-for-themselves, were immortal. Time and the Void did not exist for them, not even in a crisis, like the one happening in the Zone. Dear reader, do you not remember? This story is partly about hominids that no longer believed in angels, although the angels came without being summoned and without being expected. What is more, those angels with ponytails fell from on high, boring into the eyes of those that beheld them. Nonetheless, there is one thing we have not thought of: what if there exists an angel gland and even a God gland? A gland to produce them, to engender them, we mean to say.

ON FLYING VEHICLES OF EVERY VARIETY

Today we are going to talk about carcasses winged and wingless: airplanes, helicopters, parachutes, hang-gliders, balloons, dirigibles, zeppelins, but not rockets, which have no place here. Today we are going to discuss the genus of flying objects that are not angels, since angels may also be defined by the materials of which they do not consist. All these flying objects, whether winged or not, are neither hot- nor cold-blooded; they are bloodless. In their case we might talk speculatively about their having some kind of psychical blood, but it is preferable that we avoid such pitfalls. All these flying objects, as I have said, are the opposite of the mire qua geographic décor, landscape or stage set. They are the opposite of suffocation. Then, they are also the opposite of pipelines and subterranean tracts, since they can fly only in the upper air. Let us start at the beginning. What we can say about airplanes is that they came into being as the first form of love of the air and that they dwelled in the dawn of man's desire to float in the upper air. Resembling the backs of dolphins rather larger than the usual, gliders were worshipped because they satisfied the immediate sense of mental procreation in order to discover what everybody had always been seeking: the soul. The gliders were not abandoned until their sturdier, engine-endowed sisters, airplanes, provided the pleasures of more intense and spatially elaborate flight, including at high altitude. Almost every hominid would like to be a giant, at least ten feet high! Now is not the time for us to expound a sophisticated theory about airplanes, given that their purpose was explained from the very start: airplanes are gigantic, failed angels. The more capacious the airplane, the more of a failure the angel that serves as the model for its design. This is the logic of airplanes with hundreds of passengers on board; let us not doubt the skilled technicians that have constructed them to that end. And so farewell to airplanes, as they are only second-hand angels in the aerial masked ball. Ah, now helicopters! Ladybugs with often transparent, bulging carapaces, helicopters are akin to frogs and martins, and so we may only speak vaguely of any angelic breeze coming from them. The only insinuating thing that draws attention or even fascination here is the rotor blades: for this reason, helicopters are studied alongside windmills and this is also why they are often painted with camouflage. And so off to war with them, to a section of reality that belongs not to angels or other flying things, whether made of flesh or of steel. Parachutes are wanderers that delight in leaping from on high, without necessarily being suicidal. Of them we may say that they are akin to edible mushrooms (but certainly not to *Amanita muscaria*, the most poisonous of the poisonous and the most venomous of the venomous), and then that they resemble bare trees or succulent bald heads or (why not?) perfect lilies, albeit scentless and somehow tattered lilies, this being the only defect of their manufacture. Ladies sometimes like to make themselves long dresses from parachute material; we refer, of course, to those ladies who belong neither to high society nor the lower echelons, but to the bohemian classes, if we can call them that. In any event, parachutes are popular with the public and are appreciated as real champions, even in the face of death. As angels are not bald and do not resemble mushrooms or leafless trees, although they might look like lilies (albeit not tattered ones), in regard to parachutes we must again set them aside from our noble winged emissaries of the Lord. Paragliders are oval parachutes, but it can't be said that only hominids with elongated, oriental eyes fly with them, as the paraglider seems to be a parachute more popular than the classic parachute. After various banquets and carnivalsque feasts, today's revelers often prefer to fly by paraglider, sooner because of the intoxication that makes them believe either that they are birds or that they have reached the kingdom of heaven with souls as pure as angels'. In any event, what is for sure is that the paraglider has always proved to be less official, more elastic, more molded to the hidden desires of human beings that have no compunction about shouting from the rooftops that they feel like flying. But to feel like flying does not necessarily mean being able to do so in a levelheaded manner. Whoever falls to earth in a paraglider still ends up sensing the mist of darkness in his eyes, without any angel being able to save him. Now we come to the deltaplane: marvelous flying objects, suitable for dreamers, whose real sense functions only in the arms, hands and fingers, for it is only with these appendages that the flier controls his triangular apparatus. Flying with a deltaplane is like a furtive, throbbing kiss, with stolen glances at the sky and at what might lie hidden there. This is its only fault: it does not allow you to rest, but puts a strain on the arms greater than on an octopus's tentacles or an elephant's trunk. Perhaps angels might at a pinch theoretically fly by deltaplane, just to test their arm muscles, otherwise they would have no reason to do so. As for rockets, we shall not make any commentary here, as we already stated at the beginning, given that they resemble God more than anything else, thanks to their terrifying speed. But as a historical character dear to us (and not only to us) once said: Render unto Caesar the things that are Caesar's and unto God the things that are God's. And so, let us leave rockets in the care of the Lord and the planets among which such vehicles travel, given that not even angels fly so high. There is just one more species of flying machine for us to invoke, one very popular thanks to its special magic, even though its inflated form has nothing to do with angels: the balloon, the dirigible and the zeppelin. Balloons consist of a single sutured lung, hence their lively, sprightly, jocund respiration. Hence too the epidermal sensation given by the balloon, as well as the carousel, childhood fairground feeling it gives. With a balloon you can fly where your imagination takes you, without having to be embarrassed in front of anybody and without feeling that you have to overcome any obstacle, because the balloon is an enchanted pillow for sleep and dreaming. There is something alchemical about a balloon, something that the failed fliers of the grand Middle Ages did not know how to perceive, when they opted for wings instead of rotund, jolly bellies capable of rising to the heavens. The balloon contains the amniotic memory of birth, hence its aromatic, concentric perfection. The cousins of the balloon are the dirigible and the zeppelin: cousins full of life, for they too are full of stories, hence their elongated bellies, bursting with health. Plump, obese even, in this case the false fat is attractive, a bringer of smooth, serene flight, to be enjoyed in slow motion; beloved monsters, pampered in their construction. Their skin does not deserve to be made into shoes, handbags, armchairs or sofas, or even belts for frocks or trousers or gloves, but only flying bellies. Ah, magnificent zeppelins and praiseworthy dirigibles, blessed are you if you still exist somewhere, in some out-of-the-way corner, and you have not perished once and for all! But is there anybody we have left out of the list? Nobody at all? Where are the birds and the birdies, where are those who most closely match the angels, at least by virtue of their having wings? They have always flown and never and in no wise have they ever been born without wings. Their feathers are of every color and have silken threads within. Plenty of people have no way of knowing what goes on in the kingdom of heaven, but in the kingdom of feather many would desire to dwell. Perhaps we might also have pleasurably spoken here of butterflies, but we have decided to bring to a close this brief, melancholy recapitulation of flying things, ending with the bird kingdom and their glossy feathers. Let them be forever garbed in their wings. At least in dreams, with the aid of the angels' gland.

ON HOW GOD IS NO LONGER ABLE TO AWAKEN FROM A DREAM

Let us recall for a short space the likeable Devil-in-chief, who was wont to bleat like a fiddler and who adored Veuve Cliquot champagne. *Angelus ergo sum*. The devil's heyday had more or less shriveled away, despite his colorful jargon and verbal arabesques. In the matter of the descended angels there was not much the Devil-in-chief could do, given that there was not much that God Himself could do. Not even his page, Wee Devilkin, was not up to the task and had started to falter. For, when God dreams, the Devil-in-chief can no longer take advantage, he can no longer machinate in Heaven and Hell. Perhaps he could in Purgatory, but that is a place so ambiguous that the devil himself doesn't like to set foot there unless constrained by circumstances. And so the Devil-in-chief scratched his nose, then he tugged on his beard, and watched from his theatre box, occasionally telling a joke, grumbling, as the story that was writing itself drew to a close. As we have known since ancient times: devils stick to their own kind, and angels to theirs. But what is to be done if we are dealing with fallen angels? Well, we'll leave that enigma to the traffickers in chimaeras to solve, and in that case let us return to the dreaming God. Does anybody remember Him? He was a God who had dreamed of a train carriage packed full of angels, in every compartment, be it the Orient Express, be it a Metro train or even an experimental rollercoaster: almost every angel He had ever sent forth was there, including the three angels that had descended upon the Metropolis, although He was not entirely sure whether He had sent them or not. In any event, the latter, the three strangers, were mixed up with the angels that revealed themselves to Abraham and Jacob's wrestling angel and the angel that closed the lion's mouth in the story of the prophet Daniel and Lot's angel and Gabriel who brought the tidings to Mary and the angel that freed Peter and many, many more. They all had small, transparent wings, more like dragonfly wings than the wings of an emissary of God. Nevertheless, Raphael, Tobias' angel, as well as Fanuel and Asrael, did not appear in God's dream. Nor did the angel that had encouraged Jesus in the Garden of Gethsemane show himself in the dream of the third millennium God. What we might also recall is that God had grown melancholy, no longer knowing whether He was God or not. But we hominids know why: God is the memory of all things and all creatures. When he dreams, however, because he sinks into sleep like any other ordinary man, God no longer has any memory, His memory is deactivated, and the kingdom of heaven falls dark. In God's second dream, which we are about to recount, things were even more confused: God was dreaming, but he wasn't dreaming of anything. His dream was blank, although it was a dream, that is, it was made up of cluttered things unfolding at speed. But nothing could be made of this divine dream. Nothingness had caught up with God. And so it is no wonder that the three strangers had been left to their own devices, to get by as best they could. Even if they had been sent by their leaders, they had to forge their own destinies, the same as the people among whom they had descended. This is what always happens when God dreams. But now the dream was heavier and graver than usual: because it was a dream of and about nothing, and God was no longer able to wake up from it. His memory was congested, sick, riddled with fissures, perhaps even errors, meaning nothing could be remembered. In such a state, might it be said that God Himself had lost His memory and needed to be taken to an old folks' home? Not a bit of it. The world was waiting for him to awake from His dream about nothing, but the dream was colloidal and unending. Was it then a historical catastrophe? What would happen to Time and Space if God weren't dreaming of anything? Would they vanish or, at best, hide away in some nook or cranny? Scientists know that time and space will never completely merge, but rather they accept on loan some hideaway or carnival mask for complicated things and seasons. But when it comes to utopias and fantasies, such a dream about nothing on the part of God plays into their hands: for, when He who is highest of all dreams of nothing or doesn't dream anything, then others can do so in His stead, even striving to replace Him or exceed Him. It is not the angels that will exceed God, as they do not desire such a spectacle of light, darkness and power, but human creatures, who display the syndrome of excessive imagination. The gland for impossible worlds, in this case of force majeure, becomes more active and more voracious than the gland for angels or the gland for God. And nota bene, you need a killer instinct for such a thing. Impossible worlds never hang around to wait for inventors or discoverers, but always throb at the crossroads for those who have eyes to see them and ears to hear them. This is the wager; this is what is at stake. But is salvation really so easily obtained via the bridges of such non-existent worlds artificially made to exist, i.e. made to have a brain, blood, flesh and bones? On the market for genetic and psychical risks, the hominids have produced plenty of alarming and unbecoming golems, some of which have then destroyed their creators. And the former masters, weakened by their new worlds, have allowed them to destroy them, and even when they put up a fight, the imagined worlds destroyed them anyway, without making any show of it. We are what we are, but also what we are not. Touching verses, diamond sutras, sacred books and words, gospels, mystical epistles. Dream, God, dream! And do not awake. And so, the impossible worlds will gather together and in their concrescence they will form a chimerical kingdom, even if it wears a jester's cap on its head. Your angels are here and they will soon depart. But not to Thy house will they return. Dream, our God, dream! Hallucinations can bring salvation.

ON DEAFNESS AND SILENCE, AND THEN ON THE END OF UTOPIA

Construction of the planned ship had not got very far, and for the time being the inhabitants of the Zone had heaped up pyramids of all kinds of timber and other materials found lying around at home (or rather their erstwhile homes), in the communal dormitory, in the surrounding area, and in storerooms: they all realized, in fact, that the ship or new Noah's Ark, or reborn Titanic, or whatever it was and whatever its purpose might be, would never be launched. But the building of it had come to fascinate and obsess them, all the more so given that everybody, young and old, from the Governor, his Double, the three bodyguards, the three angels and The Nameless to the non-ranking inhabitants of the Zone, realized that the Metropolis authorities would not limit themselves to a lengthy siege, but would make some kind of intervention. And that intervention was to take place very soon. And so the hominids had decided to celebrate not only that they had not finished even a quarter of the ship's hull, after more than half the population had dreamed of the much yearned-for vessel being ready, but also, above all, that the Zone was what it was, and that the angels were there. The two former philosophers gave their consent, and so the inhabitants of the periphery prepared a banquet, if you can call it that: it was to be a celebratory meal consisting of potato soup, potato pies, and baked potatoes with a bean filling, perhaps with some marmalade pie for dessert, in other words their usual diet. The angels were to be greeted with lilac branches, after being brought thither on the last motorcycle to be found within Mile Zero (as the Zone was also known, if you remember). A motorcycle large enough for the three slender angels, accompanied by none other than the girl from the country, who had volunteered to be the main bodyguard for the occasion. Naturally, that metaphorical entry into Jerusalem or last supper (what else can we call it?) sounded rather weird: wouldn't it have been more appropriate to bring the angels on circus ponies, if asses or donkeys weren't available? But no, the peripherals preferred the ramshackle motorcycle that they had found abandoned by the artesian well one morning: in any case, there were no ponies, asses or donkeys residing in the Zone. And when they found the motorcycle in question, they thought it was a sign and that the vehicle was meant to transport special beings: a category under which the angels fell. And so they made the necessary preparations, the women cooked as best they could, the men laid the tables, and then they all gathered by the artesian well in the public square, where the children were still playing hide-and-seek and blind man's buff and other entirely normal games. The Governor made no speech, and nor did his double, and nor anybody else. On the tables could be found copies of the latest issue of *Jester*, in which the Zone's superiors communicated what everybody knew already: the periphery was about to be attacked. They brought the angels as planned, i.e. by motorcycle, and greeted them with lilac branches: and the angels seemed to give an odd smile, in fact they really did smile in an odd fashion, without just seeming to. Around the well had gathered the glow-worms and the flock of flamingos, and then the pets born with four legs and those born with three but more recently. Even the Zone's superiors' mute parrot was at the banquet, in his customary place, on the shoulder of now one former philosopher, now the other. Then, in the middle of the said banquet, something took place that could not help but take place: the angels made discreet signs with their hands, gently tracing circles with them, like windmills, thereby causing a sudden epidemic of deafness to grip all the inhabitants of the Zone, from the superiors of Mile Zero to ordinary folk. Nobody could hear anything any more; the ears of those faithful and chaste hominids were plunged into oceanic silence. Is there anyone who is not deaf that can comprehend what such a silence is like? We have called it an oceanic silence: such a silence is ashen, i.e. grey; it is a suffocating silence, inhaled by a gigantic windpipe. Whoever has experienced deep-sea diving knows full well what I am talking about: there on the bottom of the sea or the ocean, not even the water is audible; nothing can be heard, all is muffled and smothered in cotton wool. The silence there is a restrained, timid death, a death that perhaps wishes only to be a pause between multiple lives. There is nothing oppressive about it. Nothing tragic or tense. Nothing but pure, rounded, self-sufficient silence. Such was the deafness the angels brought to the hominids of the Zone, like an ephemeral and peaceful death, a death required in order to serve a noble, albeit insidious, purpose. A silence like a supple canopy, if we be permitted to be touched by pathos at such a moment of confusion. May we be permitted to believe that poetry can still be born even when its end and ours is nigh. It was a silence that emanated rays. A silence that wore lace gloves and feather down. But what was that silence to which we are now witness, without knowing its purpose? The angels had not caused the epidemic of deafness in vain, since nothing they did was purposeless or deficient. Well, that sudden silence which descended upon the population of the Zone had a strategic and preventative purpose: as they were all deaf, the inhabitants had no way of hearing the Metropolitan helicopters that were about to fill the sky of the periphery and shower the segregated, separatist, heretical space with knock-out gas, so that the rebels would not put up any resistance to their capture by the intervention forces massed by the sandbag border. The three strangers, i.e. the angels, knew one thing: that nobody should die for them; nobody should perish. This is why they did everything possible so that the inhabitants of the Zone would not hear the approaching helicopters and that after the knock-out gas had been sprayed on them they would be captured peacefully and without any violence. But didn't the angels become traitors thereby? Not at all. On the contrary. And here is why: this was the only strategy that made sure not only that nobody from the Zone would perish, but also that the subsequent incriminations and legal action would be minimal, without major repercussions on the part of the Metropolitan authorities, which were in the dark about what was happening in the territory no longer under their control. And while we are on the subject, let us say right now what was to become of the Zone's leaders and the rebels, so that everybody, readers, angels and author of the story alike, will be able to rest easy. Naturally, after the whole angeloid affair came to a close, those that were subjected to the greatest recriminations and character assassination in the Metropolitan mass media were the Governor and his Double, who were arrested, interrogated (but without being roughed up, as nobody wanted the pacifist movements to create an uproar), and sentenced to a year's imprisonment for disturbing the peace and inciting a rebellion. The Patriarch and the Pontifex Maximus themselves intervened on behalf of the two former philosophers so that they would not suffer anything atrocious. In prison, the two former philosophers were given special treatment, being allowed to receive visits from all and sundry, with the result that there were plenty of curious people, including ministers, who displayed an interest in the utopian services of the two alter egos. Even high-society ladies were fascinated by the venerable pipe smokers. But the most frequent visitors were representatives of the former Zone, who, as may be imagined, had come to no harm: what measures could the Metropolitan authorities have taken against thousands of people who, after all, had fallen victim to a subtle form of manipulation? This was the official declaration made by the Chief of Police and the President of the Sacred Homeland. No measures at all, in other words. After serving a year's imprisonment, the former Governor and his former Double formed their own political party, the Alterity Party, a name that suited them to a tee, and having been elected by the former and present inhabitants of the Zone, they became parliamentarians, defending the interests of those they had once governed in the secession. They even re-founded the erstwhile *Jester* newspaper, in which they poured out their grievances as fresh custodians of the nation and, from time to time, recollected the history of the Zone. Former presidential adviser Puma, having also been elected to parliament, since his speech-making gaffes were appreciated within the Corps of the Nation, protested vehemently against the political rise of the two former leaders of the Zone. Equally verbose and rabid was El Leader Maximo, except that nobody took any notice of him, as his rhetoric was old hat. Some media outlets cautiously declared that either of the two former philosophers might, at a pinch, stand for election as president, but we are doubtful of that, given that philosophers never become presidents, especially in a Sacred Homeland that smacked of a barracks. As for the population of the Zone, let us state yet again that nobody came to any harm, and what was more, many of the inhabitants were asked to play parts in the mega-serial dreamed up by the Brain from Metropolfilm, which serial was to tell the tale of Angels' Shanty and to be titled *Angelus*. The Brain from Metropolfilm wanted to do the filming exclusively with amateurs from the Zone, to lend his picture authenticity. Let us now look at what else went on after the eradication of the so-called heresy of the peripheral territory: the statue of the headless angel was demolished, being seen as an artistic failure and the work of amateurs. Then the lilac jungle was hacked down and cleared. The communal dormitory was abolished and the inhabitants went back to their homes. The sandbag border vanished. The trams and bicycles and few motorcars parked in garages and depots were placed back in circulation. The Zone's embalmed dead were taken to the central cemetery and buried there. But weren't all these things predictable? On the other hand, the periphery continued to be called the Zone, as the Metropolitans realized that the nickname, which was known all over the world, could never be changed. What about the bodyguards? Their story is quite spectacular in its own way: given that they had occupied their positions after winning an official competition, they could neither be arrested nor tried, despite their having played a decisive rôle in the events in the Zone. And so they were left to go free and each followed his or her own path. The girl from the country wanted to join a convent, given that her purpose was thenceforth clear: but no convent in the Sacred Homeland would take her, for reasons easy to imagine. The orders from the Patriarchate were unambiguous: they had no need for nuns whose vocation was to be leaders and who carried within themselves the seeds of revolt. And so, with the help of the inhabitants of the Zone and using donations from anonymous well-wishers, the girl from the country built her own convent: it was more a huge cell with numerous annexes, named, very logically, the Hermitage of the Three Angels. And there she dwelled forever more. And now, the Wizard. Well, this thoroughbred intellectual received a special proposal from some secret scholars living in the Metropolis, who had closely followed events in the Zone: he was offered the job of permanent librarian in a small architectural complex that housed a library of forbidden, unofficial books on religion. Obviously, this out-of-the-blue offer was to the liking of the Wizard, who accepted it without hesitation and thereby vanished from the purview of officialdom, withdrawing to an ivory tower. Now, the Roulette Player. No sooner had he regained consciousness after the knock-out gas than he was hired as the main adviser to the Metropolis Casino, a job he performed with brio until his dying day. His experience as a roulette player also meant he was in demand abroad, but the third of the erstwhile bodyguards did not wish to leave the Sacred Homeland. Sometimes, on Sundays, he even used to take solitary walks in the Zone, secretly visiting the abbess of the Hermitage of the Three Angels, with whom he would converse for a little. On very rare occasions, they would be joined by the Wizard: the three did not linger together for more than an hour, and, as might be imagined, their single topic of conversation was the Zone of times gone by. Let us now see what became of The Nameless. The patresfamilias, the grown men, that is, became the Zone's administrators, employed at a departmental town hall opened in the periphery and serving the interests of the local population. It was rumored that they were still members of The Nameless on behalf of the former Governor and his Double, who, after their year in prison, were now parliamentarians. But it was just another rumor, and nobody knew for sure. As for the junior members of The Nameless, four in number, they remained neither in the Zone, nor the Sacred Homeland, nor the Metropolis, but rather as soon as they reached the age of eighteen they joined the Foreign Legion of a country some distance from their native land. And nothing was heard of them again, although the rumors abounded and there were hints that they had risen to be nothing more and nothing less than colonels in the Foreign Legion in faraway lands. What else needs to be said? The glow-worms and the flamingos vanished as soon as the Metropolitan helicopters sprayed the Zone with knock-out gas. No more three-legged animals were born, but no harm befell those that had been born one leg short, and they were left to die of old age without being driven away or maltreated. The famous artesian well, which had sprung up inexplicably, was not destroyed, but left as it was: water has never been proven to be devilish, as we know full well, but has always been the source of life, and so there was no reason to destroy a well. On the other hand, the timber that the peripherals had gathered for the building of their non-seaworthy ship was burned in a bonfire as heretical items requiring salvation in the flames. There were even some hooded individuals who muttered prayers around the bonfire in question. The non-talking parrot vanished for a year, then reappeared and once more became the companion of the parliamentarians; it was given a special pass to allow it to enter the Metropolis's official buildings. But not even after that did it talk. That was more or less what happened to the hominids caught up in the history of the Zone. Perhaps at this point we ought to give a brief summary of the characters from Metropolis's Tower of Babel, stringing them one after the other like beads as follows: the Midget, the nez-parfumeur, the head of the advertising company, All-Knowing and All-Understanding the theologians, the chocolatier, signore Metrocirkus, the Brain from Metropolfilm (whom we mentioned just now), the cyborgs, the Censor in the asylum, the owner of the Angelina bar, the Cloner (who might well have played the rôle of the Governor's Double, if he had not in the meantime become obsessed with cloning his own right leg), the director of the funeral parlor, the Astrologer, the cryogenics expert, the Linguist, the Old Clown, the various doctors who examined the three strangers, the physicists, the mathematicians, the chemists, the Chief of Police and his team of investigators, and so on. The truth is, however, that their fate (we already know what befell some of them, those who fell by the wayside or, on the contrary, saw the light) no longer interests us; each was given a sign and did with it what he or she saw fit. And so, what good will it do us to interpret their lives, minds, souls? Let others do so if they have the time and the inclination, since we do not, as we are now interested in one thing only: where are the angels at the end of this story? Where have they vanished? What has become of them? But perhaps we might be interested in finding out what happened to the two tots from the orphanage and the fortune teller with the long, white, curly hair: but they are part of another story, which will be written and told on a different occasion, in a different book, not here and not now, and so patience, dear reader: you might meet them again one day!

THE TRIPLETS OF THE SLUMBERING ZONE

After the entire population of the Zone had fallen asleep at the little banquet after being knocked out by the gas sprayed by the Metropolitan helicopters, the three angels contemplated the slumber of the people among whom they had dwelled for a time. As so let us contemplate it too. Their sleep was like a protective cupola, flawless, dreamless, it was a perfect exodus, an exit from the exterior world via a state of induced beatitude. Probably only fetuses in their mothers' wombs or in incubators sleep such a sleep. But above all it was a naked, unclothed, unmade-up, un-travestied sleep. It was the only sleep possible without any danger of collision, an insular sleep insinuated so subtly that it might even have made all those slumbering hominids levitate against their will. The three strangers gazed for a while at the luminous faces of the inhabitants, moving among them, examining those faces as they voyaged through the subterranean tracts and the belvederes of sleep. Perhaps that was what a healed paradise looked like. I don't really believe that can be described without our using flourishes willy-nilly, and so allow us to say the following: it was a sleep without thorns, without bones, without blood, without flesh, nothing but fluid sleep, rising and falling within them. And so the angels walked for a while among those glorious slumberers, for the glory was theirs, and then all three gathered around a round table by the artesian well. It was the stone table at which they were wont to sit at dusk, watched over by the glow-worms and the flamingos, even if we forgot to mention that detail until now. Gathered together and sitting on the round stools, the three angels were silent, as was their wont. But this time, as it was the last time and their final period in the Zone, as we are about to see, the three angels no longer looked like they ordinarily did, but somehow different. First of all they could no longer be told apart, as if they were identical triplets. The mole below one eye, the missing wisdom tooth and the lack of a kidney no longer mattered. Their necks had also elongated, like pipes soaring into the sky. From their azure tunics poured bronze-colored threads of light, and their hair had turned as yellow as ripe wheat. Their hands were spread on the round table, and their eyes shone: the angel in the middle looked at the one on his right, who in his turn looked at the angel on his right. The circles between them were concentric. And so it was not only the hominids that were in a state of grace, albeit one artificially induced, but also the three angels. Let us recall, however, that angels are only bodily receptacles for a short time. When those receptacles wear out, they emerge from themselves, inasmuch as they are pure soul. We would nonetheless rather say that they are hearts of pure ruby. This is why we love and desire angels, whether they be our guardians or not. If anybody had gazed upon the three strangers from afar, she would have thought that they were connected to an electric socket, as a slight tremor, a gentle crackle could be perceived in their fingers. Not even by the end of the Zone had they been given names, as there had been no need of any. They were nameless angels, as if they had gestated in silk cocoons that they had not yet shed, but which still clung to them like vestments of infinite birth. And their elongated eyes seemed enameled and their shoulders, although wingless, seemed fluffy, and in their entirety they were comely, with the brilliance lent by perfection and the grace of being supreme messengers. And beatitude was not only promised in them, but also contained in them as voluptuousness. And sadness did not exist in them because their story ended here, given that each story once ended is begun elsewhere and differently, even if the human soul no longer knows it, but only suspects it. So, they angels gazed and were silent, and that was all: between them was woven an illuminated, branching lacework. In their bodies there was neither longing nor deceit. They knew nothing of the beasts that are found only in the soul of man. The air was so pellucid it shattered, unraveled, and then filled with soft bundles of light. They formed an intricate icon, worshipped for its gold and yellow beauty, for its iridescent velvetiness. Not even they knew what was to be, where, when, how or why. Where were they to go? Back? In the air there floated a scent of russet incense that tasted of caramelized sugar.

MERLIN, MESMAEA, ANIR AND NARKOM, OR ON HOW SAVIORS LEAVE TRACES

Merlin Stral had been the one who supplied the motorcycle on which the three angels were brought to the banquet on the last night of the Zone. He had managed to cross the border clandestinely, atop that shabby conveyance of his, and he had placed the motorcycle in the Zone in such a way that the secessionist space would make not only symbolic but also practical use of it. The man who had come up with the *Vita Alia* game on the Internet knew a thing or two. Not for nothing was he a demiurge in his own right: he had been following step by step everything that happened in the Zone, he had been monitoring the entire angelic affair, from the angle of both peripherals and authorities. It was on that motorcycle that he, wearing scuffed jeans and a denim shirt, had appeared before the strangers, still in their state of beatitude, sitting at the round table by the artesian well. Merlin waited for the silence to ebb away from the angels so that he could talk to them. It was not until the eyes of the strangers with yellow hair and azure cloaks had once more grown accustomed to human light that Merlin began to speak. And it was then that the angels spoke for the third and last time, firstly recognizing the motorcycle on which they themselves had ridden not long before:

"God is dreaming, and so you have nowhere to go back to. Up there," said Merlin, jabbing his index finger skyward, "it's closed. The gates are blocked."

"He is dreaming, true," replied the angels, "and for as long as He dreams, the kingdom of heaven is sealed. But God does not dream for all eternity. He will awake sometime and then we shall be able to return."

"If God ever awakes," said Merlin, "then humans too will certainly awake from their lethargy. And nobody knows what will happen then."

"What will happen is what will happen," said the angels. "There is nothing new under the sun. But if we too were able to dream, then we would succeed in meeting God in the middle of the dream, so that then we could go back to the world whence we came. Nevertheless, if we think about it patiently and wisely, we don't know what the middle of such a dream would look like."

"Angels never dream; they are only dreamed, whether God be the dreamer or humans. As for a dream being cut in two down the middle, just about the only place where that happens is *Vita Alia*," Merlin replied, highly pragmatically. "Only there do you find stray pieces of dreams floating around, which might be gathered, joined, and put to some use."

"*Vita Alia* instead of the kingdom of heaven?" asked the strangers, giving an ironic smile for the first time in the present story. "Then may it be so, if that is how it is to be. But if that is not how it is to be, then we shall return to the place where we must return."

"Perhaps you are errant angels, and therefore you do not need to return where you came from, but to wander for as long as you can," replied Merlin. "But our words, and yours, and mine, are empty now, and so it would be preferable to fill them with facts."

Then he peered at them and took from the wide breast pocket of his denim shirt a kind of plastic lily, which housed a small computer. He opened the lily beneath the eyes of the three angels and the toy-like computer pinged like a bell: within a few seconds the young master Stral logged on to *Vita Alia*, which he showed the three strangers, explaining to them what it was he wanted.

"I am not God and nor do I wish to take His place. Nevertheless, I can provide you with an alternative to the so-called kingdom of heaven," he told the angels. "*Vita Alia* is the name of the multinational or cosmic game I have invented. For some it is just a game, but for others it is a para-reality. I give you this latest version as a present: come with me into *Vita Alia*, where you can shelter until God stops dreaming."

"A para-reality?" asked the angels. "But what we are doing already is part of a para-reality. Even the Zone was something of the sort."

"In *Vita Alia* you can even dream or enter God's dream," pointed out Merlin. "In any case, I have another surprise for you. Just a moment," he said waggishly and then navigated through *Vita Alia* until he found an isolated room, a chiaroscuro corridor, where some objects were heaped up on the floor.

The angels watched closely. They were wings. None resembled the other, but they were wings: some were knife-sharp at the tip, others were arched, and others still were long and slender. In fact there were precisely three pairs of wings.

"They are your wings," said Merlin. "They are rumpled right now, but as soon as you attach them to your shoulders they will spread open. Which is to say, they will become part of you, as if you had always had them."

"Perhaps we do have wings, but they are just not visible," said the angels, laughing.

"You can't fool me," said Merlin. "These are your wings, and nobody else's. I know it and you know it. And I am the one who created these wings."

"What do you want of us?" asked the angels with elongated eyes and flamingo throats.

"I want to reconstruct paradise with your help and the help of Mesmaea Cuttita. Because the time has come for a new race to be born: the *mangels*. Mesmaea is the only woman capable of procreating with you to give birth to this new race. You yourselves will understand the reason why: she is guarded by two immaculate avatars, Anir Magnifico and Narkom Zarthus, her samurais."

The angels smiled on hearing those playful names and the word procreation. But then Merlin made them enter *Vita Alia* once more, so that they could see Mesmaea, Anir and Narkom with their own eyes. Mesmaea had black hair with cherry-red spots, tied up in two bunches or nests at each ear, adorned with cherry-red feathers. She had a small doll-like or geisha mouth and was heavily rouged. She had a prominent chest and hips. She was very tall, some two heads taller than the angels and even Anir and Narkom. She was wearing trousers and sports top: the trousers had white cutouts at the thighs and calves, the top at the elbows. Her gloves were fingerless. She had black lenses covering her eyes and a round microphone in front of her mouth (although she never talked to anybody). At each ankle there were two cherry-red feathers, like the ones at her ears. Anir had chestnut hair tied in a huge ponytail that reached to his waist, and two long locks of hair dangling on each side of his face; the huge ponytail helped him to fly. He had blue eyes and elven ears. He was wearing brown leather trousers, a green shirt, a brown leather waistcoat, gauntlets that reached to his elbows, boots that reached to his knees, and a wizard's cloak, fastened with two turquoise stones. The cloak had a brown stripe down the back. His hair was in fact a second clock, given that it was his means of flight. Narkom was dressed in black and wore skin-tight trousers and shirt, and a pair of boots. His hair was short and black, cut in a fringe. He had dark eyes and a long face. He was tall, but not as tall as

Mesmaea, who was a head taller. Although visibly shorter than Mesmaea, Anir and Narkom were her samurais. Mesmaea was flying awkwardly, as if buffeted by the not very pellucid air of *Vita Alia* and by the surrounding walls, which she kept bumping into, but without hurting herself. The angels giggled: Mesmaea Cuttita did not know how to fly very well, she was an odd little girl, an adult little girl, bumping into walls like a bird whose wings aren't fully grown. In fact, she did not have wings, but only those cherry-red feathers attached to her temples and her ankles. Perhaps in the past, in the Land of Mushrooms (for it was there that she once dwelled, as Merlin explained to the angels), she had been able to fly like a witch or a magician, but here, beneath their eyes, Mesmaea was flying falteringly and comically, bumping into things, hindered by the buildings, walls and pylons, which did not allow her to pass. Perhaps there, in the Land of Mushrooms, Mesmaea had eaten too many hallucinogenic mushrooms! Beneath their very eyes, she tumbled into the sea and made floundering attempts to fly up again. That grown-up little girl was so amusing that the angels almost fell in love with her. Incorporeally, of course: they had fallen in love with her the way you fall in love with a toy from which you never want to be parted. Looking at her floundering and flapping, without her saying a word, since Mesmaea was silent and focused on her imperfect flight, sulky at the knocks she had received, the angels laughed. Mesmaea was no femme fatale, nor a temptress, although her body was ripe, and nor was she a gestating womb in waiting, but rather a grown-up little girl, as I have already said. And the fact that precisely this little girl had been chosen to bear a new race did not at all surprise the three strangers. It was clear that Mesmaea herself did not know what she was going to be used for, given that she was busy with her stunted flight, as if that were all her life would thenceforth be. And then the angels understood: Mesmaea had forgotten that she had flown before, that she had been queen in the Land of Mushrooms. For, Mesmaea had reverted to the time when she was a little girl: she had gone back to her childhood so that she could wait for the angels to arrive and catch up. This must be Merlin Stral's plan. Or perhaps there was a different plan.

"Are Anir Magnifico and Narkom Zarthus Mesmaea Cuttita's guardian angels and ours, as it were?" the three strangers asked, in unison as usual.

"I don't know whether they are guardian angels. I prefer to call them samurai. It's more accurate," said Merlin. "But you can call them guardian angels. In any case, you need them, to protect you from the Negotiators of Death, and chiefly Lilih Angustias, the only one capable of eliminating Mesmaea Cuttita from *Vita Alia*."

Merlin then showed the angels Lilih. She had thick, woolly, bleached hair that reached to her shoulders and on her forehead were inscribed the letters L and H in black. Her lips were fleshy and painted brown. Her skin was dusky, artificially tanned. She was wearing a sequined evening gown and her eyes were made up in gold and black. Her ears were like a dog's and from them dangled chains. But the strangest thing of all was her hands: they were shaped like horns or whips, without fingers, consisting of one huge fingernail. The other Negotiators of Death (Merlin showed the angels just a few of them) had shaven heads and goatees and wore mauve tunics. When she eliminated avatars, Lilih deliberately pretended to be a little girl, which is precisely what she was not. After they looked at Lilih and a few Negotiators of Death, the latter not nearly as dangerous as the former, the angels were torn. For the time being they agreed to put on the wings that had been abandoned either by them themselves or by somebody else at some unknown time in the corridor Merlin had shown them, although he specifically stated that he had made the wings especially for them. In regard to Mesmaea Cuttita, the angels smiled again. She was a comical grown-up little girl who no longer knew how to fly properly, not even in *Vita Alia*. Perhaps they would need to teach her how to again. And the mission of Anir Magnifico and Narkom Zarthus was to guard the little girl's memory so that she would never forget she had flown. That's why they were samurai after all. But for the time being, the angels attached the wings to their shoulders, and the wings merged with their bodies, insofar as they were bodies and not something else, as if they were made of glue. Almost without realizing it, the strangers had entered *Vita Alia*. And there the first thing they did was to fly before Mesmaea Cuttita. Merlin was satisfied: he mounted his motorcycle, solo this time, as there was no further need for the angels sit behind him or remove them from the Zone, where, in a few minutes, the Metropolitan intervention forces were about to invade and arrest the entire population of separatist peripherals. Henceforth the angels would be able to fly by themselves, given that they had wings and had fully become part of the parallel world constructed by Merlin. And so the angels flew: at last, and for the first time in this story, they flew. At first their flight was vertical and somewhat resembled a dive, since their wings were not fully spread, but rather crumpled, folded. Even the upper air in *Vita Alia* was opaque or intractable or enveloped in something or other. But then, gradually, their wings, which resembled nothing else, since each had different wings, as we already know, opened like reincarnated parachutes; they became semi-conscious and then conscious of the action of flight, fluttering freely and consummately. And then it was that Mesmaea herself espied them, although she still kept bumping into walls and pylons, she still kept falling into the sea and emerging tousled and sulky at her aerial failures. Mesmaea espied them as they fluttered and she immediately knew they were angels. Hey, she called to them, admiring their glorious flight. Hey! Don't you want to be my flying instructors, my trainers, my mentors? Hey! The three fliers gazed in amusement at the cherry-red feathers at her temples and ankles. And above all they gazed at her unnatural flight: although she was just a little girl, she was two heads taller than them. They would reply to her soon, but not yet, as they had something else to do. If paradise had to be constructed anew, this would not be possible without a second genesis. Would it not be too much on their part? Would they not be transformed into usurpers thereby? Merlin, sitting at the control panel of *Vita Alia*, laughed: here, the demiurge could be anybody, albeit not anyhow or anytime. Consequently, the angels could recreate genesis if they so wished. But unlike the other players, they had a different kind of reality; they were not just avatars: and moreover it was fitting that paradise should be recreated to perfection, not a rushed, botched job. The vocation of the upper air, be it real or unreal, is always to shelter a territory of transformations of every kind and to be open to every possibility. Like in alchemy, Merlin Stral knew this, and now the angels knew it too, having entered *Vita Alia*. But for the time being Mesmaea did not know it, but the time would come when she would master the art of transformations. She already viewed the angels as entities that could teach her the skill of flying, without her believing that there was any miracle behind it. And nor was there any need for her to believe such a thing. With her black round glasses, it wasn't any wonder that Mesmaea kept bumping into walls or that she didn't see very well. The angels laughed; Merlin laughed too. But despite all that, only she could be the Bride, the hindered Bride, for the time being at least. But let us go back to the matter of upper air. The upper air is refined matter in which it is even possible to swim: you nestle in the upper air as if it were liquid. This is what the angels felt with their new wings, now fluttering horizontally. Speed no longer matters in such situations, because we are not talking about rockets or airplanes, but angels, and they have no engines and they don't make a droning noise. To little-girl Mesmaea it all of a sudden seemed that the angels resembled mushrooms and it was as if she recollected something from a different life. Hey! she called out to them once more, waving her long arms and legs frantically. Then she called out to herself and commanded: fly, Mesmaea, fly! Be like them, fly like the angels! Her awkward flight made the angels turn to look at her, but they did not have time to look for long, because they had not finished what they intended to do. Let me not come crashing down once and for all, thought Mesmaea aloud. Up until now I have managed to avoid such a disaster. The angels heard her once more and looked below them, at where the real world ought to be. And there it was, diminished, reduced, with God suspended above it, dreaming. The real world was as big as a mustard seed. If anybody other than Merlin had looked at them, from the real world up into *Vita Alia*, they perhaps would have seen some paper airplanes gliding at random. Angels made of newspaper. It is a good thing that in the upper air there are no oceanic swells or tsunamis. There, nobody weeps. And so the angels set out to make the world anew, gazing from above at the mustard seed of the world. Merlin gave them expert advice on how to do it. And the evening and the morning were the first day. The angels made the heaven and the earth by flapping their wings, by rustling them and clasping the void between them in wide eddies. They fashioned even the earth from the upper air. Likewise light and darkness, although these were already around them. Some things needed separating from others, but the angels allowed them to remain together. The waters were also made from the upper air, likewise the trees, the animals, the stars, the fish, the birds. And man was created anew from the upper air. And the evening and the morning were the second day. Merlin whispered to them what they should do next. The mini-genesis did not last six or seven days, but only a few minutes. The angels gazed down from very high above: the real world receded at dizzying speed. It shrank to the size of a nut and then a bean. All that remained in the nooks and crannies and at the crossroads was fiction, frothy, alluvial fiction. Yes, the time has come to draw this story to a close, just as our world itself is drawing to a close, weary, forgotten by dreaming God, our insignificant world, a world more and more distant from us, dear readers, henceforth lost in the dazzling and futile space of *Vita Alia*, the only world where we can feel alive and about which we still have the power to write.

AFTERWORD BY MARIUS CONKAN

Angels and Para-Reality

Ruxandra Cesereanu's novel *Angelus* raises a series of questions regarding the society in which we live, offering, at the same time, possible solutions to (or at least, hypotheses on) the revitalisation of the sacred and the resurrection of symbolic depth for a (post)humanity characterised by the atrophy of imagination and the hypertrophy of pragmatic reason. Taking as her iconographic model Andrei Rublev's *Holy Trinity* and proposing a postmodern reply to Mikhail Bulgakov's masterpiece, *The Master and Margarita,* Ruxandra Cesereanu, in her parable-like novel, begins with the following question: what would happen if angels were to descend upon a Metropolis one day? The novel presents the arrival of three angels who baffle, in the manner of Bulgakov's devils, the entire society there, from the president to the patriarch, from philosophers to ordinary people. After having been examined by several specialised committees to have their angelic authenticity ascertained, the three foreigners who have descended into the Metropolis are set free, each of them receiving a bodyguard. Reaching a peripheral area or zone of the city, which is about to be cut off from the Metropolis and even from the former Empire, they heal deaf, dumb, sleepwalking and cancerous people. The Zone (which could be in Moscow, Bucharest, or any city from Eastern Europe), for this is what this peripheral space will be called by a slum Philosopher turned Governor, is about to change into a miraculous *topos*. The place is inhabited by the three angels and by the hominoids who believe in the latter's angelic powers. There are also here the fireflies and flamingo birds that have cropped up unexpectedly in this mystical area. The leaders of the Metropolis decide that the three foreigners are *personae non grata* and go to extreme lengths to have the angels and the rebellious hominoids captured, while the sacred Zone is to be evacuated. Eventually, metropolitan helicopters will spray a paralysing solution over the Zone so that the hominoids may be captured without any resistance. Given that as long as God is dreaming, the gate to heavens will remain shut, the three angels have to seek refuge in a virtual world called *Vita Alia*, which has been created by Merlin Stral, who is also the begetter of Mesmaea Cuttita and her two samurai, Anir

Magnifico and Narkom Zarthus. Merlin plans to create a race of *mangels* (*man* + *angels*) by having Mesmaea Cuttita mate with the three angels. In *Vita Alia*, the latter retrieve their once-lost wings and rebuild the world through a new genesis.

Angelus is a postmodern response to Bulgakov's novel, *The Master and Margarita*. While in Bulgakov's book a host of ludic and ironic devils descend upon an essentially pagan metropolis with the intention to convert the atheists into believers (through lunacy and enlightenment), in Ruxandra Cesereanu's novel the sacred, in its classical form, envelops the Metropolis, and yet, the authorities and most of the hominoids fail to recognise it. What needs emphasising is that this sacredness is far from plenitudinous, since the descending angels are wingless and the ataraxic and indifferent people no longer believe in anything.

From the very beginning, it needs be noted that Ruxandra Cesereanu grants her angels a sacred meaning that is different from their Trinitarian acceptation in Rublev's *Troitsa*. The three angels from *Angelus* do not stand for a classical hypostatisation of the Holy Trinity, which would be consistent with theological symbolism, but for a demythologised materialisation of the transcendent in three identical forms. The appearance of the three angels in *Angelus* is based on the ideal Trinitarian type, with "identical and interchangeable figures," unlike Rublev's representation, which individualises each Person of the Holy Trinity through their apparel and gestures: the angel in the middle is the Son, the one on the left is the Father, and the one on the right is the Holy Spirit. About the garments worn by the angels in Ruxandra Cesereanu's novel, we learn only this much: "They were identical, garbed in jeans and tunics, as well as a blue cape, in fact not so much blue as azure, and their long, curly chestnut hair was tied in a ponytail". The fact that the angels in the novel are clad identically, unlike the ones in Rublev's icon, leads us towards the following possible interpretation: the "blue cape, in fact not so much blue as azure" is obviously reminiscent of the hypostasis of the Son in the *Holy Trinity* icon, so much so that all three angels in the novel may be regarded as incarnations of the descending Son in the desacralised metropolis. This perspective is also endorsed by the presence of the dreamy God as a character; as long as He keeps dreaming, the three angels cannot return to Heaven, being forced to seek refuge in the virtual world of *Vita Alia*. Through the miracles they perform in the

Zone, which is isolated from the rest of the Empire, the three angels in *Angelus* may be considered to be incarnations of the Son: through them, the prose writer resemanticises, in postmodern manner, several of the miracles performed by Christ.

Ruxandra Cesereanu's parable-like novel comprises three imaginary levels: the *disenchanted world* of the Metropolis; the Zone, inhabited by the hominoids who have cut themselves off from the rest of the populace; and *Vita Alia,* the virtual world created by Merlin Stral, the net surfer. The three angels subject these worlds to a resacralising process, although the Metropolis will remain a disenchanted space even after the angels take refuge in the second life system.

While the Zone represents the terrestrial paradise of the hominoids who believe in the founding power of the sacred, the world Merlin Stral has created becomes a virtual paradise in which the angels reveal their true divine essence by recuperating the wings they once lost. Unlike the virtual worlds that foster escapism from the disenchanted reality but are deprived of holiness, the *Vita Alia* created by Merlin Stral represents, given its paradisal structure, a heterotopia where, like in the Zone, the miraculous reigns supreme and the avatars' self-reconstruction is set into motion. In *Vita Alia*, a surrogate for the Holy Heavens, the angels are not mere *cyber-myths*; they fulfil the role of founding figures who, having reached this sacred dimension, are remythologised and reinstated as divine creatures. The race of *mangels* that Merlin intends to engender will represent not only a form of resacralising the human, but also the entrenchment of the virtual Paradise within reality.

This is the resolution that the novel *Angelus* brings to the idea of crisis: a human crisis, a political crisis, a social crisis, and last but not least, a metaphysical crisis.

54582391R00143

Made in the USA
Charleston, SC
05 April 2016